TEST OF FAE

THESE HALLOWED HILLS SERIES

Quick Quill Publishing

© 2017

Also by S.L.Mason

THESE HALLOWED HILLS

TRICK OF FAE

TEST OF FAE

THORNS OF FAE

TWIST OF FAE

TRAITS OF FAE

KILLING GODS

ALETHEA

CALYPSO

HERA

FATES

UNDERWORLD

ELYSIUM

DEDICATION

To my daughter Gillian.

She's never seen a fight and turned away.

TABLE OF CONTENTS

CHAPTER 1

No one here had seen me before. They don't know what I really look like. They don't know that my hair isn't black and my eyes aren't green. Every single one of them thinks this is me. That I look this way. Admitting to myself I'd been changed probably is the most difficult thing I have ever had to face.

Inside, I feel the same. I don't feel any different. I still feel human. But every trip to the bathroom, every glance at my reflection in the mirror, the window, or the shiny side of the car—all I see is me but alien me. I know what's causing the change, and I can't reverse it.

I can't go back to my parents' hidey hole. There isn't room for everyone. I have thirty-seven kids all looking at me—the new me, not the old me.

I dart my eyes around the warehouse, searching for Arty and hoping to spot his hair or his hunched shoulders. I catch myself looking at tables and different surfaces, seeing if he left his eyeglasses behind.

I could really use him. Arty isn't just my best friend; he's the perfect right-hand man: smart, strong, and always willing to do whatever I ask of him. The best part is that I never have to question whether Arty is on my side.

It doesn't matter what I do. If Arty wants to fight about it, he would later when we were alone. He wouldn't make me look like a fool in front of people. But Arty isn't here. Instead, I found somebody else to rely upon.

The juiced-up quarterback who jumped in the truck cab with Zoe and me. It's Nick. He's reliable, he steps up to the plate, and so far, he hasn't done anything to piss me off. He's big and beefy, and he's used to people doing what he tells them to do.

After the maze, the only person who knows what's going on, is me. Somehow, Nick got the idea I'm in charge. In his mind, I'm the top dog, and that makes him my right-hand man.

I don't know if Nick is loyal like Arty. What Arty and I had, took a lifetime to build, but Nick keeps everyone in line, keeps us moving and motivated. The Nicks of the world have their uses.

I hadn't sung anything since the moment I snapped everyone out of the enchantment in the middle of the street. To be honest, I'm afraid to sing now that I know I can create magic with it.

I sit in this dingy, filthy, grease-filled warehouse with closed eyes. I can hear its song. The rocks, every piece of metal, even the glass in the windows. They all have a rhythm, a vibration, or a tune, and they sing to me. Every now and again I feel the desire to sing back.

It has been two weeks since the maze, and we hadn't seen even one Fae. But I can feel them lurking in the background, one step behind our every move. My greatest worry now isn't just the Fae. I saw how easy it was for Janice to tame that dog, and I have seen pawprints all around the homes in my parents' neighborhood. My greatest fear is that the Fae might be using animals to hunt us. It means going out onto the street is dangerous. Even in the daylight, birds, dogs, cats, and squirrels are a threat, all enlisted to the Fae.

We don't want to draw the gangs' attention either since there are still gangs running around. I don't allow guns anymore; guns draw attention. The report of a gun carries, and the sound is even easier to hear if you're an animal. The last thing we need is a dog to follow the crack of a bullet back to us—no guns. Instead, we practice every day for an hour using bow and arrows, makeshift crossbows, and BB guns. A BB gun isn't going to kill anything, but if you can scare an animal off, it'll make it easier to get away. The animals are our real daylight enemy. They track you and then lie in wait until twilight to bring the Fae down on all of us.

I don't want to kill somebody's pet, but if it's a choice between me or somebody else's Mr. Wiggles. I'm sorry, Mr. Wiggles is dead.

"So, what are we doing today, boss?" Nick's inquiry pulls me out of my head.

"Same as we do every day. Go out. Look for food. Take only what you can carry. Meet back at the appointed place. Stick to the plan." I cocked an eyebrow at him.

He nods his head. It's plain he has something to say, especially when his nose snarls up to the side.

"Is this all we do? You know, scrounge for food and hope we don't get spotted by some Fae pet?" The toe of his boot kicks at a dirt clod.

I don't like his tone of voice, but he clearly has a burr up his ass. Rather than start an argument, I cross my arms and sit back, throwing my feet up on the table.

"All right, then. What's your idea?" I ask.

"We made a plan, it's a war, humanity against the fairies. We could go to the government and tell them what happened. We could take a whole division back with us." He's right to do all those things. Everything single one of them relies upon me. It means that I have to get us back into the Fae realm if the government doesn't decide to study me like a lab rat first.

"I got us out the first time. I'm not sure I can get back in. You don't even remember anything. The last thing you remember is some crazy, pointy-ear fucker was singing to you. Then your eyes went all milky-white, and you became a member of the Fae zombie clan. We aren't going to the government. I don't want to disappear into a black bag. And if you go to them, so help me. I will hunt you down to the end of my days. Stick to the plan, Nick!" In a flash, I'm up and leaning over the table with both hands planted into the surface.

He opens his mouth to say something. I put my hand up. "You're right, we should find some adults to take care of the littler kids. They need to be educated, loved, and coddled." I look around, knowing the only adults within five miles are my parents. I can't take anyone there. The rest of the adults are gangbangers and criminals, probably a few rapists too. "They aren't going to get any of that with us. I don't know how we would find good adults that are alive. I don't want to go over this again." I heave a sigh, blowing my bangs out of my eyes.

All of their parents are dead. I'm not going to dissuade them of the belief that mine aren't dead as well. My parents are safer if everyone thinks they are dead.

My head rolls to the side, creating a pop in my neck. My eyes slide around the warehouse. I focus in on one of the kids, Twitchy. He's good with electronics. So is his buddy, Doug, the super geek. I turn my head back to Nick, cross my arms, and change the subject. "Has Doug found anything on the radio?"

"They're still playing music. He says most of the news isn't worth listening to. The public service announcement to check in is still running." Nick gazes off to nowhere.

"We don't want to send a reply. You don't know who's on the other end of that radio. They will find us and take all the supplies or worse. I'm sorry, but I think we're just stuck with this for now. Our best bet is to keep organizing the softer teenagers to take care of the littler kids." He doesn't turn to look at me but nods his head. He stands up straighter and stomps off to the other side of the warehouse.

"Is he trying to get rid of us again?" Zoe is always nearby. The truth is she'd make a perfect spy. She moves without a sound. She's so tiny. I'm sure we could secret her away in a cupboard to eavesdrop on someone's conversations.

"He's not trying to get rid of you. He's trying to keep people safe. He knows we're not adults, and little kids need love and somewhere safe to call home. We're all so traumatized. I'm not sure we have it in us." I rub my forehead. I don't have all the answers.

"I love my sister. I help out with little kids as much as I can. You're right; they need love," her eyes plead with me. "We're the adults now. Don't let Nick talk you into getting rid of us." Fear etches her face. The same fear grips me.

"Do you really think Nick has the ability to talk me into anything? Don't worry about it. Nick's not in charge. We stay together until we find a better option." My eyes follow Nick's movements across the warehouse.

Like Nick, I want to go back, but to save Arty. I'd only been in the Fae realm for a few days, but time had marched on, resulting in three months passing on in the human realm. It has been two weeks my time since I returned to the surface, and I can't figure out how much time had passed in Fae. A few hours?

What do they say about procrastination? You may delay, but time will not.

CHAPTER 2

All my plans are taking too long.

I keep running the picture in my mind. Arty's black hair in free fall, his eye's focusing on Olive and throwing her back on the platform. The last minute when our eyes met before he sank over the side and my stomach lurched. How did Arty wake-up? Everybody else was asleep. If Olive hadn't tumbled over the side, he'd still be here.

It's not even a choice I want to think about. Olive didn't deserve to be saved more than Arty. Arty would have wanted her saved before than him. She's little, with a whole life to live. Arty would want her to live. He was sweet like that.

I said it like he's dead. He's not dead; he's stuck underground with the life-sucking Fae, I think.

No one here is capable of withstanding the Fae. They would all become entranced, and it would be a big waste of their lives. Mine and Nick's plan is the only way, and I can't stay here.

I flip through the pictures on Arty's phone, most of them of me.

"Looking at the pictures of your boyfriend again?" I grit my teeth and shift my eyes to him. Nick grates on me sometimes by pushing just the right button.

"He's not my boyfriend. I've told you that; he's my best friend," I retort.

His dry laugh always follows. "I don't know any guy who has that many pictures of a girl that he doesn't want to bone."

"You're a real Shakespearean there, Nick. It isn't like that. Arty isn't into me, more like I'm his sister or something." I close my eyes. I can hear Arty's words before we were taken. He told me to save yourself. Isn't that what I was doing? *No, you're procrastinating. Yeah, to save lives.*

"Poor Arty, friend-zoned for all time. I'm sorry, Sarah! I'm not buying it. You're good-looking and available. You like him, and you hang out with him. He's your boyfriend whether you admit it or not." Nick crosses his arms, forcing his biceps to bulge and making them appear larger than they are and they are large.

"He's not my boyfriend. Kissing Arty would be like kissing my brother. Gross. We're friends, that's it. I literally lost my best friend. Could you leave me alone about it?" I grumble, shifting my eyes from him and back to the phone before pushing the off button and sliding it back into my pocket.

"I know you just lost your friend. We all lost somebody. You never once asked me why I was there or who I went with." The chiding tone of his voice mists over me like a cold fog and my head hangs as I run my fingers through my hair. Long, thick and unruly, my hair is a pain in the ass, but it covers the point at the end of my ears.

"I'm sorry! I never asked you whom you went in with. I didn't ask you why the Fae were holding you at the tree. Who was so important they tied your lives together? I didn't ask, not because I don't care." I chance a glance at him and then around the warehouse. "Everybody's got their own demons. I didn't think it was my business to pry into yours. Want to tell me? I'd be happy to listen." I turn my full attention on him.

He looks down and away, his shoulder rises as he draws in a breath. Then everything about him sags. "My sister. I have a twin sister. I'm Nicholas, she's Nicolette. I know, cheesy. If you knew my parents, you would've understood. I'm sure based on what you told me about the maze that she made it through. Nikki's really smart. She's the smarter of the two of us. Now you know who I'm going back for—you to get your friend, me to get my sister. I don't care if you're in love with him. All I care about is Nikki. She's in there, fighting for her life alone. I'm her brother. I'm supposed to be by her side, always." Obviously, his sister is the one in charge of their relationship. He'll do anything to save her. So, if it's a choice between Arty and his sister, he's always gonna choose his sister. Which is okay because that's kind of what I would expect. If it was my sister, I would choose her over somebody's friend every time. I would choose Arty.

I dart my eyes around. "Is this why you keep pushing me? You don't want to be responsible so we can go back and save Nikki?" I tap my hands together, lightly letting the tips of my fingers meet.

"Yes, that and frankly I'm not ready to be micro-dad. Some of these kids, they look up to us like we're supposed to be their parents. I'm not ready for that. I'm not sure I would ever be ready for it. Until a couple weeks ago, the only thing I wanted to do was play football and get into a good college. That's it." His words come out hard and pleading at the same time. "I wasn't thinking about anything else other than girls. Now all I can think about is Nikki, killing Fae, and getting revenge." His right fist smashes into his left hand, flexing the muscles in his upper body at the same time. Nick likes to put on a show of strength. For a moment there, the bravado vanishes and I see the real Nick. The guy without all the brawn and he is hurting and alone. Just like the rest of us. I stand up, keeping my eyes on his, I pat his arm, and turn my mind away from all our losses.

I know how he feels. Before all of this, the only thing I was worried about was finishing high school and who I'd go to prom with.

It had all been so clear when I spoke to my parents. I had to go back in the Hallowed Hills and find Arty. But the longer I think about it, the more I realize it won't be that easy. *What if he's dead?* The what-ifs play a broken record in my head. There is only one way to make them stop. That is why Nick and I made our pact.

CHAPTER 3

Of course, it's always quietest just before the storm. That's what they say, right? The whole hindsight's 20/20, all the stupid catch-22 cliché phrases you hear from adults and on television. I just turned eighteen, and it's one of those moments where you look around and realize your parents were right about everything and then you hate it.

We do our best to make sure there are no signs of occupation in the entire industrial district. Everyone packs our trash out and leaves it at homes around the neighborhoods. We go into the houses the gangs have already raided, only taking what food is left. Most kids raid the refrigerators and freezers. I tell them to take canned goods and jars, dry beans, rice, cooking oil, and condiments.

We got lucky once and found a backyard garden. I had the kids to pick it clean and dig up all the root vegetables. We eat fresh salad and tomatoes for a few days. Potatoes taste great with salt and butter, but we only have salt. Zoe got the kids to pretend we have butter.

We cook early in the morning right after the sun comes up. We MacGyver'd up a bunch of solar ovens from a few books one of the kids scrounged up. We put them on the roof of one of the industrial buildings and then go back and check it in the afternoon. We sleep elsewhere. If someone finds the food, they won't find us.

No gas or electricity usage. I didn't want anyone walking up and checking electric meters to see if it was moving. We steal the propane tanks from BBQ grills and cook with those—no briquettes, no smoke. I try hard to teach the kids everything they need to know to be super careful and safe.

There's always something you forget. Most businesses only have one bathroom. The commercial buildings, automotive shops, manufacturing plants, body shops, and offices all just have one bathroom. With thirty-seven people all eating and drinking, it reaches a point where the bathrooms are not available. People want to take a bath, but not everybody wants a cold shower.

A couple of boys pee outside. Boys always pee outside. Boys will be boys, my dad said it enough times. I told them to stop.

Warm lips and breath arrive on my ear. "Sarah, I hear noises outside," someone whispers.

My whole body freezes up. I wasn't asleep. I didn't sleep at night. I hardly ever sleep at all.

My hands reach out, feeling for the face of the person who'd spoken in my ear. We keep everything pitch-black unless there is a night-light naturally in the building. We don't have anything on tonight. It is a girl and her hair runs down the side of her face. I move my face in closer to hers, once my fingers trail past her earlobe. I put my mouth next to it.

"Are you sure it wasn't animals?" The pulse in her neck beats rapidly under my fingers. I turn my head slightly to hear better whoever was talking.

She whispers. "No, I heard footsteps. It wasn't a dog."

I place my hand gently on Zoe's shoulder, making her body jump slightly. She refuses to sleep anywhere but next to me. How she could sleep at night anymore I can't imagine. But I guess I make her feel safe.

I hadn't slept in three days. I catch a snooze or catnap here and there. I don't know why they call them catnaps. Cats never look tired. I am tired, very tired. And yet I'm not able to sleep. Napping isn't working. Nothing works for me.

I pull Zoe's body to mine. "Gather up the little ones and head out the agreed door." Her body shifts and moves away from me. I lean back over to our informer. "Get Nick and the rest of the boys! We need to move out."

The girl's warm body drifts away.

I shift my weight onto the heels of my feet into a squatting position. I reach out and pick up my crossbow while feeling my side to make sure my gun is still there. The last thing in the world I want is to try to lead anybody out of here completely unarmed. I'm never unarmed. I always have something to defend myself with. In my case, if it isn't a sword, it's a knife, a crossbow, or any kind of weapon I can get my hands on. I'd stabbed a stick through the eye of a dog attacking me once. I can still feel the warm blood pouring out of its eye socket and through my fingers. My belly tumbles with the memory.

All I have to do if I want to stop the Fae is open my mouth and raise my voice as loud as I can and sing. But that isn't an option. Using magic feels like meddling in the natural order. It comes too easy for me, and that scares me, along with the little changes that are happening to me. Every time I use it, I become a little more Fae and a little less human.

I hear the humming of a song. The tone is familiar. I can't figure out what it is, the cadence or the vibration, but it sings to the inside of me. It has to be Janice. He will never stop looking for me. If we make it out of this, Nick is right. We can't wait anymore. I am more of a detriment to the kids than a help.

"Come out, come out, wherever you are. I've seen a princess, young and sweet, and I asked her what she likes to eat. She smiled and said mincemeat." His deep tenor song tells me everything. The icy fire flows in my veins. It is Janice; it has to be.

I hear the shifting of bodies like rats in the dark, scurrying away. I stand up involuntarily and begin to hum. At some point in time, Janice will burst through the doors. Maybe he's running around singing everywhere he goes, hoping to spook me, I don't know. He's searching for me. I feel it.

I run into a wall of man flesh, the scent of Axe and Monster energy drinks tells me it is Nick. Nobody else in our group is big enough or drank Monster. His hands rest on my hips.

I reach up and touch his face. His cheek is curved into a wicked smile. I want to smack that smile off his face. I pull his head down so that I can whisper in his ear. "Get the van! I'll sweep up the lagers and cover our backs." He pats my hip in understanding. We move in different directions in our pre-choreographed get-the-hell-out dance.

Janice's singsong bullshit fairytale rhymes fill the background. "Come out, come out wherever you are. I asked her what she wants to eat, and she smiled and said mincemeat."

I know he only says it in his singsong voice because that's how fairies entrance people. They use their music to enslave you. The only way to fight fire is with fire, and I am that fire.

I have to sing and every song costs me. What will I look like if I go back? Will I even still be human? I only got out because I figured out how the magical music works. You can't just sing a song and something suddenly happens. You have to want it to happen. It requires intent.

Fae intend to enslave those humans and then kill them. And every time I think about how they use their music to freeze people, the acid rises in my throat. I swallow even now, trying to keep it at bay. They sang those people to their deaths. I don't understand how you can be so beautiful and so evil all at the same time.

I don't care that Janice said: that he had to do it, what he is doing would save humanity and Fae. I think it's all bullshit. He looks like he enjoys it, and he certainly doesn't seem like it's a problem. If it's all about intent, he has intent. He means to kill humans. He wants to mentally enslave them. It's the only way the magic works.

Warm, little fingers wiggle into the palm of my hand. I glance down to see the moonlight glinting off blonde hair. My stomach tightens as if every muscle in my body coils up in anticipation. There are only three blondes in our group, and two of them are tall. Only one of them is little. Olive. I whip my head left and right, looking for Zoe, but I don't see her anywhere. All that comes back is the shuffling of feet on the other side of the warehouse and sniffing of little noses every now and again. The intake of breath from a yawning mouth as their lips open and close. My eyesight in the dark has improved tremendously in the last few weeks. But I still can't see through the deep gloom. I don't have to. I know where the shuffling feet are going. The little yawning mouths are going exactly where I sent them.

The soft padding of Fae footsteps drifts to me from on the other side of the doors. Fire with fire, the rumbling starts in the back of my throat bone-deep and low. One of those little ditties that you hear people mindlessly humming as they work.

Magic isn't about the song; it's about intent. It doesn't matter what I sing or whether I sing it out loud or whistle. All I have to do is listen for the tone. It is the first thing I do everywhere I go.

Every object sings and I listen to their tunes. The different vibrations they live at. Some are high and sweet, some low and sharp, a few flat as winter snow. Steel. Steel is a chorus, an entire chord. You can hear it as a clear F major. Beautiful. If I hum it just right, I can convince the steel in the doors to merge with the steel in the frame, creating a magical weld by merging the door from being a separate part into a solid single object with the wall.

Don't get me wrong, I know it will not hold long. I just need it to hold long enough.

So, I let the notes reverberate in my vocal cords, keeping my mouth shut. I picture exactly what I want the metal to do. I want it to blend, to merge, to become something more than what it is. No longer separate parts but one solid entity.

The shifting of the door handle stops. Then for good measure, it twists again. Obviously, someone was turning it from the left to the right. But the only thing moving is the handle. Even the bolt doesn't slide anymore.

Oops! Oh darn, I guess, I welded that too . With my arm stretching out behind me and still holding the warm little fingers, and move swiftly across the room. It is easy to maneuver around the various tools. They are the modular cases for Snap-On tools. Auto mechanics keep all of their tools in these big boxes. They lock and roll. It's easier to roll your tools from one vehicle to the next, and all I have to do is dodge around them like a dancer.

With every song I sing, it becomes easier. My body is light and agile. I bend like a willow or jump like a note. Every now and again I feel myself floating as I come down. As if I am a feather.

A clang slices through the air, jarring me and I freeze mid-step and turn to see the saucer-shaped eyes.

"I'm sorry I didn't mean to." Olive's lower lip puffs out.

I don't reply. There is no point. Olive didn't mean to knock the wrench down. I scoop her into my arms and leap across the room.

"Now, Mary, Mary, aren't you being contrary? Open this door and show yourself." Janice calls.

Really, he can't even get one fucking nursery rhyme, right? He twists them around and fucking them up. My feet know the way to go. I exit the back door of the warehouse and into the yawning opening of a van where little bodies are stacked one on top of the other. I smell the sweet breath of children along with sickly sour of fear, then drop Olive on someone's lap and step in myself, crouching down to shut the doors as quickly as possible.

"Hit the gas, Nick! Let's get the fuck out of here. Now!" I shout, as the roar of the engine and the heat replaces my voice. One of the older boys sits in the passenger seat —Stephen. He's smart, good with a crossbow, big and strong, and most of all Nick trusts him. The vehicle jolts forward. I put my left hand out, steadying myself on the headrest as I reach out with my right to lock the side door. I gaze over the others and then turn around to get a look at our six.

Nick's voice cuts the tension. "What's behind us?" He demands.

Steadying myself as best I can, I lean over the Lincoln log pile of children's bodies, and survey the scene outside the driver's side windows. "The Fae are already behind us," I reply.

Janice jumps down off one of the abandoned vehicles, landing light as a feather in the back alley. I have to admire his abilities. He is almost like a god with his long white hair fanning out behind him. As his hair falls down to his shoulders, his clothes highlight the tips; they're black, that's new. His skin is opalescent in the moonlight, his smiling teeth gleam. That isn't what gets me, it's those violet eyes. The windows on the van are tinted, but he stares through them, right into the heart of me.

My chest clenches. Is it excitement or fear? Part of me longs for him to come and find me and end this game of cat and mouse. I feel it in my chest, the increase in my breathing, a flush on my face. The other part of me cringes away. the part of me I think is still human and it's stronger one, for now.

That's when the revulsion always hits and the burning bile rises in my throat. My instinct is to do anything to get away from those evil creatures.

Everything about the Fae draws you in their beauty, their song and mostly the way they stare at you as if you are the only creature in the world. But for me, it is almost as if the human in me, the survival instinct that we all intrinsically have, rails against their attempts to ensnare me. All I want to do is get away from them. My internal war lasts as long as I allow my eyes to stare into his. It could have been an eternity or only a second.

The van shifts turning a corner. Our gaze is broken, as is the spell. I sag against the release, part of me jubilant, I'm free. The other part of me cries out for the loss.

CHAPTER 4

Nick drives around in the city for twenty minutes, circling several times and criss-crossing down streets. I keep my eyes sharp out the passenger's side windows.

Our lights are off. All of them. Stephen, our gearhead, has even managed to unplug the fuses for the brake lights. I don't know how stealthy you can be in a huge cargo van with thirty-seven kids piled all over the place. Muttering and sniffling abound, along with all the wide eyes. I have to keep tearing myself away from their deep stares.

Terror, when you're around children, it's a palpable thing. They reach out for the adult, seeking the solace they can't find within themselves. They climb all over Zoe. They love Zoe. She's kind, patient, and calm for a fifteen-year-old. She's great with kids. Try as I might, they steer clear of me. I have my moments. Truth is, I think most of them only cling to me because they see me as a source of power, thinking maybe I will keep them safe.

In the daylight, they don't want anything to do with Nick or I. But as soon as the sun goes down, they cling to Nick and sometimes me. They're scared. Hell, I'm scared. But you can't be scared and in charge. Children—people, aren't looking for a crybaby. They want to know you can save them. You must be all-knowing; you can't have self-doubt. You must know the answers to all the questions, and if you don't, you fake it. That's what people look for in a leader. I have to be ten moves ahead, planning for the next ten. The unknown and indecisiveness, they're killers. They allow chaos to creep in and cut your group to pieces bit by bit.

The van shifts back and forth as it turns, jostling my body left and right. We drive serpentine down many roads to avoid the dead bodies—the human logs. They lie all over the residential neighborhoods on the road, on the sidewalks, across yards and porches. The stench of death still fills the air and filters through the vents into the van. That sickly sweet scent of rotting meat coats the back of your throat, gagging you until you taste the vitriol rising to meet it. I swallow it all back, breathing through my mouth.

The driving rocks the van back and forth, soothing sleepy little bodies. The smacking of lips and exhaled breaths from little yawns reaches my ears and the tense pile of children's bodies sag into a relaxed sleep. My eyes trail over them in envy. I wish I could find that kind of rest.

Finally, we enter another industrial district. Warehouses line the roads around us, some of them the dark gray of CBS block, others the rusty red of steel buildings. Nick drives around in circles before he turns left, heading down a narrow lane to the last building on the line.

There's a bay door open enough for the van to slip inside the workshop. The gloom envelopes us, and Nick switches the engine off, allowing us to glide to a stop. The door handle clicks as Stephen jumps out of our still moving van. His door doesn't quite catch to close. He trots back and lowers the bay door with the chain, painfully slow.

"All right, kiddies, we made it to our next destination. If everyone would like to exit the van to the right, we will move into our next hovel," Nick snickers under his breath. He thinks he's clever.

Glaring at Nick through the darkness, I bit my lip. The last thing in the world these kids want is his smart-ass comments, but I keep my thoughts to myself; no point in having an argument out in the open. I don't care if we are inside a van. We're still out in the open. Every moment we waste here is a risk.

I unlatch the two doors, slowly pushing them open with the utmost of care. Then I lower my feet to the floor with my crossbow shouldered, my right hand on the trigger, and my left hand holding the tip up. I move it from the left to the right, scanning the room. the vibrations around me are normal, but I trust my eyes more than my new ability. The soft foot falls of Nick's shoes come around from the driver side.

He squats down in front of me, placing his fingers into the grate in the floor. This warehouse has an unusual feature. There is a large rain drain towards the back of the building as if the building had been built over a parking lot or street. I'm sure a lot of people thought it was for drainage. They used a lot of water in this building, water jetting small machine parts.

When I had first found this shop, I was hoping for an entrance to the sewers along with an exit. Water did drain down to the sewers. However, when I explored it two weeks before, I found a door. It was unlocked and opened into a shelter of some kind. Who knew? That was the beginning of the plan. To train our band of escapees to fend for themselves.

Nick and I both groomed Zoe and Stephen to take over. All our plans were to get here, where the kids would be safe until we got back. If we got back.

I see the gaping hole in the cement floor and nod my head to Zoe in the dim light while snapping my fingers. The kids move like waves, parting to let her by. Nick grabs both of her hands around the wrist and swings her down into the hole, slowly lowering her. I watch her, inch by inch, disappearing into the inky blackness. A few moments later a dim glow comes from the pit. She'd found the light in the shelter.

"Let's get the hell out of this workshop." Nick's voice reverberates off the steel walls. The double meaning isn't lost on me, he's desperate to leave.

One of the other little girls urges children forward, lining up next to Nick. The teenagers jump down by themselves. Nick lowers the little ones, one by one, to the bigger kids. Stephen moves over and stands next to the edge of the pit. He gives me a scout salute and then steps off the edge into the blackness. Nick hands the smallest children down to Stephen. I keep surveying the area. No one is here. I can't hear anything. It's only the sounds of insects and wind, the scurrying of a rat or maybe a cockroach. I don't want to think about the last one too much.

When the Fae come, all sound ceases. Everything goes to sleep or disappears, scampering away desperate to not be noticed. Even the rocks die. It's as if the world freezes at their will. All, except me. I don't freeze for them. I will never freeze for them.

Finally, only Nick and I remain. "Ladies first," he smiles.

I cock an eyebrow at him.

"You know the gig. We've already practiced this. It doesn't work that way. Go on! I'll be right down." I reply.

He jumps down into the hole, and I hear an umph and a splash as he hits the bottom.

Stepping to the edge, I squat down and lower my bottom to the floor. I don't want to think about all the dirt and grime on the floor. I'm wearing jeans. There's no way in hell it's ever gonna reach my panties or any other part of me. However, my hands are thick with mud. I lean over and pull the grate to me, covering half the hole. I'm left with enough space to slip through.

My feet dangle down into the dark gloom. I turn over onto my belly, sliding down blindly into the hole. Nick's large hands wrap around my ankles. Using his hands, he guides my feet until I meet the reassuring firmness of his shoulders. I settle myself, and his strong hands clasp my calves, bracing me. It's the only way I can keep my balance. My arms reach up high enough for me to slide the grate into place.

With my hands trailing along the moist wall, I lower my right knee and then my left to Nick's shoulders. I rub the grime off my hands onto my jeans. Nick's hands slide up my hamstrings over my butt, reaching my waist. I take both Nick's hands in a climber's grip. I straighten both legs, allowing my body to slide down his back. My feet dangle until they reach the floor. Nick and I had only practiced this three times.

I never thought I'd be doing any kind of acrobatics, truth be told. When I stand on Nick's shoulders, I'm scared to death I'll fall. The only thing reassuring me is the likelihood of me falling is extremely low in an enclosed tunnel.

As soon as my feet touch the floor, I allow the humming vibration in my throat to fill me with an intense desire. I picture the entire grate welding into the metal frame surrounding the entrance to the sewer system. I let it go long enough, picturing the metal merging in my mind. There's a point where the magical creation and the Acappella sound fills you. You feel the intent flowing, and then it pops. Whatever it is you meant to do, it succeeds, requiring nothing more. When it reaches the crescendo, I let the sound drift away.

All I want is to close the door to the shelter, twist the locks, and sleep. Three small screws hit the top of my head. My face turns up to the grate, revealing two eyes gazing down at me. They are wide and frightened.

"Don't leave me, Sarah! I didn't mean to oversleep. I'll stay awake next time, I promise. Please don't leave me behind." Olive pleads.

My eyes dart down the tunnel, but Nick has already sauntered away. I dash down the hall, grabbing Nick's hand.

"Little girl, little girl, are you lost? Have you forgotten where you live? Where are your parents? Do they live?" Janice's sing-song voice reaches down the dark depths of the tunnel to me.

Ice fills my veins. They waited until we were out of the van. He'd waited—Janice.

How did he track us?

CHAPTER 5

Blue eyes peek over the edge as moonlight glints off the blonde trendles trailing down at me.

"Where's Zoe?" The pitch of Olive's voice scrapes over the butterflies in my belly, killing them all.

My heart jumps into my throat. Nick's large hand wraps around my bicep, pulling me back into the shadows. The gloom of the light down the hall is gone, Nick must have shut the door. The tunnel lines with inky blackness. I know stepping into the shadows isn't going to be enough. If even one of those creatures' peeks over the side, they might very well pick Nick and me out of the dark. I push him farther down the tunnel. He pulls me with him.

"Hide and seek is really neat, especially if someone has what you want to find," Janice announces.

A bloodcurdling scream slices the air. I watch in horror as the head of the little girl above us disappears from the grate. A muffled whimpering is silenced.

Janice continues, "I know you're here somewhere, Sarah. I have something you want. This little girl. If you want her, then you know what you need to do. Just because you left the competition doesn't mean you're done competing. The Fae need you. Humanity needs you, and if you don't come, you will regret it and so will this little girl, along with the rest of humanity. Do you hear me, Sarah? You want Olive to live? You know where I am." His voice becomes as deep as the caverns the Fae live in.

Nick pulls me deeper into the darkness.

I strain against Nick's restraints. *Janice, you fucking bastard! Why couldn't you just leave us alone?* The singsong sound welcomes me, caressing me. I want to cry out, but I can't.

Nick's large hands drag me through the door of the shelter. He turns the lock and the cylinders shoot home sealing us in.

"Why didn't you just leave me out there? I'm the one they want. They don't want you." The tears are already running down my cheeks as my hands beat his chest. Nick grabs my wrist, holding them to his chest. I desperately work to wrench free.

"Are you kidding, Sarah? We have a plan. What did he mean you're a contender? Why do they want you bad enough to follow you no matter where you go and take small children?" His eyes bore into my mine. I haven't told him everything. The pressure in my chest grows.

"The Fae are having some kind of sick fight or contest. What do I give a shit what for? They kill us indiscriminately, steal children, and chop off the heads of parents." I give him a dry laugh. "But they don't take the ugly ones, Nick. Have you ever noticed that?" Hysteria is close hovering just under the surface waiting to bubble forth. "Is your sister pretty? Are you strong? Because that's all they take, the pretty and the strong. Everybody else is expendable to them." I shout.

His fingers dig into my arm. his thumb separates the muscle between my triceps and the bone creating a burning sensation. It hurts, but it's a welcome relief from the pain building inside of me. The moment I turn around and walk away from Nick, I have to go into the next room and Zoe will be there. Her big blue eyes will stare at me, asking why we were shouting, and I'd tell her. My chest burns, and a big lump forms in my throat along with hot tears running down my cheeks.

"Let go of me, Nick! Let me go out there. Let me get Olive back."

If I give in, maybe Janice will take me to Arty. Then I can save them both.

Nick's face closes in on mine, breathing over me. Our noses are practically touching, and his hazel eyes bore into mine. "If you think they're going to give that little girl back because you give yourself up, you're a bigger fool than I ever thought. They won't give her back; they'll keep her. And yes, my sister is beautiful, and yes, I'm big and strong. I did notice that's all they take. Which is why we made the plan." He says.

My head presses into the wall behind it. I can't lean back anymore. I have to face this.

I push my forehead into his. It is something I'd seen male dogs do when they wanted to dominate the others. The alpha pushes his forehead down opposing the opponent. With my eyes directly in line with his, my eyebrow and hairline combine into his.

"Arty isn't my blood, but he is my brother and I love him. If you think it doesn't burn me every day that you're standing here and not him, you're wrong. I would've kicked your ass right off those goddamn rocks and taken him instead if I knew what I know now. If I'd had to sacrifice one, it wouldn't have been him. That's why we made the plan."

Nick pulls back his fingers, releasing my arm. I instinctively move my shoulder and flex my bicep a couple of times, swinging my arm back and forth to get the blood flowing.

"Everything we've been doing was to get here. Somewhere the kids would be safe without us. A place Zoe and Stephen can work from. I won't let you throw all that away." Nick's words sting me.

I reply, "Yes, that was the plan. But if we move quickly, we might be able to save Olive. If we leave now we won't and I'm not throwing this opportunity away."

The meaty paw that a minute ago had been tearing the shit out of my joints scratches his face. He rolls his head around on his shoulders. I hear a vertebra pop, and he turns his head and locks his eyes on to mine.

"Okay, smarty-pants. Now that you're ready, I'll go help you save this kid. We bring Olive back while we're getting my sister and your stupid friend." Nick's voice is low, and the words come out as a whisper.

I can't lose Nick; I need him. He helps keep the mob in order and has my back at every turn. I'd misjudged Nick. I don't want him to leave. "Yes, we're going back."

A gleam fills his eyes as a wicked grin scrapes across his face. He crosses his arms with his hands underneath his biceps. You know, the big guy pose, the one that always makes their biceps look bigger. "About damn time." He replies.

There are backpacks dumped all over the hallway. The kids had divested themselves from their excess weight before they went into the shelter proper. I scavenge around until I find a few bottles of water and a couple of energy bars. I throw a couple at Nick. He catches them and shoves them into his backpack. I sling my pack over my shoulder.

"Okay, let's go!" My heart hammers in my chest.

Zoe's voice cuts through the blood roaring in my ears. "You're leaving? Why are you leaving? You're just going to abandon us?" she demands.

If I had been a sail, every breath of wind within one hundred miles would've disappeared for me. Her words deflate me, and my shoulders sag down. My eyes drop to the floor. Nick turns and looks away with his hand on the locking mechanism.

"They took Olive. I think she fell asleep in the van. We didn't go back and double-check. I'm going to get her." The words tumble out in a jumble.

A strangled cry is muffled by a hand. "You left her in the van?" Zoe accuses.

I move my head up and down; I can't look at her.

"You left my sister, my six-year-old sister, in the van, and now the Fae have her again?" Zoe's voice cracks.

Nick steps in. "Yes, Zoe. Your sister got left behind. It could just as easily have been any other kid in this group. Don't scream at Sarah; she was ready to go out there alone. I'm going with her. You and Stephen stay here and take care of the kids. Sarah and I will seal the door from outside. We'll make sure they can't get in from the sewers. Keep the other end of the tunnel open. Be ready to leave if you need to." Nick moves to my side, facing Zoe. "Stephen and I stocked this place up with enough food to last a year for ten people, so you

~ 50 ~

can probably stay here for three or four months, maybe longer if you guys ration." He finishes.

The muffled crying doesn't stop. Keeping my eyes on the wall, I turn around and hug Zoe. I feel the wetness of her tears on my neck, and they burn hot like the rage I hold inside.

"I will come back with your sister. I swear! I will never return without your sister." My voice quavers as I leave the unspoken *alive* floating in the air.

"She's all I have left. Our parents are dead. If you don't come back with my sister, I'll stab a knife right through your heart. Just like you did mine." She whispers.

I pull back from the force of her words. I'd never heard Zoe so mean. She's a runner. She isn't a fighter. She's sweet, kind and gentle. What she said, cut me to the bone. My veins fill with the ice of the cool, calm, and collected threat issued by this sweet girl.

Zoe's words kick me in the ass. Nick is willing to do anything for his sister. All this slow planning has robbed me of the will to kill whoever I need to get to Arty. That fire I'd had when I left the Hallowed Hills, it rages back, pushing the fear away and leaving only the determination I need.

I turn without meeting her eyes and nod to Nick. He turns the handle, unlocking the door. Zoe, tight-lipped, closes the door in my face. The humming starts in my throat, reaching out to the door and fusing the metal into one massive lump, locked in concrete.

Under the grate, I hum my song, separating the metals and dividing them into two pieces as if nothing had ever happened. Nick locks his fingers together, forming a basket for my foot. He hoists me up, and I place one foot on his shoulder and then the other. I angle the grate out of its seat, moving it so it only half covers sewer entrance.

My eyes peek above the edge, surveying the floor in the warehouse. It is empty. No one is here. Of course, they wouldn't be here. Why would Janice stay? He already succeeded in his mission. His dogged attempts to find and corner me had paid off. He'd gotten what he wanted. I'm sure he was surprised when I didn't return for Arty.

Clearing my throat Nick's hand releases my ankle. He cups my foot with his hand. I press down as he pushes up, locking my leg straight. It gives me enough height to place both of my hands on either side of the floor, and I press myself out of the hole and roll onto my belly and hoist my legs out.

Reaching underneath one of the workstations, I pull out a rope I hid there. I tie it around one of the wheels of the van and throw it down the hole. Nick climbs out, eyes darting left and right.

"They're not here. He got what he came for and left." I sigh. "We can't risk opening the roll-down door. We'll have to leave the van here and go on foot." I hoist my backpack over both shoulders and reposition the crossbow strap.

After my mistake with Arty, I'd never been caught without good shoes. Last few weeks I'd done more walking than my entire life. My legs had grown strong and muscular. I'm in for a long walk, but it will take my mind off what comes next.

Closing my eyes, I listen to the tune of the building and the surrounding area. There are no disruptions. They use music to create their magic. If I can somehow follow them using their magic against them, we can snatch Olive back. Using slow steady steps, we work our way to the nearest exterior door with a big, glowing exit light over the top of it. One of the cool things about commercial buildings and commercial spaces is there's always a big glowing sign pointing to the way out.

We depart the building, following along the exterior, keeping to the shadows as much as possible. Not that I think keeping to the shadows like teenage ninjas is truly going to help. My eyesight in the dark has improved, but the Fae must be markedly better. For me, everything has become glowing colors of varying shades of green. There is no black and white at night. It is like having my own version of night vision naturally. I can see Nick relatively clearly. Fae probably see us as clear as day. But sticking to the shadows does make Nick feel safer. I can't very well explain to him how I know that it doesn't help.

If I tell Nick my eyesight was better and why, for all I know he might kill me himself. That certainly isn't going to save Arty or Olive. The footsteps behind me are soft and steady, as is Nick's breathing. None of that wide mouth panting. For such a big guy, Nick moves with some serious stealth. Even I find him barely perceptible, and he's right behind me. From a distance, if you didn't see him, you wouldn't know he's there. Maybe all those years playing football taught him how to breathe better and tiptoe around.

We cross an alley between two warehouses, and there is something here. A vibration in the air towards the center of the street. It's different, and it shouldn't have been there. I step out of the center of the alleyway, moving beyond. The vibration disappears. I take one step back without looking and right onto Nick.

"We're supposed to be going forward, Sarah, not backward," he whispers in my ear.

"Sorry, there's something here," I reply. He doesn't ask any questions. I take one more step back and move around in a circle, turning this way and that. The vibration goes to the left down the center of the alleyway. So, I follow it.

"You got your cotton balls in your ears?" I inquire.

A dark laugh follows. "You're kidding?" Nick replies.

It's all I need to know, just making sure he isn't going to become entranced and run off or start fighting me unwittingly. The vibration in the center of the alleyway tells me this is the way to go, a musical fairy-trail. There is no way in hell I'm gonna stop following this sound, whatever the hell 'IT' is, the invisible musical notes. My body picks up into a jog, and my breathing grows heavy.

"Sarah, we're out in the open. We should be off to the side where the shadows are." His voice is nervous, imploring me to change my course.

"No, this is where the trail is. We have to follow it. This may be the only way to get back into the Hallowed Hills. Either I take us or they do," I retort.

"Well, I'd rather get there under my own speed if you don't mind." He grumbles.

The reply slides off my back like water on a duck. "Me too, but at this point, it doesn't really matter how we get there as long as we get there. It will be just as easy for me to save Olive and Arty if they've already taken me where they are." I'm tired of arguing all the time with Nick, but a deal is a deal.

"They're not gonna take you to wherever their captives are. They'll keep you separate. Don't be stupid!" Nick quips.

I hate when Nick calls me stupid. "They're only going to keep us separate if I don't make any demands. And I won't participate in their stupid competition if they don't let me see Arty, Olive, and Nikki in the flesh." It sounds good, but I'm not certain it will work out that way.

CHAPTER 6

My feet pound into the asphalt as pressure on chest muscles strains my lungs. I'm doing my best to throw it down the road, and following close behind me is Nick. He'd probably pass me if he knew where he was going, but he doesn't.

The humming of my fairy-trail grows louder with every step. We exit the industrial district and move past a shopping plaza before I'm left standing in the street with the trail screaming in my head from every direction. No matter which way I walk, it doesn't lead away. I smack my hand to my head because of course, it doesn't lead away. They hadn't gone anywhere else; they left.

I still pick up the trendles of the music as it reverberates in the air. Glancing around, sound waves drift up into the air.

The skin around my eye's wrinkles in frustration. "They left. They jumped on their platform here and left." I kick at nothing on the road. "Goddamn it!" The scream tears at my throat.

An unfamiliar cough breaks the silence. The hair on the back of my neck stands up as I turn towards the sound. Nick shoots to my side in an instant.

"So, you're interested in killing fairies too?" Two steel-gray eyes and a crew cut issue the words. He has an earpiece. I give him the once-over, typical fatigues, combat-style boots. All the gear my father stored away ten years ago in a closet.

"Yeah, I'm tracking fairies too. They took a little girl." I toss my head back to scan the sky.

Two other men, probably weekend warriors, flank the jarhead. "You're a very interesting looking woman." One of the weekend warriors' comments then lets his tongue hang out.

I reach up and run my fingers into the hair at my crown, fluffing it around my ears. My eyes had become an unusual shade of green, but so far, I think that was the only telltale sign other than my ears.

"You know, there aren't that many of us humans left. The Fae like taking us. I haven't seen a pretty girl in quite a while now." He tilts his head down to stare at me through bushy eyebrows.

Nick steps forward, but he doesn't touch me. I get the distinct impression he's there to defend me. Not sure how I feel about that. "Yeah, my sister's pretty. What of it?" He lets his arms hang loose at his side, flexing his hands.

Oh, that's his game. I'm his sister which certainly makes more sense.

"Look, we're hunting fairies, your hunting fairies. Why don't we work together? We escaped from the Fae with her help. We're trying to figure a way back. Either you want in for the ride, or you want to be an asshole. Make your choice." Nick retorts.

I'm not sure how smart Nick is. After all, there are only two of us, and I'm a girl. There are three of them. They're bigger with guns, and I don't think he can fight off three dudes—men who clearly look like they hit the gym pretty regularly.

"You mean to go where they go." One of them laughs, leaning back with his tongue out, while Capitan Steel rubs his chin with his free hand.

"Yeah, they live somewhere. We were there and got out. Now we want to get back, so either you're in for the ride or you're just a fucking asshole standing in our way. Which is it?" Nick puffs up with his comeback.

I'll give it to Nick. He has a set of brass ones for sure. Mouthing off to three jarheads isn't smart, but then again, guys like to show who's got the biggest...

"If you guys are going in, we're going with you." The leader, Capitan Steel, stands stock-still, his eyes still boring into me.

"Whoa, whoa, Nick. Backup. First of all, we don't know these guys. Don't know anything about them." I let my eyes drill right back into Captain Steel. "Why would we trust them? If I'm going back to the Hallowed Hills, I only want to take people I can trust." I say while lowering my voice.

Capitan Steel cuts in. "I hear what you're saying. We're all that's left of our crew. Everybody else in our squad's dead. Fae cut 'em down. They lock us up with their voices and then bleed us dry. There's no way I'm staying here. If you have a way to get wherever they live, I want to take the fight to them. My name's Jake. This here's Will." He tips his head to a man to his right.

"My name's Tom," The short guy with his tongue out supplies. Tom looks like a short version of Joe Pesci, with a New York Little Italy haircut and all.

Nick puffs himself up in a man stance, the one where they try to make every muscle look as big and bulging as possible. "We get on the other side, she's in charge. I don't give a shit who you are, or what you think you know. The only reason why I'm alive is her." Nick's proclamation isn't what I had in mind.

They lower their weapons, enough to show they aren't a threat for now. Will's eyes never find me. Instead they scan the area.

"You know how to keep the Fae from entrancing you?" I inquire.

"We filled one ear with cotton balls, and we got an earpiece in the other so their singing doesn't work," Will replies.

"Or you could be like me and be completely tone-deaf so their music doesn't mean shit to me." Jake is funny. I can't help it. I crack a smile. I suppose being tone-deaf would do it if the singing works on vibrations.

Perhaps they haven't noticed the peak of my ear and the unusual shade of my green eyes. Or am I naturally compelling everyone at this point in time without even realizing it? When I compelled Lavender in the Hallowed Hills, I yelled. I was angry. I didn't care if she was supposed to be a Fae lady's maid-type person. She changed my hair color without my permission. It isn't that she changed my hair that bothers me anymore. Now it's growing out the same color, and my hair was never black. It's brown. Boring brown. That's me, boring, brown Sarah. Now I have black hair and green eyes.

I feel like everyone who sees me can tell that there's something not quite right. They can see I'm different from them. Olive's the only child that doesn't shy away from me. They feel it on a deeper level, like when all the hair on the back of your neck stands up. Or you don't know why you turn to drive home a different way than normal. Then you find out there's an accident on the other road.

"You don't have any other friends?" Nick's voice takes on that note of suspicion you get when you're being set up.

"No, we're a three-man crew now. There were more of us but not anymore." Jake locks his jaw down hard on the last word, pressing his lips into a thin line.

"Yeah, they killed Reilly real good," Tom says. "One purple-eyed motherfucker cut his head off. Right in front of me, Reilly didn't even raise his hand. He knelt down in front of the pointy-eared bastard. Then he chopped Reilly's head right off. It rolled away like a soccer ball. I guess the only blessing in the whole situation is Reilly's parents are dead. So, they'll never know, there's no next of kin to inform. Just us." Tom's assessment is cringe-worthy, to say the least, but it explains the blood splatter on their faces and clothes.

I hadn't seen Arty's dad get his head cut off. I'd only seen the aftermath. It didn't change the fact that someone had walked right up to him and cut his head off. Phil was a nice guy. I wouldn't wish that on anyone. I guess, the only consolation is he went quickly.

Those poor kids at my youth group sure didn't. They bled out slow. I can't stop the scene from filling my mind. Pastor Rollins' torn shirt and swollen eyes, kneeling in the grass with the arrow through his chest and dry blood crusted around his lips, and all those bloody hands in the grass.

Nick hadn't seen it. I hadn't told anyone about it. What's the point? Everybody has their own little story about how the Fae fucked up their family or their lives.

"We need to get out of the open," Jake announces. "This group might be gone, but there could be others running around. They're still scouring the towns. According to the squawk on the street, they're moving into the cities. Cleaning them out pocket by pocket." Jake's tone of voice is no nonsense and in charge.

"Why do you suppose they started out here in the burbs?" Nick asks. "I'm sure the pickings in the city are better than here." Nick's question surprises me.

"Fewer people, less resistance. Who knows?" Jake's steel-gray eyes clock the area.

I take one step toward the other side of the street. All four take a step-in unison, shadowing me. I stop and turn to stare at them. "Well, I wasn't creepy or anything." I laugh nervously.

Nick smiles. "Sorry. You take a step, I take a step. I'm with you. You're my only chance of saving Nikki." He says.

The other three guys don't say anything. I lift my left foot while eyeballing the jarheads off to my right. I want to see if they are going to mirror me again. They don't. The moment I set my left foot down and lean forward, all three of them take a step.

Nick doesn't. "Okay, that is creepy. What's up with you dudes? Why are you mirroring everything she does?" Nick asks.

They're following me, but I don't think they realize what they're doing. In their minds, everything is normal. I compelled them, but their eyes aren't glazed over. I took their free will and somehow compelled them to follow me unquestioningly.

Nick shrugs.

The desire to free them wells up in my throat. I swallow it back. I don't want to sing, but it has to be done. They need free will and the ability to control their own bodies. Not follow me step-by-step. I need them fully cognizant and making their own decisions. It's our best chance of protecting ourselves.

We are still in the middle of the street, so I head for the nearest tree. It's easier to sing closer to nature. Man-made structures block the vibrations. The humming of life is sweeter, it changes with soil. I heard someone say when you're in contact with nature, that's where the magic happens. It's true. When I stand on the grass with the soil beneath my feet, I feel the magic. I feel their songs. They rise up through the ground, seeping into my skin and saturating every part of me. I'm compelled to react, to sing.

The Three Stooges follow me step-for-step.

"You three stay here." I leave them by a couple of trees. Reaching out, I grab Nick's wrist and drag him about ten feet away. He doesn't resist my pull. He's a big guy, so making him go anywhere is difficult.

In a low voice, I explain, "I've compelled them. Not like you were." Looking from Nick to the three jarheads, then back to Nick. "You don't remember anything. But they're forced to do whatever I do. To follow me. I have to stop it, so I'm going to sing. They will have their free will back. I need you to not freak out, and if they freak out, I need you to stop them." I stare into Nick's wide eyes and nod, he in turn slowly begins to nod with me.

Ridges form between Nick's eyes as his arms cross. He tilts his head and opens his mouth a couple of times to say something. I hear air escape as he frees one of his hands to point at them. "I'm not going to begin to understand. I'm not going to try to understand what it is you just said to me, or how it is you know that. You've never told me what happened to you in the Hallowed Hills. But if it gets me back to my sister,

I will defend you to my dying breath. I told you that." He finishes.

I return, "I know you have my back as long as we get your sister, but I may have to do things that I can't explain, or don't want to explain, and it's gonna change me. It's been changing me, and all I need you to do for as long as you can is please help me. You want Nikki; I want Arty and Olive. We both want to get the fuck away from the Fae. Those are our objectives. I don't care what their objectives are." I wave my hand in the direction of my shadows.

"Once I have my sister, if you're a little too weird for me, I'll take her and leave," Nick says. "Until then, yes. I have your back unequivocally. I'm never gonna side with them. You're my best hope for Nikki." He locks his jaw down, re-crossing his arms.

I don't know why I need to reassure myself of Nick's intentions, but hearing his affirmation comforts me.

CHAPTER 7

Standing in front of the Three Stooges, I let the magic begin. My chest rises, and air fills my lungs, the feel of oxygen flows into my nostrils. My eyes close, and all around me, the low hum of the natural world rocks with my breathing. I coil in my mind.

The memory of Janice enslaving Arty plays over. It's the key to unlocking everyone's mind.

The notes rip from my lips in a gentle C, followed by an E and G. The chord resounds off the trees and the soil.

The men in front of me visibly sag with release, each rubbing their foreheads while shaking the fog away. Magic is a drug; it fucks with your mind. Their eyes dart around in fear and shock.

"You made me stand here." Jake unholsters his sidearm, aimed at me, with a finger on the trigger.

The force of Nick's hand splays over my chest, thrusting me back. My heart speeds up. Had I done the right thing?

"Take it easy, Jarhead. She just freed you and your pals." I step out from behind Nick to the three sets of hard eyes.

Jake growls out. "How did that happen?"

I shake my head. "I don't know, but you're free now and that's all that matters. If the Fae try to compel you, I can stop them. That's what's important." I offer.

Jake still has his weapon trained on me. "How do I know you aren't going to compel me again?" he demands.

"She didn't do it on purpose. Do you want to kill Fae? She's our best chance." Nick's voice hardens as he moves back into a protective stance in front of me.

"It's okay, Nick. They're not going to hurt me." I step out from behind him again.

I know a change has happened. There's something different about me, a little bit less human. Every song and note facilitate that slow transition from day to night, where the sunlight bleeds away, and the darkness creeps up on you slowly. Until all at once, you realize you're standing in the dark and Fae.

I continue, "Either you trust me and you'll follow me, or you don't and you'll kill me. Make up your mind!" I lift my chin to face their choice, whatever it was.

Jake grips his M9 Beretta tighter. I see the flexing movement in the tendons on the back of his hand. As the muscles in his head tighten, the blood vessels in his neck bulge. He's exerting an effort to restrain himself; he wants to shoot me. I can almost taste his desire.

All of nature around me is silent with anticipation as if they are holding their breath. Jake pulls his arm back and runs the fingers of his left hand through his hair. The grip of his sidearm presses into his skull.

"I'm not gonna kill you. I feel like I should, but I can't. I don't trust you, but if you get me where I can kill Fae, till my own death comes to me, that's good enough for now." He holsters his weapon. Tom and Will take a step back and relax.

It isn't an allegiance, but I'll take it.

"Since you seem to have all the answers. What's your plan? How do you get us where they go?" Jake locks both hands back on the M4 carbine hanging from his shoulder strap.

That is the $64,000 question, isn't it?

I keep going over in my mind what I'd heard Janice do when our rafts lifted. He'd sung a haunting song, one of Fae. His desire to go home had been deep and aching. The sound of it had resounded inside of me. I'd felt the pull. His desire had become my desire, and I could taste in my throat his love for the beauty of the Hallowed Hills. The melody of the song still rang in the back of my mind, haunting me. When I slept, I would dream of it and long for that place.

"We have to go back to where we came out. I have to go home, to the maze stones." I chance a glimpse at Nick and dart back to Jake.

Nick claps his hands together, rubbing them. "Great. Let's go back to the pile of rocks."

I move my head up and down. I said as much as I wanted to say for now.

"Where's home? How do we get there?" Jake is direct and to the point.

"Across town," I reply.

Without a word, Jake turns and nods to Tom and Will, and we head deeper into the shopping district.

Human logs fill the parking lots next to cars. The air is filled with the stench of rotting flesh. I pull my bandanna around my neck and up over my nose and mouth to block out the bugs and the stink. It might've done a better job if I'd rubbed it under my armpit first.

The real secret to traveling around is to not look down at the bodies. Otherwise, you get a full view of maggots wriggling around in torn flesh, on eyes, and out of mouths. The sound of clicking claws and scurrying feet meets us at every turn. If I don't watch the ground, I miss the places on their bodies where rats, dogs, or birds had pecked, torn, or ripped the flesh away. The hot sun burns down, turning different parts of bodies from a soft white and pink to dark brown. In some places, the skin is cracked, swelling open with maggots tumbling out.

Traveling on foot is like driving: check your mirrors, left, right, up, down, behind looking for Fae. Jake and his crew do that. Jake takes the lead with Tom on the left and Will on the right. Nick brings up the rear, and somehow, I end up relegated to the center.

Tom reaches out and pats Jake on the shoulder. With his left index finger extended, he points to a big four-wheel-drive truck. A GMC Sierra with a crew cab and a human log lying not far from it. I can't think about the bodies any other way.

Jake brings up his left hand in a fist, giving me enough time to get a very close look at the high and tight haircut on the back of Jake's neck before I run into his spine between his shoulders. I hadn't noticed the signal for stop, so I guess I deserve a face-plant into a sweaty back. My heart rate speeds up. I can't see anything. I'm boxed in by four massive pairs of shoulders. I'd become taller but not enough to beat out these guys.

"Tom, check the body for keys," Jake orders. "Nick, you and Sarah get in it on the passenger side. Will, take shotgun. Tom, you ride behind me."

I move to Nick's side as we execute Jake's orders. I hear the rattle of keys and the clutching of a hand as they're caught. Nick yanks the door open, practically shoving me to the center of the truck. The roar of the engine and the closing of doors all hit it once along with the sandwiching between big shoulders and beefy arms.

Why do they say these trucks can seat six people? I'm sitting here between two men, and there is barely enough room for the three of us. Are they talking about three Leprechauns?

Because there's no way you can fit three full-grown men back here, ever.

CHAPTER 8

I guess Nick must've told Jake where I lived or at least where we'd come out because Jake never asked me for the address. I suppose I could've just leaned back and enjoyed the ride, except there isn't anything about this entire situation that's enjoyable. Everything has taken a turn for the weird. I obsess over the road with my eyes glued to the windows. Truth be told, if we're attacked, I don't want to use magic to save us. I'm not in a position to do much until I get out of the goddamn vehicle. So, I lean back and let it all come at me.

I move forward in my seat as we pull down my parents' street. I don't know what I was expecting. Something is different. Somebody moved the bodies maybe? But it's all hauntingly familiar. There are the same dead bodies, with more decomposition than last time I'd seen them.

The revulsion still creeps up my throat. I can't think about them as my friends and neighbors, or as the woman who lived down the street and used to give me candies for Halloween. Or the old guy who screamed at me because I stole the flowers from his flowerbed. Those people were all dead. All that's left behind are husks of what they'd once been. Humans.

In the center of the road, just as I'd left it in front of my parents' house, is a perfectly round circle of cobblestones in varying shades of gray and brown. I even spot a red or pink one nestled neatly in the center of the road. The truck jostles as Jake rolls over one of my neighbors. Nick's hand squeezes mine. I don't know if I made a sound or not. I swallow the bile as it burns a path up and down my throat.

"Hey, Jake! You want to not drive over Sarah's dead neighbors?" Nick asks.

Heat burns my eyes. *I can't think about this.* I shove the pain back down into my belly, desperate to push it out.

"Oh hey, sorry, man. I didn't realize you guys actually knew this neighborhood." Jake's eyes meet mine in the rearview mirror. He shrugs.

"Yeah, this is where Sarah brought us back. Her parents' house is right there." Nick's hand waves off to the right.

I try to pull my eyes away from the dashboard. I can't seem to snap out of it. My stomach rolls over several times as the rock in my belly grows to a brick. I push back mentally at the brick but it doesn't budge.

"Shit! Open the fucking door, Nick! Before she yacks on us." Tom's words lodge in my throat, holding the dam.

"Hit the Breaks?" Will yells.

Stumbling, I practically fall out of the truck. All of the lovely acidic with its glowing yellow colors spew from between my lips. The muscles in my body clench and unclench, as my hands hold on to my kneecaps.

Rough fingers move over my brow and pull my hair back. "It's okay. Get it out. You'll feel better." Nick's tone is soft and soothing "They're just dead. Remember the Fae can't hurt them anymore." He pets my hair back and rubs a hand up and down my spine.

Moisture drips down my nose as every orifice in my body seems to open up the floodgates. I'm just happy I didn't wet myself.

"Sorry, I didn't know it was is your parents' house." Jake's voice comes from far away. "So, your dad's over there?"

He's talking about Arty's dad. I shake my head to try to gather some more saliva in my mouth so I can spit out the last of the bile. "No, my mom and dad aren't here. Those are Arty's parents."

Nick goes all big brother on me. "Sorry, guys, back off! Give her some air. Let her catch her breath. Here, Sarah, take a swig of this. Swish it around and spit it out. Get the acid off your teeth. You don't want to lose your pretty smile."

Half-cocking a smile to myself. If Arty were here, he'd be the one holding my hair and telling me to go ahead and throw up. Instead, I'm surrounded by a bunch of strange guys and Nick.

Tom throws out, "Lordy, Nick, tell your girlfriend to suck it up, and let's get going." Whatever pity party I was having, it instantly passed.

"He's not my boyfriend, dickweed," I say and spit on the ground near Tom.

"I'm not her boyfriend. I'm her... we're allies. Just like you, we banded together for a common cause." Nick's retort isn't as convincing as mine.

"Ha, told you so. You owe me a twenty there, Jake." Tom laughs, letting his tongue sneak out from between his lips.

Will barks back. "You're a real asshole, you know that? You don't have to bet on everything. I mean, honestly, of course, they're just allies. Shit, look at him. Of course, she doesn't dig him, he's a big *roid* baby." Will shakes his head.

Nick puffs up slapping a fist into his open palm bristling at the idea that I wouldn't want him.

I want to lunge at Will and smack him in the face. There's no reason to hurt Nick, just for fun. But the truth is, I can't fault them. I'm not into betting, but there isn't anything to take the edge off of the reality we're all living in now. More power to him. Everybody needs something. I need a good cry. Nick needs a fight. Jake and Tom need to bet. My question is when did they make the bet? As we were walking up? I hadn't heard them talk about money.

I walk over the grass. It's fresh, green, and singing its sweet song. It draws me in. I don't need to be distracted. I take the tip of my shoe and wipe the puke off. The song sours slightly. Apparently, the grass doesn't like yak either.

"You popped out here?" Jake asks as his steely eyes burn into me.

"Yeah. This is where we touched down." I wave my arms around.

"And you saw this?" Jake points at Nick.

Nick shakes his head. His eyes wander down to the ground. "No, I don't remember anything until I woke up standing here." He tilts his head back. "We were already on the ground. I had the sound of Sarah's voice ringing through my mind, and suddenly it was like waking up from a long nap to the radio playing. I felt groggy like I'd been asleep for a long time, but my body was tired like I'd been running in my sleep. Other than that, I can't remember a thing." Nick shakes off the memory.

Jake swings around to look at me. "Which house is yours?"

I point to the walkway without a dead body in front. "Don't go up the walkway. My father planted Claymores on both the front and back doors." I reply.

Tom pokes around the front yard until a thin wire creases the leg of his fatigues. He squats down and runs his index finger across the line. "Fuck me, she's not kidding. Her old man did." Tom has such a way with words. He lifts the debris covering the box and then replaces it.

I turn my attention to the cobblestone circle. The pavers are surrounded by mushrooms, little brown ones and tall skinny peeked white ones. Some are flat while others are round. A clump of pointy umbrella-like mushrooms dots the circle along with oyster, white button, chanterelles, and grand morel mushrooms. They're all in varying shades of sepia tones, yellows bleeding out to a delicate ivory white, earthy reds, dark browns tipped in purple. Their song calls to me.

The grass and the trees make a chord, they sing in C, E, D, a B-flat here and there. The mushrooms are different, and the air around them is distorted as if they give off heat in a desert. A circle of magical distortion.

"It's a fairy circle." I don't bother to look up at the gasp heard off to the right. "I think we need to stand in the circle, and that's the way back," I remark, then tilt my head to the side.

Will raises his hands and waves us off. "No, I'm not going. You guys go ahead. This is too creepy for me. You're telling me you came back from wherever the Fae live on this pile of rocks, surrounded by mushrooms. No fucking way. I'm sorry. Keep your fairytales to yourselves. I'll stay in the human world. You go wherever the fuck they went without me." Will runs his fingers through his flaming red hair. He promptly turns around and marches down the street with his head held high. I see him shifting his head from left to the right to see if anything is coming.

Jake jumps in. "Okay, William O'Brian, you don't want to play with fairies; that's fine."

"Hey, Will! If you want to help a few kids stay safe, I could point you in the right direction." Nick's voice carries enough for him to hear.

Will stops, turns, and taps his foot on the ground. "I'm listening."

Nick rushes on. "Go to the edge of the Sanburg Industrial district at dawn every morning and wait. Either a little blonde or a bigger guy with brown hair will appear. Tell them Nick and Sarah sent you."

I hold my breath.

"Yeah, I could do that. They friends of yours?" Will inquires.

"Yeah, they are," Nick says.

I'd never heard Nick refer to anyone as a friend. I nudge his shoulder, and he shrugs.

"I suppose I could keep an eye out for a few kids. I ain't goin' with you. I'll do my part from this side." Will turns his back on us and keeps walking back the way we'd come. I heave a sigh of relief.

I don't blame him for leaving. The fairy circle is kind of creepy. If I was still human, I'd feel it was totally creepy too. But whatever I am now, I know I'm not human. I'm not one of them, but I'm not one of us either.

The song of the mushrooms pulls at me, making me smile. Air slides through my nostrils, and the taste of clean air comes from the land of Fae. Deep down inside the pull is like gravity. I want to step through into the circle. The hum throbs with my pulse.

I don't realize I'm leaning forward until Nick's hand locks around my arm.

"Are you okay, Sarah?" he asks.

I glance down at his hand and up into his face. The moment of peace and tranquility emanating from the Fae world lifts from my shoulders—gone. Suddenly, gravity locks me back in place. "Yeah, I'm fine. Anybody who wants to go to the land of Fae, please step inside the mushroom circle." I avert my eyes from the circle. The moment I spy the mushrooms again, I hear their song, and I'm not sure I can stop myself from following it.

Jake announces, "I'm going too. Tom, are you going to run off with Will?" he eyes his friend.

"Well, there's no way I'm gonna win that twenty back if I walk away now. Will doesn't like to gamble. Guess I'll just have to go with you. It's the only way to get paid." Tom replies and shrugs.

It's a shady excuse, but maybe that's his way of saying, 'yeah, I'm going but not for the reasons you think.'

My eyes dart over to Nick.

"You don't have to ask me," Nick says. "You know what my answer is. Let's go! We're burning moonlight." The songs of the mushrooms will diminish as the sun rises. How Nick knows is beyond me. If we were going in, we have to go now.

I step to the edge of the ring, and their song fills me again. It isn't as powerful as before. I'm able to control it—a bit. It fills me, but instead of drawing me to it now I can bend it to my will. "You guys step inside first. I have to go last." I supply.

I watch the magical distortion ripple like a stone in the water as each of them steps over the fungi-covered edge. The three of them take up a triangular position within the circle, oblivious to the magical wall or their disturbance of it.

I insert my right foot through the wall of magic, feeling a squeeze and a tingling as I step down. The song that had drawn me to it changes from a pressing hum into a blazing orchestra. The music is all-consuming. My left foot follows suit. As soon as my body clears the wall, the mushrooms' desire pounds into me. All they want, all they've ever wanted, is to go home. I'm submerged in a lake of magic. The circle's desire becomes my own. I want to go home to the Hallowed Hills.

A vision of iridescent plants in the phosphorescent lights comes to me. I move to the center of the circle, and I feel the notes pour from my mouth. Focusing on the vibration of the notes emanating from my vocal cords my jaw opens wide to let the notes out, and my voice rises with a chorus of mushrooms, singing the beauty of Fae. Deston's castle, evil pixies, rainbow horses, honeysuckle, morning glory, baby's breath, all of it wrapping around me in a sonnet woven of spider silk notes. Thoughts and visions I'd never seen in the Hallowed Hills loosen from my lips.

My eyes register that we've risen into the sky, but I don't feel the gravity of Earth anymore. The human world falls away from me as I sing.

My skin burns with liquid acid, melting away my humanity. Music streams from my throat, covering the screams under my skin and in my bones. Changes race through my body. The sun dawns in the distance, blinding me to the world I've always known. My back arches with my arms spread, balancing on my tiptoes.

When I'm done, I won't be the same. I never will be the same, but I can't stop. The magic is a drug, and I'm addicted. I reach the crescendo of my song, begging it to take me home. A loud crack splits the air. The sun disappears, leaving the day-glo lights in the air around me.

My hands now carry the iridescent markings of the Fae. The pressing need to sing vanishes. The round softness of my humanity disappears with the music, leaving only a sharp point that angles away from my skull. My fingers trace the new shape of my state of being.

Nick's eyes go wide, and his pupils dilate as his lips part slightly to say something.

Hot tears race down my cheeks. "Don't! I don't want to fucking hear it." My body quivers and trembles.

Nick's mouth snaps shut, and his jaw muscle grits as he grinds his teeth.

The fairy circle slowly lowers us down. I shift my gaze around to get my bearings.

CHAPTER 9

After our circle lands, I don't just see the day-glo colors painted across everything. I hear their sounds too. Vibrating music, and waves emanate out from everything around me, intersecting with each other. The waves touch, mingling and changing and wake out like waves in a pond to meet others and repeat. The world is a pond with millions of thrown pebbles, all waking at the same time. When you throw pebbles onto a lake close to one another, their wake waves flow out from each other in circular perfection, outlining whatever shape they are. They meet each other and reform, creating a whole new wake wave with a new shape. Fae is the lake, and everything is a pebble.

One way or the other, I will never see the world the same.

I reach out and touch a wake with the tip of my finger, pushing back and changing its shape. My companions have wakes too. Jake and Tom's wakes are weak and smooth.

Nick's is stronger and rippled. They don't radiate like the plant life around me, strong and vibrant.

Fae appear different and yet the same. The sound waves flow everywhere, altering my perception of reality. It's brighter, the colors more intense, vivid, and domineering; each one vying for attention and dominance over the other. It reminds me of my brief time at the Fae court, all of them vying for attention. The plants aren't much different. There are ferns and climbing plants with big leaves. Something that resembles a day-glo version of an elephant ear. Delicate flowers, butterflies, large and small in a rainbow of color. I can see and hear all their vibrating sounds.

"Sarah?" Nick snaps me out of it. I'm staring at him, entranced by the sounds waking off of him. I turn to face the three of them.

You know the moment when you can tell something is wrong? Like there's a giant piece of lettuce caught between your teeth, or maybe your hair is sticking out in twelve different directions, or you rubbed your nose and now there's a booger hanging out.

"What are you?" Jake voices the thought on everyone's mind. It's a neon sign across their faces.

In slow motion closing and opening my eyelids blink. Time shifts for me. I'm moving in slow motion while they are fast. Humanity runs at a different time span from Fae. The Fae are eternal, immortal. Humanity is not. Now I can actually see how quickly their time is spent.

"I don't know what I am. Something else." The muscles between my brows pull together at my frustration. *How do you explain the inexplicable?* In the pit of my belly, the brick lodges deeper.

"You looked human before. You don't anymore. You look like one of them, but not quite." Jake's response is laced with confusion.

I see the shift of Nick's body, repositioning himself between Jake, Tom, and I.

"You wanted back into the land of Fae, I've brought you here," I retort.

Jake and Tom's weapons train on me. Their wakes change from smooth to sharp thorn-like peaks.

I think quickly. "You didn't ask me how I was going to do it. You didn't ask me what it would cost, or if there even was a price to pay. There is always a price. The price, me, little bits of my humanity have been slowly cut away. I figured out how Fae magic operates. They call on music to weave the magic around themselves. They sing it into being, and every time I use Fae magic, it changes me." The wake around me changes as I speak, interacting with my words. "You wanted in here. As for explanations, I don't owe you shit." I throw the last part out there.

Nick posies himself like a sentinel next to me, silently defending with his arms crossed and his jaw muscles working.

Jake scratches his chin and replies, "You're right. There is always a price to pay. No, we didn't ask you what the price was, and you offered it for free. So, touché. Now we're free to run off and get ourselves killed. Tell me what your objective is, and maybe I'll help you achieve it." Jake says then shifts his eyes to Tom and back to me.

"We're here for three reasons. Nick wants to save his sister. I want to save my friend Arty and a six-year-old little girl, Olive." *Don't tell them they took her because they want me. Bad idea.*

"Olive. Why is she so important to you?" Jake looks up at me through his bushy eyebrows.

"She's my friend's little sister. I promised I'd get her back. Zoe stayed to help the other kids. I left to go save her sister." I say, simple and to the point, no need to get bogged down with extraneous details.

"So, can we get on with it? We're standing out here in the open, and we're burning whatever the fuck you call this moonlight; mighty stupid," Tom says. He has such a way with words.

"Burning moonlight? You're even starting to talk like them?" Jake joshes him.

"You're very funny, Tom," I snap. "You're not in charge. Just because you have a gun doesn't make you the big baddie here. Your job is not to question why, but to do and die."

Both of them recoil from my words.

I know they've heard those words before, but not from an eighteen-year-old. Tom moves toward me; it's slight.

Jake raises his arm, blocking Tom's path. "Let it go! She knows what's going on here. She had operational knowledge; we need to follow her. Once we decide it's not worth following her anymore, we'll go our own way." Jake lowers his weapon.

"Yeah, she's got operational knowledge; it's true. She's been here, and she got us in just like she said she would. She could be holding back. She could know more about what's going on here. We need to cut the head off the snake, Jake." Tom's gun never leaves me.

My mind races and my hands are moist with how I'd react if that gun goes off.

"I agree. She's probably holding out on us," Jake says. "She's a teenager; they hold out on everybody. But she's got two brain cells to rub together, and she looks like one of 'them'. She can say she entranced us, and we can all slip by a lot of Fae. Don't look a gift horse in the mouth for what it is. She's using us, we're using her." Jake's simple reply does the trick.

Tom looks away and nods his head. "Yes, sir!" Tom gives Jake a half-hearted salute, lowering the tip of his gun. His hard eyes say it all. He doesn't trust me and never will.

I don't blame him. If I looked anything like I feel, I wouldn't trust me either. It's the Fae. For all I know, the land masses shift around. Nothing about the land of the fair folk is forever, except the Fae. Everything here feels as if it is in constant motion, moving with the music and the magic.

Nick breaks into my thoughts. "Do you know which direction to go, Sarah?"

I glance down. Nick's dirty broken fingernails lie gently cupping my shoulder.

"I'm not really sure. I think one way is as good as another right now. So, I say we go that way." I wave my hand off to the right. The plants look familiar—sort of. I really picked randomly, so it doesn't matter which direction we go until we run into a road or some kind of structure. Or maybe another fairy castle. We don't have any idea where we are. The guys move into their triangular position, and I hoist my crossbow off of my back, carrying it low in front of me.

"By the way, guys, I think we should try to avoid using the guns as much as possible. First, there's no replacement ammo here. Second, if you listen, Fae is quiet. It's peaceful. No loud cars or machinery. Anyone within hearing distance of a gunshot will wonder what it is. A lot of the Fae have never left this realm, ever. Only a small handful actually go up to the surface and kill humans."

Jake doesn't turn and look at me. He nods his head.

"Like I said, Jake, operational knowledge and a holdout," Tom mutters.

I liked Tom better when we were on the surface. Now, he's just a dick, cementing problems.

We trudge through day-glo green phosphorescent underbrush, which looks like what Astroturf would if it grew it under a black light and reached mid-thigh? I'm sure Fae have no idea what a lawnmower is. Unless they have special fairies with scythes to mow the lawn.

The rainbow foliage and array of colors resemble a scene out of Jurassic Park with that pungent, funky scent of slightly decaying greenery and earth, overlain by a heady perfume weighing down the air like a mist of flowers.

Tom reaches out to touch a vivid, orange orchid-looking flower.

"Don't touch that!" I snap.

He freezes mid-air. The wake flowing from it is jagged and cruel.

I squat down and pick up a stick with a flat wake line. Moving in front of Tom, I lightly tap a petal. They puff out a yellow mist and a sour scent. Like lightning, I move Tom ten feet away. The mist lingers with its sickly sour wake over the flower before the petals fold in on itself.

"Holy shit! what the fuck was that?" Tom's exclamation mirrors my thoughts.

"Just another way the Fae can kill you. Everything here is beautiful and deadly. Got it?" My eyes take a turn piercing each guy to reinforce my point. They need to understand you can't trust anything.

I turn on my heel away from Jake and Tom's murmuring. The tip of my crossbow pushes leaves out of the way.

"You ever seen that flower before?" Nick's shoulder bumps into me.

"Nope." My eyes search the area for more pretty death.

"Anything you want to share with me?" he inquires.

I chance a glance at him out of the corner of my eye, only to catch him doing the same thing. He gives me a half-smile as I shake my head. He mouths, 'Okay.'

From a distance, I spy a towering rainforest of umbrella-shaped trees. The closer we get, the more certain I become it's absolutely not a forest. The wake line coming off the forest don't resemble trees. They remind me of a stronger version of humans or Fae. The tree line doesn't follow the horizon like a forest either. The umbrellas range in size from tall and narrow to squat and round, not a tree but—mushrooms.

CHAPTER 10

"What are those?" Tom's a gambler, not a thinker.

"Mushrooms. Giant mushrooms. Can't you smell the funk in the air?" I smell and taste them.

"Yeah, I thought I smelled mushrooms. Gotta be the biggest goddamn mushrooms of all time." Jake scratches the back of his neck. "If I didn't know any better, I'd think Jules Verne had actually been down here. Maybe his journey to the center of the earth was real."

I throw a sharp glance at Jake. He's right. A lot of this does resemble Jules Verne's *Journey to the Center of the Earth*. Giant monster-like creatures, oversized plants, and now we're looking at a mushroom forest.

Were all of those writers trying to tell us something? Have they known all along? Alice in Wonderland, she went somewhere else, down a rabbit hole where magical fantastical things happened, and it was ruled by an evil queen. The queen who wanted all the roses to be red. It's not just that she wanted the roses to be red. She wanted to rule everyone and have them kowtow to her. *What if they were talking about the Fae?*

Whether they encountered Fae themselves or regurgitating somebody else's story, it wasn't important. What if humanity has been encountering the Fae over and over again for our entire existence? All these stories of people going on fantastic journeys and running into monsters, being trapped in underground worlds, lost civilizations. *What if they were all the Fae?*

That's crazy. It's all fiction. But here I am underground in the Hallowed Hills. The Fae had been pushed down here after losing a battle. There's a giant day-glo mushroom forest. I think Jules Verne left the day-glo part out. But they are mushrooms nonetheless. I'm sure if everything here hadn't been lit by fairy light, they'd look like normal mushrooms.

Of course, the only way to test that theory is to go up to the surface and create my own fairy light and see what happens. We are on the same planet, and we have the same soil.

The sound waves waking off of the mushrooms should be a perfect outline, but they aren't. Instead, they're moving squiggly as they wake out like a beating heart. They meet up with other mushroom wakes instead of reforming into it a completely new wave. They curl around one another into spirals. This is a different type of magic. I see the difference, and it's amazing. I look up, down, and all around. The muscles in my face pull back into a smile of fascination.

"What are you seeing that we aren't seeing, Sarah? You got a big smile on your face?" Nick's more observant than I give him credit for.

"Once I was asleep, but now I'm awake, and I see through the eyes of a waking person. Humans are asleep. We can't see the magic; I can." Wondrous awe laces every word.

"Yeah, that's just kind of creeping me out, boss lady," Tom says. He has to piss in my cornflakes.

"I really don't care if I'm creeping you out. Want to place a bet on the next time I use magic? I have almost zero experience, and I'm just barely beginning to understand what goes on down here. If we go to battle, there is no guarantee I can actually save your dumb ass. If I have to choose between who I save and who I don't, I'm afraid you are quickly falling to the bottom of that list." I hear the cuff of laughter.

"See, Tom? Making friends already? I think she likes you," Jake jeers.

Tom laughs. "You don't like me. Women despise me. I got a big mouth. No, I think she likes you, Jake. I mean we already know she's not boyfriend-girlfriend with Nicky over there. He doesn't have a chance, being friend-zoned and all." Tom sticks his tongue out and laughs at his own joke.

"Yeah, but she wants to save some guy name Arty. Maybe that's her boyfriend," Jake shoots back.

I shake my head.

"No, he's not her boyfriend either; he's been friend-zoned just like me," Nick retorts.

I shoot Nick a dirty look.

"I don't have a boyfriend. I'm not interested in a boyfriend. Don't you guys think I'm a little too freaky for you or anybody?" I smile back at all of them, turning the tables on them is fun.

"No. Fairy looks good on you." Nick's words strike me speechless. He'd been walking behind me most of the time. What part of me is he talking about? My butt?

"Well now, that wasn't weird or strange. So, you're into alternate species or inter-species relationships?" Jake laughs as he says it, but Nick doesn't.

Tom pulls his tongue back between his teeth long enough to spew out, "No, I figure part of you is still human. Maybe the most important part." Tom leers at me with his dirt brown eyes, tongue still lolling.

"Yeah, somehow, I don't think he's talking about your heart, Sarah," Jake says. "I think I'd stay away from Tom. He seems like a piece of shit." Jake smiles over at Nick. I think Tom's a pig and Jake just likes to antagonize Nick.

"Well, whether I'm still human in the most important parts, you're never going to find out because you aren't even in a friend zone; more like the asshole zone," I shoot back.

All three of them chuckle. "Tom, I guess she burned the fuck out of you." Jake laughs.

The dry laugh issuing from Tom's chapped lips remind me that I hadn't eaten or drank anything all night. There are low-lying plants around us. One of them is shaped like a calla lily, although I'd never seen a purple one. The flower resembles an upside-down wine bottle with the bottom cut off. I pull it down, revealing a liquid trapped inside. Judging by the moisture in the air, it accumulates there. Mushrooms like moisture.

I assume it's water. If anybody can attest to it and survive, it will probably be me. I listen but there's no sound wake coming off the liquid itself. The flower is happy and healthy, carrying a beautiful G minor. I tilt it over and let it pour some into my mouth, swishing around. It tastes like water.

"Don't drink that." Nick slaps the flower out of my hand.

"I'm thirsty. I don't have any water, and it tastes just like water. I think if a fairy wanted to kill us, water from a calla lily wouldn't be their first choice. They have plants here that will simply jump all over you and stab you to death with a neurotoxin and then chew your body apart. I think the water in a calla lily is the least of my worries." I cover my mouth. I didn't mean to snap at him.

"We don't know whether it's a poisonous calla lily or not." Nick's brows pull down as he grinds his teeth.

"Yes, I did find out. The flower told me it wasn't." The words leave my mouth. It's true, the flower had told me it wasn't poisonous. Clear and pure, it isn't tainted. There are no minor tones or heavy chords about its song, only perfect harmony. It can't be poisonous; I just feel it.

His eyebrows shoot into his hairline. "What if it's only drinkable for you?" I examine the flower and its contents again, but it all comes up sweet and innocuous. I open my mouth to reply, but Tom cuts me off.

"I don't know about you guys, but I'm thirsty." Tom tilts the nearest calla lily over, pouring it down his throat.

Remembering my encounter with the hedges in the maze, I warn everyone. "Don't break them, and don't kill or hurt them. Just drink the water. They'll collect more, that's what they do. When they get too full, they tip over and pour it onto the ground, but they keep the water for other living things, okay?" I don't want to run the risk of pissing off a flower and having it try to kill me or stop helping us.

"Don't worry, we won't damage the plants," Jake reassures. "We need some water to fill the cantina. We left in too much of a hurry." Jake finishes his understatement of the year.

The closer to the giant mushrooms we get, the deeper trepidation enters my belly. The trees feel wrong. They reach out to us, pushing and pulling at our own wakes. The base of the fungi on the outer edge begins small and grows to epic proportions. The mushroom grows in clumps, each grouping to its own. A gloom settles over us the deeper we trek. The gloomy silence follows us, growing deeper with each step. My fingers itch to reach out and trace the stocks of the massive fungi. They call to me mournfully with a sad song. The gloom falls into a deep purple haze. Wrapping around us, the mist murmurs in my ear. The sharp edges of whispers pull at my hearing, cutting my eardrums with terror. I whip my head left and right, but the wake lines reveal nothing. They pulse with the forest, creating a magical void of pain.

"Can you feel that?" I can't be alone in my trepidation.

"You mean the heebie-jeebies? Yeah, I got that." Tom replies, as his body trembles to shake it off.

Jake's boot slips on the side of a mossy white rock, throwing him off balance. "Watch out for the rocks." He orders.

I watch the mushrooms and the moss-covered ground. My eyes dart. My breathing grows loud in my ears. My heart rate speeds up to become a pounding boom of a canon. My eyes lock on the amethyst mushrooms up ahead. They sway and shift with the hammering in my chest like dancers at a rave.

Windy whispers whip by my head, dragging my hair with them. A scream escapes, but it isn't my own.

Jake turns to face me, his hand in front of him. He takes on the stance of a sword fighter with no sword. His eyes gleam silver in the purple gloom. "You wish to dethrone my queen? We shall see." He shouts.

I watch in horror as he raises his invisible sword to strike Tom.

"Nay, we shall triumph over you and your evil queen. Her reign of death must end." Tom retorts, then thrusts his invisible sword into Jake's chest.

Nick stepped forward to join Jake. I grab at his arm, pulling with all my might.

This isn't real.

"Stop, this isn't happening!" I shout.

Nick freezes in place. I dash to Jake's side, pulling at the sleeve of his dungarees. He shoves me to the ground and raises his invisible sword to slice down at me. His silvery eyes are milky with enchantment.

My lips press together to form a whistle, only to have the wind knocked from my chest. Jake's boot smashes down on my belly, crushing the breath out of me.

"You'll not use magic on me, pretender." He raises his boot again. I watch in horror as it gains speed.

"I'll save you!" Tom's body crashes into Jake's torso, and both tumble to the ground, thrashing about. They roll over and over, each turning for the upper hand. However, Jake's bigger and stronger. He gains dominance over Tom, wrapping his hands around Tom's throat. His thumbs press into his windpipe. Tom's eyes roll around as his fists beat at Jake's arms, pulling at his wrist. His legs kick and scuff. He digs with his fingers into Jake's grip, attempting to break Jake's stranglehold.

"Stop! Stop, damn it!" I roll over to my knees and climb on Jake's back.

The voices swirl around me, urging me to kill him. Others want me to torture him and cut him to pieces, bit by bit. One screams 'traitor' in my ear. A warm stream runs down my neck into my shirt.

I beat my fist into his shoulders. He shifts underneath me, but I hold on tight. With every ounce of breath in my being, I whistle Dixie in his ear. He freezes and then sags, falling onto his side with me. Tom coughs, drawing in a ragged breath. They don't move. I scratch my neck, only to have my fingers come away with blood. The voices swirl with their clamoring desires. *We have to get out of here.* My arm is trapped under Jake's torso. Pushing his back with one hand, I pull the other, but I gain little purchase.

I cry out, "Get off of me!" Curling my leg up, I plant my foot in the small of his back and push, freeing my arm. The voices continue to swirl around me, tearing at my hair and clothes. The wakes are undefined and pulsing. My companions are frozen, locked in this enchanted forest. Nick has little cuts on his face and arms; Tom too. I watch in horror as a wake passes over Jake, drawing a line of blood as it goes.

I dash to Nick, pulling at his hand. Maybe they will follow me like in the maze. He stumbles forward, feet dragging along the peaty ground. Tom is stock-still, lying on the ground. He stares up at the mushroom canopy towering over us. I grip his arms, dragging him into a sitting position. It's like moving a giant, sleeping child. I lock my arms under his and pull with all my might to no avail.

"Get up, you stupid jarhead!" My foot connects with his tailbone. He doesn't even grunt. I can't move him.

Jake lies on his side with his legs under him. I pull one leg until his knee reaches his chest, leaving the opposite leg where it is. Kneeling behind him, cupping both hands under an armpit, I pull him into a half-kneeling, half-crouching position. I move into a squatting pose, and using the strength of my legs, I strain to stand. He moves to stand, with me pulling for dear life at his back.

Two up, one to go. I turn back to Tom, sitting in the loamy soil. His milky honey-colored eyes meet mine.

"Watch out, my lady." He jumps up and charges behind me, heading for Jake. I whip around. Nick shoulders me to the side. Nick's large frame tumbles on top of me as the sound of steel crashing together fills the air.

"I'll make pixie meat of you." Tom's angry words ring out in a singsong tone.

"You have never been my equal. Pixies will feast on your flesh before mine." Jake holds a real sword pressed against Tom's own.

I push up with my hand, and Nick rolls to the side into a crouching position over me. He pushes me back into the dirt. My cheek stings pressing against a hard edge. I roll over to my side. Nick's fingers trail over my breast. I slap Nick's hand away. Digging my elbows under me, I lift my back off the ground. Light sparks off the ground where I'd been a moment before.

A wake moves off the long narrow object covered in forest debris. My hands brush the soil and peat aside to reveal a sword, next to a metal bracer and rings. The whispering voices tear at me, pulling me this way and that. The pounding in my heart forces adrenaline to my extremities, but the blood drains from my face as realization dawns on me. *It's a graveyard. We have to get out of here.*

Nick and Tom are protecting me from Jake. They all hold swords, and my eyes search for my crossbow. I spot it on the forest floor behind Jake. My hand runs over my body. My knife is gone as is my gun. All I have left to defend myself are the bolts for my crossbow. My hands frantically sift through the loam and leaves, landing on the pommel of a saber. My fingers curl around the hilt, bumping into a metal circle as I tighten my grip. I pull it from the ground. My groping reveals jewelry and weapons along with armor; they litter the forest.

Everywhere my eyes land the remnants of war abound for those with eyes to see.

I whistle Dixie in a hope they will cease their fighting. They carry on as if in another world or time. The waking waves around them change color along with their eyes. Tom appears to grow long black hair as does Nick. Jake's dark locks turn to long white braids flowing behind him with every swing. The clashing of swords rings in the air around me as if an entire army fights around us.

I grab Nick's arm, pulling him away from the giant mushroom and the graves they hid.

"We need to leave."

Tom turns away from Jake to follow us.

"You can't run from me, you coward!" Jake shouts "I always knew the Seelie court was weak. You don't have the stomach to fight. Blood is the only way to win you fools. This is why you will never win." Jake hacks at Tom's back. Tom throws his sword over his shoulder in time to block the blow.

The three of us run with Jake in hot pursuit.

"Even your pretender has no stomach for what must be done. How can you expect her to rule if she can't even lead a battle? You are lower than flutterbys, so weak are you." Jake footfalls stop.

Tom shoves me to the side and groans. I glance back only to spy Jake throwing his head back to laugh. He picks up the chase once more. So tight is his grip no the sword his knuckles glow white in the dim purple light.

The screaming voices and tearing whispers lessen the farther away from the graves we get.

"Where the hell are we and why are we running?" Nick's voice cracks the air. I chance a glance at him and then back to the ground jumping over roots and smaller mushrooms.

"Is Jake still following us?" I ask, my breathing is heavy with a dry mouth.

"Yeah, why does he have a sword? How'd you get the cut on your face? Why is there blood running down your neck?" Nick doesn't miss a beat running.

"The forest is a battleground graveyard. He's possessed." I retort.

"Sarah, what's going on? Why do I have a sword?" Jake's lucid words call out to us. "Come on, guys! Don't ditch me."

Jake pleads, then waves his arms around and tosses the sword to the forest floor.

I slow to a walk and bend over to catch my breath. The dark gloom lifts to a shady mist. The mushrooms thin up ahead. I quicken my pace.

"I have a terrible pain in my shoulder," Tom complains, his words tear at me. He might be hurt, but I don't want to stop.

"I want out of this forest of crazy before anyone tries to kill me again," I shout, pumping my arms and legs, I make for the edge of the tree line.

CHAPTER 11

In the shadow of the Mushrooms, Tom turns and surveys the surroundings. I watch in horror as Tom reaches over his shoulder and scratches above the knife protruding from his shoulder.

"Stop!" I move to Tom. Nick freezes mid-step.

"I'll be damned! You weren't lying, Tom. You do have a sharp pain in your back." Jake laughs, then pulls a gauze packet out of one of the many pockets in his jacket and hands it to me. Tom cranks his head to look over his shoulder.

"There's a knife in my back. How in the hell did that happen?" Tom looks from me, to Nick, and back to Jake.

"I think Jake threw it at you." I lower my eyes and bite my lip.

Jake splays one hand around the wound. With his left hand, he pulls the knife, and his right-hand pushes Tom's body away. A fleshy sucking sound follows, and the blood oozes out the moment the blade is free. Tom unbuttons his jacket and Jake cuts the undershirt at the neck. I pour water over the wound and cover it with the gauze. Jake pulls a roll of duct tape from a leg pocket and rips a strip off. I move my fingers as he presses the tape over the top.

"Well, Tom, now you can tell everyone how I'm a shitty friend and stabbed you in the back." Jake smiles.

Tom chuckles.

"Wish Will was here. I bet him twenty bucks you would, over a woman." Tom chuckles.

They both laugh. I don't see how that is funny. I help Tom pull his jacket over the wound and button it up. His eyes meet mine.

"You going to tell us what happened back in that forest?" Tom's mirth drains from his face, leaving only the cold eyes of a killer.

"I don't know. One minute we were walking along and laughing. The next you and Jake were fake sword fighting with Jake trying to kill me. Then you found real swords, and the real fun began. My guns are gone and so is my crossbow." I look down and away. I don't want to tell them where the swords came from or what I fear.

Tom's eyes never leave me. I'm haunted; maybe he is too. His lips smile, but his body never relaxes. He is always on the defense. He knows I'm holding back, but for some reason, he holds his tongue.

We come out in a wide-open meadow. Off in the distance is a barn. Something about it is familiar. This is Fae. Every building can look like the other although I know that isn't true. Everything here is brought into existence by whoever wants it. They morph and alter everything around them to suit their needs. If the barn looks familiar, it means I'd seen it before. There's no other answer.

The night I'd been taken, this is where Janice left Arty.

I offer, "I think that's the home of the Puca." I announce. Lavender had shuttered when she said his name—Puca.

"The Puca? What the hell is that?" Tom demands and regains his composure.

I fill them in. "It's some kind of Fae creature. It takes young, strong guys. It's probably where you were held, Nick. I know that's where they had Arty before. Maybe they brought him back. Once you belong to the Puca, he generally doesn't relinquish his property." I say.

All three of them quiet down. Whatever chitchat or playful banter we had died in the mushroom forest. There's nothing to hide our approach. No bushes or trees. But daylight in the human world means bedtime here. The Puca is probably asleep, as are his charges.

There are a few horses out front. They paw at the ground, blowing air through their nostrils. They wear no halter, harness, or saddle. They are tame and realized this is where they should be. Horse is merely a term I use quite loosely. One's blue, and the other's lilac.

Twisted sound wakes pore off them, their genes had been manipulated to create the colors. Their bodies are lighter, bones stronger, someone had altered their genetic makeup.

So beautiful, I ache while gazing at them. Long, fluffy eyelashes open and close as their intelligent opalescent eyes peek out at me. I can't help smiling. I'm like a little girl in a fairy dream.

Before when I'd been here, I was terrified. Everything was a threat. I was constantly on the lookout for an attack. Even when I made it back to the surface, threats loomed on all sides.

But now, at this moment I don't feel that; it's all wondrous. There are still threats here, but somehow, they don't touch me. Whatever threatens humans doesn't threaten me. I no longer fall into that category.

I shake my head to throw off the fog; it's an enchantment. I refocus on the ground between the funky horses and I. Up ahead looms a wake wall spiked with sharp edges. I follow the shape with my eyes, a perfect ring around the barn. My hand pushes Nick back.

"Stop, don't take another step! You too, Tom! Don't move," I shout. The wakes gather closer together at our location.

I watch the wakes dance up into the sky. It's some kind of a warning line. Is it there to keep people out or something in? I make a nickering sound and a simple whistle. I'd never been around horses. I'm like every little girl, I wanted a horse or pony. Something I could ride to call my own. My mother was against them. She demanded my father promise to never take me riding. She preached the dangers of strange horses.

The blue horse at the barn turns and flicks its tail up in the air, letting the carnelian colored hair float down, spreading out like a sheet. He turns and tosses its head, making a snorting sound. He paws the ground with one of its hooves and moseys towards the line and stops short. I take several steps closer to the wake wall. Tentatively, I reach my hand out, I don't know what will happen when I cross the line, but I'm going to find out. If Arty's there, I have to try.

The horse snorts and tosses its head. He doesn't want me to touch it. I feel its fear almost as if it's repelling me and telling me—no. I tentatively pull my fingers back, clasping them to my breast. We need to get to that barn. The sound wake goes up, and it never stops. It doesn't seem to lose its effectiveness the farther on it goes. It doesn't interact with other sound wakes, allowing them to morph and mix. It continues exactly the same. The wall breaks the wakes around it, separating and dividing them. It cuts them in half.

I take a deep breath, scrunch my eyes closed and thrust my hand into the wall of magic. The sharp thorns cut into the tender flesh of my palm. I scream, yanking my hand back. My palm blisters, and blood wells from cuts. The sharp edges of the wake glint in the Fae light, almost laughing at me.

Stupid, Sarah! Look before you leap, dummy.

"We can't cross this line, and I don't see a way through. I'm going to have to sing it down or cut an opening for us." My belly bunches. *I can do this, I hope.* No one speaks.

As I listen for the discordant sound pouring from the security line, I hear notes that should never be together. It's a war between a chord and discord. My survey of the ground reveals no obvious reason for the line or where it emanates from, or its creation. Nothing more than a white powdery substance.

I pick up a stick and throw it. It passes through without a hitch, same for a rock. Objects pass through, but flesh cannot. Obviously, wind can.

What about fire?

"Jake, can I have your lighter and canteen?" I ask.

He unclips the canteen and places it in my hand. Tom tosses me his Zippo lighter, and my fingers clasp at the raised seal on the backside. I turn it over the medallion and reads 'Semper Fidelis' along with the Marines' crest. I flip the lid off and run my thumb over the roughened wheel. The flint sparks and a flame catches. I toss it over the line.

"What the hell? You are going to get my lighter back, aren't you?" Tom bellows. Nick moves to block Tom's approach.

"Yes, but we need to get through this wall first." I don't bother to glance at his face and unscrew the top of the canteen and throw a little water across the wake. The thorny wave disappears. The water goes through as well.

But why had the wake disappeared?

I examine the wet spot in the grass. The powder was washed away. It creates an opening in the security perimeter. Next to the water droplets sits Tom's lighter. I pick it up and toss it at him.

"I'm sorry, Jake. I think we need all your water," I say. "It's the only way to create a good-sized opening to get a horse through. I don't know about you, but I'm over walking." I announce.

Tom flicks the lighter, reigniting the fire, and closes the lid on his pant leg a few times before pocketing it again, all the while throwing me a hard stare. All three take up their point positions around me as I splash water, dissolving the powder. As soon as there's enough space for the horse to put his head through he does. He's a stallion and magnificent. He rubs his nose into my hair and blows air out his nostrils in my ear.

"Yes, you're a good boy." I patting his fuzzy cheek. He bends down outside the security line. Using his strong lips, he pulls up some of the grass. I smile to myself because the grass is always greener on the other side of the security fence. I run my hand up and itch between his ears. I whisper, "Wait for us! I'll be happy to ride you if you don't mind." He snorts acceptance and tosses his head up and down. It seemed like a yes to me.

"Now we need three of his friends, and we can go wherever we want," Nick remarks, he has a one-track mind, move forward.

I scrunch one eye shut and gaze up at Nick. "I want to see what's in that barn first." We move in unison, and my blue stallion follows alongside. We tiptoe up to the stable proper. The other two horses standing out front come and rub themselves on me too. I pat each one of them in turn, and they go and stand next to their blue pal.

CHAPTER 12

Janice hadn't said the Puca was dangerous, but he'd implied it. The security perimeter wake is spiked, to dig into your skin and claw at you. The Puca clearly put it down to keep things in. Or is it to keep something out? I don't remember the wake wall from my first visit, I only remember Arty blindly following Janice into the barn. The stamping and snorting from the other horses beyond the door drag me out of my past.

The barns sliding doors mock me with their seemingly peaceful appearance. But everything in Fae is deceptive. You can't rely on it to not squeak, alerting anyone nearby. For all I know the, wood itself might sound the alarm by touching it. I don't see small critters running around. That doesn't mean there aren't alarms here somewhere. The Puca clearly doesn't want anyone to get out, but doesn't mean that I can't get in.

The guys crowd behind me, waiting for me to make the next move. Their presence comforts me. The horses don't stay behind, the blue stallion is right next to me as if laying a claim. He rubs his shoulder against me and then lifts his head and snorts at the wall, nodding to the opening. It's encouraging. Still, I'm tentative. He picks up his front hoof as if to kick the door. My heart freezes in my throat while I grab for his hoof.

Why would I trust a creature of Fae? They're pretty and deceitful.

I don't want to be heard. This won't be a clandestine infiltration if we alert them to our presence. In slow motion, the dark blue hoof lowers to the point of contact. I squint to avoid the vision, but my eyes refuse to block the visage before me. The sound of a hoof scraping down wood never arrives. Instead, the tip disappears into the wooden door.

It's a mirage, a *trompe l'oeil*, there to fool my eye, and it fooled me. It's a magical illusion the Puca had woven to keep others away. I thrust my hand into the wooden illusion, and it disappears.

I turn and smile, but none of the guys smile back. Jake nods his head with a big knot of wrinkles between his eyebrows. He tilts his head to the left, indicating we should move in. I pat the blue stallion on his cheek, rubbing down his long neck. I step through the illusion.

On one side of the interior, a rainbow array of horses line the stalls. Some turn to inspect the newcomers while others busy themselves facing the opposite direction. A few nibble the hay hanging inside their stalls. The other side displays a similar layout, but the stalls house humans. They are given only knee walls with the split stall doors, a water dispenser, and a tray for food. It's more cage than stall.

Twenty-two men. My eyes trail down the line, desperate for the broad shoulders and dark, tossed hair that Arty sports. My heart sinks. At first glance, none of them catch my eye. It doesn't mean he isn't sitting down or maybe asleep. I start by the door, walking past each stall. I eat up the interior. With each pass, the knot in my throat grows. None of the guys are awake. They are physically present but mentally asleep. I peek over the top of a half wall into a stall with two guys. One sits on the floor with his back against the far wall. His legs splay out in front of him as he sits on top of a mound of hay. His friend faces away from us in the other corner. A metallic ring of liquid hitting the side of a bucket cues me in. He's peeing and completely unaware of anyone watching him.

A water bucket sits near the door with food, a couple of bread-looking rolls and some fruit—similar to the fruit at Deston's castle. I don't see a protein. Neither of them gives me one iota of attention.

Nick also searches the faces. I never asked myself if he might know someone. I shake my head. Arty isn't here. My steps slow at the last stall for a cursory once-over of its occupants. Mahogany-colored, matted, hair frames a vacant face, normally etched with a snide half-smile—Brad. He and Camille had been taken, or at least I thought they had been. They weren't dead with the other kids at the church, and Brad would never have left his car.

On instinct, I whip my head left and right. If Brad's here, Camille is in Fae too, somewhere. She could very well have been in the corral with me at the maze. My heart speeds up with burning eyes. I don't like Camille, but I don't want her to die. I pace from one side to the other, turning at the stall doors.

In the maze, they took us all in pairs. If Brad's still alive, she probably is too.

Brad stands up next to the door and hangs both hands out between the bars. He stares out, unseeing into nothingness. I move into his line of vision. Maybe if I catch his eye, he might see me.

His eyes carry the white, milky-glaze of enchantment. Brad's eyes are normally those pretty clear baby blues, the kind the girls always swoon over. Now they resemble an old woman's cataracts.

"Brad, can you hear me?" I lay my hand over his. He's unresponsive. What did I think, he's going to wake up just because I spoke to him? If I sing the song, would that pull him out of his enchantment or would I wake everybody in the barn? I obviously hadn't thought that far ahead, this isn't going to be easy. Neat is what we need. Either I'm here to get Arty and Olive, or I'm here to free everyone. I can't have it both ways.

If I free everyone and the Puca comes back, he'll notice. All of the Hallowed Hills will send out some kind of an alarm and start looking for us. My palms moisten. Damp sweat forms under my arms. I don't want to be caught. I don't want Nick caught. Jake and Tom are too old; they'll die. Puca might not notice one, but he'd notice two.

"Aren't you going to wake them up, Sarah?" Nicks prodding claws at my resolve.

I bite my lip. I can feel the crinkling around my eyes as the muscles in my forehead pull down. A tingle grows in my nose, the kind when you think you might cry because you know you have to do something and you don't want to do it.

"No," I reply.

His pupils dilate, and his eyes open wider. He shakes his head.

Nick plunges in. "Why not free all these kids? I know you can. You did it for all those other kids." Jake puts his hand on Nicks' arm, pulling him back a step.

"They will send a lot of somebody's out here," Jake interjects. "They'll know someone is here, and then they'll hunt us down. No, she's gonna leave them asleep. Don't get me wrong, I want a firefight. These are all just kids like you. What are you, maybe eighteen?" Jake inquires.

"Yeah, I'm eighteen. I'm old enough to go to war and carry a gun alongside you, jarhead." Nick retorts and grinds his teeth, his jaw muscles work over the bone. He stares Jake and Tom down, his eyes shifting from one to the other.

Tom laughs dry under his breath. "Well, he's got you there, Jakey." Tom's fingers dance over the trigger guard of his carbine.

I take a deep breath, pushing the quivering in my chest back. "Nick, he's right. I can't wake them all. Puca might not notice one. If Arty was here, I would take him and go. But he's not, so we take Brad and go." That's my compromise, the choice I can live with—the needs of the few.

Nick looks around. "You know this guy?" then points at Brad.

I nod, yes, "Yeah, he is in my church group, my frenemy's boyfriend." I make my rounds of the rest of the stalls, desperate for a glimpse of Arty's black hair or the reflection off his glasses, but he isn't there.

I know he isn't gonna be here. They have him somewhere more secure. They want me bad enough to kidnap Olive so they definitely have Arty. I think maybe together with Olive somewhere. *As bait for me.*

"He's not here, let's go." I approach Brad's stall and unlatch the door. Brad puts his hands down to his sides as it swings open. He steps out as if it's the most natural, normal thing in the world for him, to be exiting a horse stall as a piece of chattel himself. His stall mate stands up in preparation to leave as well.

"Not you. Sit back down!" I order.

He freezes and then turns around. He walks back to the far corner and sits back on his hay pile as if nothing happened. He registered the command in my voice, but that is it.

Brad's hand is warm and moist as I lead him out. "I can't wake him up here, or it'll affect everyone," I inform no one in particular.

Brad's appearance isn't dirty, but he isn't clean. He probably could use a shower, but he doesn't smell bad. The only thing about him I find odd is the giant leather belt over his jeans. I could be a weight belt. There are two rings on either side, just above his hips. I don't think much of it. It's odd, but this is Fae. Everything's a little odd here.

I pull him along behind me, exiting the barn through the illusion. I place his hand on the horses as the blue horse moves forward. So does Brad, giving me the ability to stop leading him around like an infant. I'm not anybody's mommy, and I'm not ready to be one.

"Where to now, boss lady?" Tom's nickname irritates me.

I roll my eyes and give Tom a hard stare. He really is a dick. I liked him better when we were still on the surface. "We follow this road this way. You guys want to get up on a horse?"

I exit the barn, and everything falls into place. I'm standing in the same spot where only a few weeks ago I watched Arty's vacant stare disappear over a hill. It could have been a lifetime ago, but it picks at me. I turn to face the barn and envision Arty standing obediently next to the door. Now, I know exactly how to get to Deston's castle from here.

Following the road, I wait until the barn is out of sight, and then I sing the notes to awaken Brad.

Jake and Tom shift on their feet, eyes darting around on watch but avoiding me. I make them uncomfortable. As the last note rings from my lips, Brad's eyes clear away the milky white enchantment.

"Where am I? Where's Camille?" His head whips left and right, only to settle on me. "I know you…Sarah?" His face contorts in pain and confusion.

"I don't know where Camille is. Do you remember anything at all?" I ask. Hope and dread fill me. Hope that he's seen Arty and knows where he is. Dread that he remembers the carnage at the church all of it rolls in my belly.

"You are, Sarah, aren't you?" His eyes squint, focusing on me. I realize I look different, but he seems know who I am.

"Yes, it's me, Sarah. You remember we went to summer camp together every year for the last twelve years." I hope he remembers me. He's the first boy I ever kissed. It was a dare.

"It is you. You look different for some reason. Did you to dye your hair?"

I heave a sigh. "I did dye my hair, but it's not important. Do you remember anything?" I prod.

Brad rushes into his story, but he never stops glancing around. "Yeah, we were at the church and ready to leave. You left a little while before. Then there were all these announcements on TV about these creatures coming down out of the sky. Pastor Rollins locked all the doors and turned the light off. We hunkered down for the night. The next morning Arty took off to your house. Camille and I stayed. Both our parents were out of town. When the sun set, Javen, Steve, and Ross ran outside. They wanted to see the creatures, Pastor Rollins tried to stop them, but they wouldn't listen to him. I followed Camille. She wanted to see them too. She really is a pain sometimes." He scratches his head. "Anyway, I went to pull her back inside, and there they were. Pointy ears, shiny eyes, tall." His words are slow as it dawns on him what I look like. He steps back, raising his hand to his mouth.

"Are you sure you're Sarah? I mean you look like Sarah, but you look like one of them. Where's Camille? They took her. They started singing, and I don't remember anything else except for Camille screaming in the background." He looks down at his hands.

"There was blood. A lot of blood. Steve, they killed him. They killed Steve, they killed my best friend." His eyes redden, and a film of sweat covers his face. He leans over, holding his mouth. His body convulses, and he spits.

"Aw man, he's gonna yak. Five bucks says he yaks." Tom's need to jeer at everyone while making a buck goes beyond the pale.

I roll my eyes and turn to shoot Tom a dirty look. "Shut up!" I bark.

Tom shrugs his shoulders. The heat in my chest is crushing me. I wasn't there; I'd only seen the aftermath.

Brad stares at me, unblinking. "The creatures looked, they looked like you. But a guy, he was tall. He started singing. He had blue-green ocean-colored eyes with orange irises. I remember staring into them thinking, 'Wow, what fucking drug did I do to see that shit?'" his voice trails off.

"Okay, so where'd the blood come from?" Jake demands.

Brad shakes his head as he puts his hands over his face. His body crumples to the ground wailing.

"It came from Steve. He had a big arrow sticking through him as his blood sprayed all over me. It was like a hose or something. It was awful." Brad pulls his hands away from his face. He looks up at me, heavy with tears running down and his cheeks. His eyes are bloodshot. I'd never seen Brad in so much anguish. "He's dead, isn't he? I know he's dead. There was blood coming out of his mouth." Brad moans.

I can't lie to him or give him false hope; it'd be more of a killer.

"Yes, he's dead. I saw him." I confirm, then close my eyes to shut out the vision of Steve and all the other kids at the church.

"How are you alive? Where's Arty? Is he here? Who are these guys?" Brad points at Nick and the guys. I put my hand on his shoulder, patting him and swallow back the lump in my throat, and the tears stinging the back of my eyes.

Brad would be like Nick. All I have to do is help him save Camille or get him back to the surface.

"They took Arty. These guys are here to help me get Arty, Nick's sister, and a little girl named Olive. We can help you find Camille." I choke on the last word. I never liked Camille. She's always such a bitch, but I can't leave her down here. I don't want to leave anyone down here.

"You'll help me find Camille?" Brad asks, on his knees, grasping at my hands.

I nod my head.

"Really? But you guys hate each other. You'd still help me find her?" he replies. The ridge of muscles crinkles between his eyes in disbelief.

"Of course, Brad. I don't like Camille, but she doesn't deserve to be down here or be treated like one of their playthings." I shake with anger, images flash through my mind of Zoe and I, running away from the fire in the maze. The eyes of the girl I watched vines eat alive. The Fae had been watching. They had stadium seating outside the garden maze. For all I know, they ate popcorn. Rage shoots through my veins at the thought they were laughing while I watched that girl get torn apart by pixies.

"What do they want us for?" Brad's eyes fill with terror.

I shake my head.

Jake cuts in. "A workforce. They always take the young and strong. Women for breeding, men for labor. It's pretty standard practice in Africa and the Middle East."

"Thanks for the vivid detail, Jake. I'm pretty sure I'll have nightmares about it." I retort.

Nick demands. "Did they try to touch you? Do you think they touched Nikki?" Nick's fear is palpable; the worry he carries for his sister is sweet.

I puff my lip up a little bit and shake my head. "No, as a matter of fact not one person tried to touch me. They fed me and dressed me up like Fae Barbie and then forced me to go run through a weird maze while other girls died." My hands clench, as my nails dig into my palms.

"They had you running through a maze?" Jake scratches his chin.

"Yes, I'm a contender. They didn't say what for, and I really don't care. They said the prize was everything, the world. I'm competitive. I want to win." I shrug it off.

Brad starts laughing. "Sarah, competitive. That has to be the understatement of the year. If there was a competition, you joined it and won. You like to win."

I bristle at his words. *Am I that transparent?* "I always won fair and square. It's not like I was running around cheating, like Camille." I retort.

"Yeah, that's the funny part. She would cheat to win. You would play by all the rules and just magically take the brass ring. She hated you for that... hates you." The muscles between Brad's eyes bunch up again. He realizes he spoke about Camille in the past tense.

I pat him on the shoulder. "You need to get up. We have to move. Staying in one spot is dangerous. We need to keep moving." I offer Brad a hand up, and he takes it.

Jake announces, "I came down here to kill Fae. Said I'd help as long as I felt like it. You only have Tom and me until we're tired. If you want to find your friends, do it quickly."

Somehow, I'm pretty sure Jake isn't going to abandon us. It's this feeling I have. He always puts that 'I'm leaving' on the tail end. Like 'I'll kill ye in the morning' crap to look like a badass. He would cave and become a softy; I can feel it. Tom, on the other hand, I believe he'll bail in a heartbeat.

The horses are still following us, but I haven't seen anybody touch one of them except for Nick and myself. Brad cringes away from the horses. They come up to rub their noses on him, but he swats them away. His absolute abhorrence of the horses is bizarre.

"Are you afraid of horses?" Nick asks.

"No. I don't know. They give me the heebie-jeebies," Brad says. "No, I like horses. I just can't stand to be near them now." Something about Brad strikes me as odd, and the farther we walk along, the more there is something not right about him. If someone comes up from behind, he flinches a leg like he's going to kick. Instead of turning his eyes from the right to left like most humans would, he turns his head from side to side.

"Hey, Brad, when as last time you had your haircut?" I ask.

"Like three days ago why."

Three days ago is really three weeks ago, but Brad wouldn't know that. He always wears his hair high and tight. It hangs over his shoulders. There's no way his hair would grow that much in three weeks. I'd seen Brad without a shirt on lots of times at summer camp since the guys always took their shirts off to go swimming. Sometimes they'd wrestle or lift weights too. It was always fun to watch him. Brad had been one of those guys that didn't have a lot of chest hair, just a smattering at the top between his pecs. *Okay, why do I remember these things?*

Brad's hot, I mean, hot guy, no shirt on, lots of bulging muscles—hot. Sorry, I remember. It's like Nick. I know Nick has a fair bit of chest hair for an eighteen-year-old; he's pretty hairy. But he isn't like out of control. Something about Brad isn't normal. He isn't a hairy dude. He has long dark brown hair. I know his great-grandmother was Native American. We always teased him because he couldn't grow a full beard. Even if he wanted to, it was all patchy. The guy I am looking at now almost has a full beard.

"Have you seen yourself in a mirror?" I ask.

Brad turns his head to the side to look at me. "No. Do I look bad?" he inquires.

Jake taps his ring on his carbine. "Hey, Tom, toss me a mirror." Jake catches it with one hand and hands it over. Brad's eyes grow wide as his hand reaches up, running his fingers through the thick beard growing on his face.

"How long was I there? Where is here?" His head turns to the side to look up at the Fae sky.

"About three weeks, here in the Hallowed Hills. This is the land of Fae, the fairies, fair folk." I tilt my head forward so I look up at him with my green eyes.

"I thought they were elves with the pointy ears." His side glace unnerves me.

"Yeah, no elves. Fairies, the Fae." I sigh.

"Three weeks and I grow a beard?" The hair on the back of his neck is as thick as on his face. The only difference is it's the same length as the hair on his head. The closer I examine him, the more I realize all of his hair is that dark brunette like on his head. And he's walking funny.

"You don't remember anything else?" I inquire.

"No, nothing." He shakes his head loosely.

"Is that your belt?" I point at the leather strap covering his midriff.

"No." His hands reach down to remove it, but his fingers don't seem to have the dexterity necessary to take it off. He paws at it. His fingernails had thickened in different places, giving them a blocky look. The wakes coming off of Brad go from frightened to absolutely terrified. They wiggle and squiggle before spiraling up and away. They slam into

~ 145 ~

anything they can, creating even more chaos. The belt isn't giving off wakes towards me; they move inward toward Brad. It's doing something to him.

Nick reaches out to touch the belt, but he yelps, snatching his hand back.

Nick blurts out, "I don't think you should touch that, Sarah. There's something wrong with it." He informs me.

I nod my head. We have to get it off of him. Whatever it's doing, it's changing him. It's working some kind of magical spell on him. I stretch my fingers out, tentatively poking the belt with one hand. It singes just a smidge. While throwing out a shock, I pull my hand back. It's like touching an electric fence. I move my fingers over the tail of the belt. Maybe I can push it through the buckle and loosen it enough to slide off. The singeing becomes a burning, and I suck air through my teeth as it cuts into my flesh.

"I think you should let go," Nick says, his voice is filled with worry. A whisper of smoke rises up from my fingers.

I release it only to look down at the black and crackled flesh still attached to the end of my digits. "We have to get it off of him," I reply, then bite my lip.

Brad's eyes stare up at me. They're still blue, but they've changed somehow, larger, more almond-shaped, and less round.

"Get it off of me! Whatever it's doing, it's doing it faster. My eyes are funny I can't see right," Brad yells, as his hands paw at me.

"Give me your knife!" I demand of Jake. He hands me a Kbar. I take the tip of the knife and begin sawing into the leather. It hardly makes a dent.

"Maybe you should sing something," Nick suggests.

I give him a pinched smile. "Every song costs me. I want to try everything else first."

Nick presses his lips together tight and nod his head. He'd seen how high the price is. He's scared, we all are.

Brad's eyes roll around in his head, and he kicks his feet to the ground several times, pawing at it.

CHAPTER 13

"You know what it costs me every time I sing." I retort.

A gurgling sound rises from Brad's throat. I look from Nick to Brad. The Adam's apple in Brad's neck works up and down. He swallows his words away.

"I don't know what's happening to him, Sarah, but if you can stop it, you have to try. Look at him!" Nick waves his hand over Brad's twitching form.

What I see will soon no longer be human. His eyes roll around in his head, and the shoes on his feet split open—if you can call them feet any more. His legs start to turn as the bones snap and reform, changing position.

"Ppplllleaaaase hellllppp!" A bloodcurdling scream wrenches from Brad's throat as he falls to the ground. His back rounds with raised muscles. The horses surround Brad, nuzzling him. His arms elongate, and his fingers curl up, hardening and reshaping themselves.

"There's nothing you can do for him, Sarah," Janice says.

I whirl around at the sound of his voice, but I don't need to look. I already know who it is. My eyes narrow as I take in Janice.

"You did this to him. You took him. This is all your fault." I raise the tip of Jake's sidearm to take aim.

"I didn't say he couldn't be saved." Janice returns.

I feel myself wavering as I look into his violet eyes and grind my teeth.

"You did this to him, Janice. You better fix it. If you know how to stop whatever is happening to him, do it!" Dragging my eyes from him, down to the withering form that was once Brad.

"I can't stop what's happening to him either," Janice announces. "There's only one way to help him."

The sound of three guns being cocked and pointed at your head can change your point of view and how you do things.

Most people freeze in terror, but Fae apparently don't have emotions like humans.

"I think you better do what our little boss lady here wants you to do. Before I blow your pointy-eared fucking and head off." Jake growls his threat out between clenched teeth.

Janice never breaks a sweat. He doesn't even take a breath. His chest rises as I put my hand up, waving the guys back.

"Do it or I will let them kill you. Or I'll kill you myself. I will find a way. I don't know how you found me or what you want from me. But if you hurt anyone here and you don't help Brad, I will spend the rest of my days finding a way to fight you and kill you. Even if I have to cut you apart piece by piece and the only sharp object, I have are my teeth. I'll do it." I move in nose to nose with him. His height is no longer such a difference. I burn with my bravado. The heat under my skin stains my face. His face blocks my view. He too moves closer as every gun leans into him.

"Yeah, now that right there, Mister. That's what we in the Marine Cor. call a threatening maneuver," Tom says as Captain Obvious. "So, if I was you, I'd not make any more moves. You know how to help the kid, help him. Otherwise, you're about as useless to us as tits on a bull." Tom spits on the ground not far from Janice's feet.

All those other times when I said I didn't like Tom, this is one of those times when I understand why Jake keeps him around. He's a threatening, trigger-happy gambler. I don't want them to kill Janice because a part of me feels drawn to him. My heart rate speeds up when I'm around him. It isn't fear. There is another part of me that wants to see him dead and bleeding. Those two sides war with one another. I sigh with resolve and then tear my eyes away from his full, serious lips.

Janice carries on with his negotiations. "The only way to save him is exactly what you were doing. You have to get the belt off of him. Even then, it might not slow down the change. The more you fiddle, the faster the magic works. If he fights it, it closes in on him. If you had left him enchanted and asleep, he might not have changed for months. By waking him, the enchantment moves ten times faster." His violet eyes bore into me. I pull away to glance from Nick, to Jake, to Tom, and then down to the withering form of poor Brad.

Janice's voice raises the melody creating the enchantment. I watch Brad's eyes begin to milk over, and his fidgeting and whimpering quieten.

I urge Janice on. "It's working! Keep going!"

Janice's voice rises even higher, sharp and determined. His eyebrows draw together as he slowly allows the music work. He abruptly cuts the notes off. "I can't. He won't let me." Janice searches my face with drawn eyebrows and a clenched jaw.

"I thought we didn't have a choice. You guys sing and we're fucking zombies. What do you mean he won't let you enchant him?" I demand, crossing my arms and uncrossing them, waving my hands around.

"Let me clarify, I can't enchant him. He's been blocked." His violet eyes trace my every move; it's irritating. It reminds me of a cat how their body and face never move, only the eyes.

"He can't be blocked? What are you talking about? You enchanted him before. Do it again!" I step over to Janice. I'm ready to slap him as hard as I can. My body wars within me.

He doesn't flinch away. "You took the enchantment off." It's a statement, not an accusation.

I retort, "You know I did." I feel the exasperation growing within me. "So, what, I took the enchantment off. I sang what you sang with my own twist." I shrug.

Brad hardly looks human anymore.

"Sarah, you blocked me out. If you want him enchanted, you have to do it yourself. I can't beat you." Janice's face goes deadpan as the importance of his words washes over me.

Jake leans in, pressing his gun firmly against Janice's temple "Well, that there is the wrong damn answer," he informs Janice.

Tom snickers in the background with his tongue hanging out. Tom demands, "What 'cha doin' out here all by yourself there, hey pretty boy?" Once again, I like Tom's style.

Cool as a cucumber, Janice replies. "It doesn't matter why I'm here alone. We need to put Brad under before he finishes changing."

My eyes are drawn to Jake's hand.

Nick breaks his silence, "Give Sarah your gloves. Maybe they'll stave off the burning long enough for her to pull the belt off."

I have my doubts, but anything is worth a try.

Jake removes his hand from his weapon and thrusts it toward me.

"You take the glove off, boss lady," Jake's eyes never leave Janice's face. "We don't want our pointy-eared friend getting any ideas, do we?"

Janice tilts his head to the side, raising one eyebrow. "Why don't you just sing, Sarah? You can end his pain right now. All you have to do is sing a song and entrance him." The logic of his words isn't lost on me, but neither is the cost.

"Yeah, I don't think we're going to be takin any orders from you here, pointy boy." Tom's finger twitches over the trigger guard.

"None of your business why I won't sing." I pull the Velcro from the back of Jake's hand. I begin to tug the glove off. The inside of the glove is coated in sweat. The glove slides off. I take the leather portion and do my best to fold it around the tongue of the belt. It's no good. It still burns through the leather. "Okay, I give up. How the hell do you get this thing off of him?" The tips of my fingers are tender and red from my attempts.

"I told you, Sarah!" Janice nearly shouts. "I can get it off, but I will have the same issues you're having."

Why doesn't he just say what he means? "But fairies can heal themselves," I interject.

"The more he fights the enchantment, the hotter it burns and the faster it turns. You must put him to sleep before we can get it off of him. I'll take it off myself. I swear by the blood of all the Queens, and Danu herself, I will do this. I will not fail you, Sarah." I've never heard a Fae oath, but Janice makes it sound pretty solemn.

"If you're lying to me and this is some kind of gimmick, I will find a way to..."

Jake pushes me out of the way. "Yeah, yeah, yeah, Sarah. We heard you threaten him the first time; it was actually better the first time."

I gaze down at what's left of Brad. I push the head of the orange stallion out of the way. The blue stallion nuzzles the back of my head, urging me on.

I feel for the music inside of me, the same music I used to unlock the kids and Brad a little while ago. I sing it in reverse. My voice rises, and I watch the eyes of the half-man half-horse in front of me roll slowly then milk over as he falls under my spell.

"That's it, Sarah. Keep going." At Janice's urging, I continue.

My focus never leaves Brad's withering form. He quiets his whimpering. His body settles, and he stops twitching.

"Okay, humans, I'm going to move slowly over to your friend. I'm going to take the belt off of him, and afterward, Sarah's going to heal me," Janice says as a matter of fact.

"I didn't say I was going to heal you. I said you can heal yourself. Don't put words in my mouth." I bark.

"I cannot heal myself. It is against the rules of Fae. If you're injured, someone else must heal you. They have to care enough about you for you to be healed. Otherwise, my healing takes time just like every other living creature." Janice says, then his eyes move from my mouth to my eyes.

"Come on, Sarah! Just let him do it. Just say you'll heal him," Nick pleads.

"Fine, I'll heal you," I huff at Janice while blowing my bangs out of my eyes.

Janice is by Brad's side in two steps. I watch his hand take the belt off. Smoke rises from his hands. The muscles around his eyes grimace in pain. He pulls air in between his teeth, creating a hissing sound. Finally, the belt loosens, releasing its hold. It falls to the ground.

The flesh around Brad's belly is blackened and withered. The belt's magic digs in, chewing on him and willing to rip him apart in order to change him into a horse. His hands are already altered to hooves. He's reached the point that he's no longer a man, but he isn't yet a horse either. His head and neck haven't changed.

He was always so good-looking. Bile rises up in my throat, burning me.

"Take a long look, Sarah. This is what Puca does to his stable boys. He uses humans to create Fae horses." Janice's solemn voice rings with the truth. The other horses nuzzle Brad, rubbing their scent on him in acceptance.

I turn on Janice. I want to pummel him. "And you let him. You just let him do it, don't you? All you Fae you sit down here and have your little soirées, eating your vegetables and looking at your day-glo plants. Then every now and again when you get bored, you go up to the surface, killing as many humans as you can on a spree because someone told you to. Isn't that what you said? Someone told you to do it?" I spit the words at him like my threats from before.

He reaches out as if to touch me.

I draw back in disgust. "Don't you dare fucking touch me! I don't know who you think you are. You're some crazy creature that lives under the ground and stole me away from my parents." Blood pounds in my ears, racing through my veins. "You left Arty here at this very barn so he could turn into a horse with the rest of these humans." I choke.

It hasn't really struck me, but Janice is alone. I whip my head around, searching the area for additional Fae only to find none. "Where's your reinforcements? How did you find me? Why did you come here alone?" My lips pull back in a grimace of anger.

"I didn't bring anyone. It's me, just me." His hands open wide.

"How did you find me?" I move to him.

"I didn't put an enchantment on you, if that's what you mean," Janice replies.

I want to scream. "Is that how you found me in the human world?" It comes out as a whisper. I already know the answer. It had taken everything I was to get into the Hallowed Hills. When I left the Hallowed Hills, I'd left anything from Fae at my parents' house. I'd bathed since the maze, even if it had been something as simple as an enchanted lotion it wouldn't have lasted long enough for him to track me. He'd followed my magic trail, just like I'd followed his. The one thing I couldn't wash away or erase, magic. It lingers in my blood.

"I knew you would run away from Fae as soon as you figured out a way. After you left, I figured you would go to your parents. I went there and found the maze stones. You left Fae without the mushrooms. That's impossible. There's no way to return to Fae without a mushroom circle. So, I grew one for you. It works like a homing beacon."

I should've known better, shaking my head in disbelief. "Is that why I was so drawn to it?" I ask.

He closes his eyes, tilting his head back. My eyes are drawn to how truly black his hair is becoming. "Yes, did you hear the song of Fae?" His face gives nothing away.

"The mushroom sang to me," I whisper.

"Without that song playing through your mind, you would never get back into Fae. I knew you'd return for Olive, but I thought Arthur was with you." Janice looks from me to the others.

"It's just another fairy trick. I wouldn't believe him." Nick's words stick in my mind. Nick places his hand on my shoulder to physically support me.

"Being as I don't trust you, Janice. I don't believe you either." I reply.

"Don't you see what's happening, Sarah? I came here alone to find you. I knew you were with other people. I also knew you would never come back here without somebody helping you. I don't have Arthur, Deston doesn't have Arthur. I don't know who does. I do know this—you need allies. You can't keep fumbling around and expect to not be discovered by someone or worse, taken hostage. All of your friends turned into the very thing you've just witnessed. And Fae will turn them. Fae won't feel any pity or sorrow for you or for them. If you want to help your friends and help yourself, you must come with me. Let me help you. Do you see what's happening to you? Do you think what's happening is normal?" Janice implores.

I know he's playing on my uncertainty and fear so that I'll go with him.

"I don't believe you." My resolve falters. *Can he help me?*

"I'll go get Olive and bring her back to you. Olive is a scared little girl. The Fae are protective of their young too. Let me bring Olive back to you." Janice is too eager to help me.

Nick breaks in. "Terrible idea. If you let him leave, he'll come back with an army and take us all." Nick shakes his head.

No matter how much I want to believe Janice, the nagging in the pit of my stomach tells me I can't. Fae aren't to be trusted—they're murderers.

CHAPTER 14

"Why don't we waste him and go on about our business?" Jake presses the muzzle of his gun into the base of Janice's neck. He pushes Janice forward, forcing him down on one knee.

"Stop!" I cry. I'm angry and scared, but I don't want to become like one of them— the Fae. Seeing Jake hurt Janice bothers me. It isn't just about being better than the Fae. My heart leaps to my throat at the thought of Janice in pain or suffering. Bravado aside, I do care. My eyes had lit upon his hands blackened and burnt the skin cracking open in places and oozing.

I somehow, I expected that with the Fae's connection to nature, their blood would be green. The viscosity of the liquid comes through the cracked skin, resembling blood but the color is all wrong. Some fantasy writer once wrote about unicorns having silver blood. The truth is so much more mundane and yet frightening at the same time. His blood is blue, dark royal blue. As it drips out onto the ground, small mushrooms sprout with every drop. Something in my chest flutters, I'm not even sure why, but my eyes meet his. "Is that how you made the mushroom circle?" I whisper.

Janice grimaces and replies, "Fairy circles can only be made with fairy blood. It's usually somewhere a Fae died. It takes a lot of blood to create a fairy circle. The bigger the circle, more blood." He informs me.

"Did you bleed yourself or did you bleed someone else for hours?" It comes out harsh. I don't intend it too.

"Ryan, one of my underlings was already dying. I simply made his blood useful. He'd bled a great deal before we ever got back to the maze stones. He only had enough blood left in him for maybe three-quarters of a circle. I bled the rest myself, for you, Sarah. To give you a way back and a way out." He offers.

"He could've used any of the Fae blood. They have no allegiance to one another." Nick sneers, he's blinded by his fear for Nikki.

"Yeah, it's just another Fae trick," Jake says. "Don't believe the *fairy*. They don't do anything but lie." Jake wants to blow Janice head off. Another untrustworthy source.

"How much of the circle did you bleed before Ryan?" I watch Janice's body language.

He smiles. "I could tell you anything right now, you wouldn't know." That isn't true. He's lying. The ring of the lie is there. Is it a tone or a note? Either way, the magic tattles on him.

"Oh no, Janice. I would know if you were lying. How much of the circle did you bleed before you found Ryan dying?" I prod.

"Full quarter. We fanned out in your parents' neighborhood, checking every house over and over to see if you were hiding in one of them, being clever. You are clever, Sarah. Ryan was shot in the kitchen of some house, but we couldn't find anybody there, and no trace of you."

"Did you search the house for the culprit?" My heart is in my throat. *Please say he didn't find them!*

"Yes, I couldn't find a trace of anything. The dogs just sat in the kitchen and whined by the back door." His eyes watch me carefully.

New fear grips me. It had to be my dad, but why did he leave the basement? Unless the Fae discovered the safe room and he shot him to keep it safe. That's the only explanation. The door to the safe room is by the back door of the kitchen. Of course, the dogs sat there and whined. It could've been any house. Just because the dog was whining by the back door doesn't make it Sorenson's.

The ring of truth reverberates. He'd bled for me. I had made a promise. I said I'd heal him. I meet his violet eyes, so expressive, so beautiful, and his eyelashes jet black. His eyebrows slowly fade from white to black. As my eyes follow down the white hair on his head, I see the long trendles fading from white to black. The last time I'd seen him only the tips were black. Now it's spreading. Over half of his hair has turned from the bottom up as if the color is changing in the reverse. His lips are full and firm. His jaw is chiseled, coming to a slight point with high cheekbones and a high forehead.

Creases around his eyes are the only telltale signs of pain. He quietly keeps it hidden behind a façade of control.

I resolve within myself. "Tell me what I have to sing to heal your hands. A deal is a deal."

A smile breaks across his face. "I knew not all of humanity had lost their honor. You only need to keep thinking in your mind, 'your healing is mine.' Sing a B-flat." He instructs.

It sounds silly to me, I can't really do that. I try to find the B-flat with my voice, but it doesn't come. His version of healing won't work for me. Instead, the song that keeps coming to mind is, "Rain, rain, go away, and heal Jan-i-ce today." I sing it several times, and the parched skin on his hand fleshes out, knitting itself closed. The blood crusts flake away into the grass.

"How did you do that?" He turns his hands over, observing the changes.

I shake my head. "I sang and healed your wounds. What's the big deal?"

Nick clears his throat and thrusts his hand into his hair, slowly running his finger around the edge of his ear. I stare at him and down at the ground. My hand finds the peak of my ear, the point has elongated. My eyes go to Janice's ear, even as my fingers trace my own.

"You created your own healing song. Amazing!" Janice's eyes dart to my hand as his pupils dilate. "When did you start changing?" he demands.

"Since I left the maze and the Hallowed Hills."

Jake and Tom pull their weapons back. They are still trained on Janice, who kneels on the ground eyes wide with wonder.

"I swear my allegiance to you. I am yours to command," Janice exclaims.

Jake growls out. "Don't believe him! He's a pointy-eared liar. They're probably raised to be liars their entire life."

I tilt my head to the side and cock an eyebrow at Jake. "Really, do you think I'm stupid enough to believe the words that come out of the mouth of a Fae? I've been down here longer than you."

Jake tears his eyes away from me to stare at the back of Janice's head.

"You can't swear allegiance to me. Aren't you sworn to Deston?" I demand.

Janice replies, "I relinquish all fealty to anyone but you. I am yours to command."

I laugh out loud. What a ridiculous idea that I'd have some Fae under my control. They did have a say in my control. I'd already had one Fae swear allegiance to me, Lavender, but I'd compelled her.

"Did I compel you?" I raise both brows this time.

"You are capable of compelling?" It's his turn to look shocked.

"Yes. Well, that's what you guys did to us, isn't it? You compel us. Did I compel you?" There is no need for him to know that I'd compelled Lavender. She's more useful if she's still a secret.

"No, my Lady, you did not compel me. I willingly give myself into your service." He spreads his newly healed hands, exposing the tender flesh.

Tom does a little dance and picks up the edge of his shirt, pretending he's prancing. "Oh, it's 'my Lady' now. I absolutely am at your service."

It's kind of funny watching Tom dance. I snicker. "Stop it!"

All of the guys guffaw.

"I'm sorry, Sarah. It's pretty funny. I mean, swearing allegiance. You can't fucking believe him." Nick's eyes are hard, his jaw locked and flexing.

"I'm not that stupid, guys. I know you can't believe him. All Fae are a bunch of liars. I realize that. However, if he is actually telling the truth by swearing allegiance to me, he could be more useful to us."

"What, as target practice?" Tom spouts.

"That sounds like a great idea, Tom. Why don't we let him run as fast as he can and see how far he gets before one of us shoots him?" Nick guffaws and Tom laughs with his tongue between his teeth.

"You're both assholes," I sputter.

Nick stops laughing. He explains, "No, Sarah, we're just realists. If you really think he is telling you the truth, you're being foolish. I wouldn't trust him with a dog I liked."

Tom and Nick have a point, but I'd seen what allegiance means to a Fae. We can use that.

"I wouldn't trust him with a dog I like or don't like," Jake says. "Mostly because the Fae enchant animals, dumb ass." Jake isn't going to be convinced.

"Really doesn't matter whether I trust him or don't trust him or whether you guys trust him or don't. The whole point is we have his sworn allegiance. If I accept that, he's in my service. Apparently, in Fae, they're kind of big on this whole IOU my allegiance shit." I cock my head to the side, putting my hands on my hips. I reach my hand out, and I touch his shoulder.

"I accept your allegiance. You are now in my service until such a time as I release you, you die, or you request to be released." I heard that in a movie; it sounds right.

He offers me his sword, handle first. "You have to take my sword and touch me on either shoulder with it." He lowers his head, the long white hair on his scalp separates to either side, baring the back of his neck.

I clasp the pommel in my hand, it's heavier than I thought it'd be. I lift it as high as I can, which is barely above his shoulder. The muscles in my arms strain and shake with the amount of exertion necessary for me to raise such a heavy weapon. When I saw him wield it, it all looked so easy. He'd swung it around and chopped people's heads off, cutting them down as if it is a butter knife and weighed almost nothing. This thing has to weigh easily fifty to sixty pounds. I'm strong enough to pull my own body weight up, but I'd gotten lucky in the maze. He flipped this thing around as if it were a baton. If I'm not careful as I lower it onto his body, it'd slam into his shoulder, cleaving him in half.

I settle it gently on one of his shoulders, turning it to the flat edge as it touches down.

"You must say in the name of Danu," Janice instructs.

"In the name of Danu," I repeat.

Janice continues, "Now you have to touch it to my other shoulder and say in the name of Oberon, the first king and queen of Tuatha Dé Danann, I accept your fealty."

"Is that all?" I exclaim.

"In the name of Danu." I barely clear his head, laying the sword gently down on his other shoulder. My arms continue to strain. "In the name Oberon, the first king and queen of Tuatha Dé Danann, I accept your fealty." I finish with a huff, blowing my hair out of my eyes.

"I accept your fealty into my court," Janice instructed.

I feel my shoulders shift down as the weight of the sword becomes too much for me. "I don't have a court." I bite my lip.

"Not yet you don't, my Lady." Janice quickly replies.

"I accept your fealty into my court." I take a deep breath, filled with exasperation, fairies, and their bullshit little games.

"Now you're supposed to tell him to rise and be recognized," Nick interjects.

I turn my head sideways, raising an eyebrow at Nick.

"Who made you an expert on fealty?" I wave my right hand around in Janice's general direction.

"I'm kind of a history snob." Nick ducks his head to hide his embarrassment.

I lift the sword, but I don't make it far enough. It touches down on Janice's forehead with the sharp edge. It's just enough to draw a small drop of blood at the very center of the widow's peak in his hairline. It runs down between his eyes and off the tip of his nose. I watch it in fascination and sorrow as the words flow over my lips. "Arise and be recognized by my court," I whisper.

All the sounds of Fae nature around me goes silent, holding its breath. In slow motion, the drop of blue blood slowly falls to the ground. Part of me is fascinated, the other part of me revolted. I'm expecting a mushroom to form, but instead where it touches the ground, something else sprouts.

A green bud slowly rises up, rearing its head in the direction of the Fae sky. It's a flower bud in variegated greens. The casing of the flower bud opens, peeling back the outer layer until it finally reveals pedals underneath. They are white with a velvety fuzz, causing light to refract off the iridescent petals. It shoots in a thousand directions at a time. One by one, the petals peel back like fingers from a palm. It exposes itself as the purest white rose. My breath catches. I wait to see the color of the heart. All of the Hallowed Hills holds its breath. Nothing moves, and the sword becomes light as a feather. When the final pedal spreads into position, its heart is as black as night. With one touch of a golden ray in the center, it beams out. The last petal falls into place, creating a giant shock wave that bursts forth.

My hair pushes back from my face, and its wakes form out from us. Janice's hands fully plant on the ground as he sags into his kneeling position.

"I have found you, you to have come." He sounds like a crazy person. Janice grabs my hand. The heat from his lips meets my skin, searing me. It burns and entices all at the same time. The fire blows through my body. I don't want him to just kiss my hand. I wanted him to kiss everything.

"Okay, lover boy! I think you've had your fun kissing her. Let go of her hands, now." Tom has his sidearm pressed firmly against Janice temple, indenting the skin into the soft depression on the side of his head. Janice releases my hand, putting his hands up on either side of him.

"I forgot myself. It won't happen again."

"Why don't you gather yourself over there and stop fawning over me? It's making me sick." My sharp tongue covers how he affects me.

Janice gathers his feet underneath himself and stands. I'm not able to tear my eyes away from the beauty of the flower. It stops blooming, but it isn't getting any smaller. It's getting larger and growing. The longer it exposes itself to fairy light, the blacker it becomes, fading out from the center to the white petals. It reminds me of the color of Janice's hair.

I want to pick it and take it with me. The beauty calls to me; its sweet song reaches into my soul, mirroring me. The moment I lay my finger upon its velvety soft petals, I know it can't be touched by anyone else ever again. A clear note rings out in recognition.

"Don't touch it, Sarah!" Nick says. "It's probably just some fairy magic. He's trying to trick you. You probably touch it and fall into a deep sleep like the Wizard of Oz or something." Nick reaches out to stop my hand. I pull my hand back. It's still beautiful, and I don't want to leave it there. I don't have any more water, but I need to nurture it.

"Ever seen a flower like this before, Janice?" I inquire.

"Yes, my Lady, once."

"Did it change colors?" The flower fills my eyes, enchanting me.

"Yes, they all start out black-and-white before they settle into their true colors," Janice replies.

"Their true colors?" I'm starting to sound like a toddler with a million questions on my tongue.

"Yes, these flowers grow and bloom very rarely. They turn out either black or white, depending upon what their true colors are."

"Well, now that is really informative. So, what is its true color?" I demand.

"Only the flower decides." Janice supplies less information than a Chinese instruction manual.

"I guess it's about as clear as dirty dishwater," Nick scoffs.

"I want to take it with us. Give me a shovel. I want to dig it up," I say. Janice grabs my wrist.

I look down at his hand and up at his eyes. "You want to let go of me?" I ask.

"Don't. You cannot dig the flower out. You will kill it. You must leave it right where it is," Janice says.

Tom leans in and quips. "Hey, listen, loyalty boy. You want to get your hand off the boss lady? Looks like she doesn't like you touching her." Tom's reliable. I give him a small smile.

I gaze at the flower one last time and tear my eyes away. "Okay, I'll leave it there if it's that rare. I don't want to kill it."

Janice picks up a few loose branches. "We want to protect it by hiding it from others whom might kill it." Janice moves branches and bushes into a protective circle.

Jake cuts in. "You're welcome to do whatever you want there, pointy ears. We'll be leaving. Something tells me that shock wave that went through here will tell everybody where we are." He begins strolling down the road.

Janice grabs more bushes, moving them around the flower. He creates a protective bubble, hiding it. His gaze takes on reverent awe, moving his hand as if there's an invisible bubble protecting it. His eyes stray to me, the muscles working in his face. I think he wants to smile. It would've creeped me out if it weren't for the fact that my heart twisted in a way I'd never experienced before. I smile at him, and he returns it. No one had ever smiled at me that way.

"Let's get to Deston's castle and get Olive." Nick hurries us on.

CHAPTER 15

Just because he pledged himself to me and some weird flower grew out of the ground doesn't mean he's loyal. It also doesn't mean that I trust him. He still has pointy ears, and his loyalty will always be to the Fae, never to humanity. No matter how much I resemble Fae now, it doesn't mean I'll ever be Fae on the inside. I'm always gonna be me, and I hope some part will still be human.

We crest a hill, and it's probably the same hill for all I remember. There's a ridiculous fairytale style Fae Castle, Deston's castle. He's probably in there, lording it on high with all his Fae minions and sycophants. Every one of them is jockeying for position with their multi-colored hair and their light eyes, wrapping themselves up and leaves and pretty flowers. It makes me sick. It doesn't change what they are, which is fucking evil.

"So, do you have any idea of how are going to get inside?" I examine the portico.

"My lady, I would walk all of us under the archway into the forecastle, but they're heavily armed." Janice pointed at Jake and Tom. "They would need to leave their weapons behind. If you could pass for being enchanted, we could all walked in. My lady, you resemble Fae more than human."

His words sting me. I don't want to pass for Fae. Even if it did save Olive, I'm human.

"Well, I'm sorry, but I don't think Tom and Jake are going to give up their guns. You need to come up with a better plan for rescuing Olive. Maybe we should just float in," I query.

"That will never work. Protection lines surround the castle, and the enchantment on the walls disallows flying over, you must find a way through a valid entrance. The only person who can fly unencumbered is Deston himself." Janice responds.

I broke the last protection enchantment that was supposed to keep people out. I don't how difficult a spell that was. It seemed pretty easy to break to me, but that's me. The only truly intricate spell I'd seen was Brad's, and I'm not sure I'll be able to do anything for Brad and his half-horse problem.

I look over at Brad, he can't remember anything, he is more horse than man. With the belt gone, he won't change anymore, but that doesn't make him what he was. He can't go with us.

"I got my own plan, and here it goes: Jake and Tom, you'll stay outside the castle and find somewhere to hang out. Don't go killing a bunch of Fae, like rogue humans who magically got in here. No one will buy that shit. Nick and I are going inside. Nick's our enchanted human." I release the breath I'd been holding and wait for the push back.

"You want to enchant me?" Nick exclaims.

I bite my lower lip and nod my head. "Yeah, do you trust me?" I ask.

Our eyes meet, and Nick stares me down.

"If I hadn't met you on the surface, I wouldn't trust you now. But yeah, if it gets us inside and puts me one step closer to finding Nikki, that's the only thing I came for." Nick thrusts his hand at me. I take it. He doesn't shake but cradles my hand, closing his other hand over mine. He then drops them and runs his fingers through his hair. He isn't thrilled.

I raise my voice and sing the notes to enchant him, watching his eyes glaze over. They turn milky-white as his mouth goes slack and his shoulders relax. His arms lose their tension and slide down thoughtlessly to his side.

"You're very good at that," Janice comments. "You managed to focus it directly on him so it wouldn't affect anyone else. That takes true talent. There aren't many Fae who have the strength to do what you just did." Janice's words irritate me. I don't want to be talented.

I shoot him a look from the corner of my eye. "Yeah, I'm real thrilled. I'm better than most of the Fae. I already knew that." *God, I sound like such a bitch.* Biting the inside of my lip to hold back the 'I'm sorry' that naturally wants to follow.

"As you will it, my Lady," Janice replies.

I roll my eyes. This whole 'my lady' talk is annoying. *I'm not nobility. I'm some regular girl from nowhere Texas.*

"You sure you really want to go in there with this pointy-eared bastard?" Tom looks at me through his eyebrows at me.

"Yeah, it's the only plan that'll get us in with the least amount of resistance. That is what we're looking for. We're trying for stealth, not brute force. I mean, you are the only two soldiers around. Nick doesn't really count as a soldier. He'll fight as hard as he can and he's strong, but let's face it, you're trained and there are only two of you. Better off leaving you here and doing it my way. I'll leave the horses with you. If I were you, I'd find a stand of trees and hide in it. Not mushrooms!" I arched an eyebrow at both of them.

"Now, that little lady sounds like a good time. What do you say, Jake? We go hide in a stand of trees and pick up off some Fae from a distance?" he chuckles.

Jake takes his turn at bravado. "That does sound like a good time, Tom. Twenty bucks says I get the first."

"The hell you will. It's fifty that I'll get the first Fae." Tom retorts as they move away.

I shake my head and watch them bickering. I touch the blue stallion on the side of his face, rubbing it and scratching between his eyes.

"Go with them. They'll protect you. If anything, you'll be free in the forest to live as you want." The blue stallion snorts and tosses his head up and down. He turns and walks away with his friends following him.

Brad wouldn't go anywhere unless I instruct him to. I place my hand on what is left of his shoulder.

"Brad, you have to go with the horses. They'll keep you safe and show you what you can eat in the forest. Listen to them and Jake."

He mindlessly turns and canters away. I watch the shift of his hips and his hindquarters. My throat swells with the lump lodged in it.

I need to figure out what's going on here, and Fae have to pay.

Rhyming crap, I hate that.

I want to kill someone. I want them to pay for all the pain and suffering. I know it's not going to resolve anything. You have to kill the right person, and maybe that might fix the problem.

I swallow back my rage, "Lead on, let's get this done. I want Olive and Arty, and then I want to get the hell out of here."

Janice nods his head and steps in front of me, taking the lead.

It's another ten minutes from the hills to the castle proper. I trudge ahead while Janice takes everything in stride as if it's just a stroll in Fae and nothing to be remarked upon. We approach the moat and the giant arched entryway with the spiked portico.

Everything in fairy is natural. From a distance, everything appears man-made and normal, but up close you can see it's different. The stones of the castle could've grown there, but the texture is all wrong. The stone is white marble-ish, but it glistens and glimmers in a crystalline fashion.

The portico itself could've been metal, but the truth is if you look closely, you can see the dark vines of some plant interwoven, making it harder than stone. The sharpened tips glisten as if they are metallic and capable of slicing you to ribbons if the portico comes down.

The archway is perfect, but it's as if someone sang it into existence. Its design is unusual. Instead of being a smoothly rounded circle at the top, it's in waves, scalloped with a Moorish slant.

In the forecourt, we will be safe when we were inside the wall, first hurdle down. Two armed Fae cross the forecourt having spotted Janice. They make a beeline for us. The first man draws his brows together, staring at Janice in a hard manner. The second man gives me a once-over.

"Kar-ol, how goes your time?" Janice inquires.

"My time goes well as does my human hunting. How goes yours? Is this one a plaything?" Kar-ol's eyes inspect Nick.

"He's strong. I thought it would make a fine addition to our kitchens." They all three look him over and nod their heads. The second man continues to examine me with his eyes.

"You look familiar, do I know you?" His vermillion eyes crawl over me inch by inch.

I, in turn, sneer back at him.

Janice, he cuts them off. "No, she's a recent convert from another court."

"Well, that explains the hair."

I don't understand what he means about my hair. It's black. *What's the big deal?*

I want to open my mouth and say something, but what if it's wrong?

The wake waves surrounding us fascinate me. I can't stop staring. An overwhelming sense of heaviness fills the area. More Fae, more wakes, each one strong and decisive. Every one demands my attention, like a meat grinder trying to mix and cut you up into small bits and then mix you into everything else, constantly turning and changing.

Kar-ol remarks, "I have not been to a Seelie court in a long time. I find them boorish fodder for goodie-goodie behavior. Did you not become bored with all their goodness? How it oozes from them like honey out of a beehive?" He snarls one side of his face.

"Yes, I was bored. No good can come from too much good. I was raised there and tired of it." I give them the best reply I can dig up.

Janice steps in. "I must take her to Deston. He will want to meet the newest member of his court. So, I will say my farewells."

"We are heading to see Deston ourselves. Shall we travel together?" Kar-ol offers.

Internally, I groan. We're trapped. If we say we want to stop by a room and pick something up, they'll come with us.

"I must drop this pet off in the kitchens. Go on ahead of us. We will catch up after. I'm perfectly happy to let you see his Grace first."

They nod their heads and cross their fingers, touching their foreheads in some kind of weird Fae salute. I do the same in return, mimicking Janice's movements.

Janice ushers me through a small side door to the castle, along with Nick. I hope we somehow reach Deston's room using the elevators, but that isn't going to happen. Nevertheless, I'm still hopeful.

"We are not leaving Nick in the kitchen or anywhere else here," I whisper.

"No, we'll leave him in your old room. No one will look there. They think you're gone. The room is clean. It'll be the safest place for him." Janice returns.

I breathe a sigh of relief. "Well then, I'll remove his enchantment. He doesn't need to be standing in a room alone, brainless." I murmur back.

Janice doesn't even turn his head. "If you do and someone does discover him, you will have given him a death sentence. Leave him enchanted. This way they'll think he's lost or someone misplaced him on purpose as a joke. Enchanted—he's protected." Janice returns.

I grind my teeth. I don't think it's a good idea. I don't care what Janice thinks even if he says he's loyal to me and wants to be in my service or a vassal or whatever the hell all that crap meant. I don't believe him. I just don't believe people.

I think most of them are liars. Nick's only with me because he wants one thing, his sister, and as soon as he gets that, he's leaving anyway he can.

"You better not be lying to me," I say between grinding teeth.

"Yes, because you'll hunt me down to the end of your days and kill me slowly with a spoon digging my heart out? Perhaps you'll thrust bamboo skewers into different parts of my body and slowly split them apart, watching me rage in pain before I bleed to death? Yes, yes, I've heard it all, not just from you. Others too, my Lady." He throws a side smile at me. "You are not the first person who has threatened to kill me. I've been alive a long time. I've had many enemies threaten to kill me in a thousand different ways, all sounded extremely painful. None have come true. I'm not saying you wouldn't succeed. I believe you would. However, let's not waste time blathering on about threats." His hand brushes mine.

I snap my mouth shut. He sure does make me sound petty.

All seven hundred of the servants' stairs mock me. With heavy feet, I begin the slow, circular climb. It's a good thing Janice and I are separated by Nick's bulky form. Otherwise, he would've seen the daggers in my eyes, trying to stab him in the back of his head for making me walk up all these stairs. Finally, we reach the seventh floor. My feet know exactly where my room is, and I unlock the door with a whistle. Quickly pushing Nick inside, I double check the corners and cupboards to make sure no one is lurking in hiding. After, I close the door on Nick's milky, vacant eyes.

"You could've escaped from your room at any time?" Janice exclaims.

I raise my eyebrows and give him a half-smile. "Yeah, but where would I have gone? I looked human." I reply.

"Yes, but you no longer look human. How is that possible?" he inquires.

"Well, isn't that the question of the year?" I sneer.

CHAPTER 16

I leave Nick behind. I added an extra note, one octave higher, to the locking song. I left it in the background as if it is part of the reverberation, making it barely perceptible. No one can unlock the door. The only person present is Janice. If he noticed, he certainly doesn't let on. I had to do it. If they start looking for me, the first place they'll check is my old room. So long as no one realizes I'm here, Nick is safe there. And as long as no one can get in the room, Nick is safe.

I hope.

Janice leads me to the elevator.

"Is this the way to Olive?" My eyes dart either way down the halls.

Why didn't we take the elevator in the first place?

"We have to go see Deston. We can't run the risk of anyone looking for us. Kar-ol is on Deston's campaign. The likelihood of him mentioning my return with a recruit is high. Deston will want to meet you. We can't get around this. Hopefully, he won't recognize you. I don't think anyone who has met you before will recognize you." Janice doesn't sound convicted.

"I don't have to look into a mirror to realize I look nothing like my former self. Everything about me has become a stranger. I'm taller than before. My eyes aren't even the same color. Deston will recognize me, or he won't. There's nothing we can do about that. We get Olive and Nick and go." I

"No matter what, we must go to Deston. It's the only way to get Olive." Janice slowly says.

"I don't understand. When I talk with you face-to-face, you seem normal, like you have a conscience. As if you really do want to help me and humanity. But the moment I'm not standing in front of you, confronting you, I hear you repeating nursery rhymes; incorrectly I might add. You stole Olive on purpose. Now you're willing to get her back with me, for me. I just don't understand. It's like there are two people living inside of you."

"There are two people living inside me, and I don't have time to explain. Standing in the hallway like this to have a discussion isn't normal for Fae. We don't explain ourselves to each other. I took Olive; Deston ordered me to. I say the rhymes because Deston makes me. He was my liege lord. Now you are. Only you can force me to do anything, but we mustn't allow Deston to learn of this." He explains.

My mouth goes dry. What if Deston can force me to do something? If he can enchant me, then we are nowhere. Deston is obviously stronger than Janice or anyone else around here.

"What makes Deston so powerful?" I'm playing toddler again, asking a million questions.

The doors to the elevator slide open. "He is a prince." Janice shrugs.

"Yes, but even princes are beholden to a queen or king. Very few princes rule in their own name and answer to no one," I reply.

"You're right, but here without a queen present to rein him in, he is ruled by wild. Wild is the power. What he requires is fulfilled. When you swear allegiance, you swear to do what your liege lord demands of you. They tell you to go, you are compelled to go. Like humans are compelled by fairy song, we are compelled by our vassal ties." Janice has an unnerving ability to stare into me.

I shift from one foot to the other. *And now he's sworn to me. If I say go, he must go.* "It's not just a feudal system or a caste system?" I inquire.

"Every living thing answers to someone. There is always someone above you unless you're queen. No one is above the queen." His words ring with finality.

"What about the king?" I inquire.

"No one is above the queen. The king is merely there to amuse the queen. He's not there for any other reason." That doesn't make sense. Humanity has always placed a king above a queen.

"Is he her lover or just a political alliance?" There has to be a reason.

"He can be both. He helps enforce the queen's dictates, usually leading her armies. But she could also decide to relegate those jobs to a prince or even lower nobility, depending upon who she feels is most capable of handling her requirements. It's a typical feudal society. Humanity adopted our version of rulership a long time ago. Why do you not know these things?" He side-glances at me with a raised eyebrow.

I cross my arms, cocking a hip to the side. My eyebrows pull together. "Humanity has not been ruled by high feudal society in hundreds of years. Most of those fell away with the advent of democracy and the republic. Everyone having a vote, rights, and free speech. Have you ever heard of free speech?"

The doors to the elevator slide closed. Janice's lips tighten. "The ability to speak freely is not new. It is a dangerous practice freely speaking one's mind." He retorts.

Every time we speak, it rakes over the last nerve in my body, irritating me. I refocus on our surroundings, the elevator. It's a box, a beautifully decorated box. Don't get me wrong, but it's still a box. It makes me feel trapped by beauty. Listening to Janice describe Fae society's interworking's, I honestly believe it's an inconceivable idea to me. Humanity has moved on from this form of rule, but the Fae are still stuck. Feudal states still exist, but most of the monarchies had already moved on to constitutional monarchy with a crowned figurehead or dictatorships, because who wants to rule if you don't have control of the Army to back you up? Those were in places like Africa and South America. That kind of rule doesn't exist in the Western world. Now I'm standing face-to-face with someone who just told me he expects me to know all about it because they gave it to humanity. *And that makes it all okay?*

"This idea of freedom the Greeks postulated, how did that work out for them?" Janice's voice is laced with smug satisfaction in his knowledge.

"Not very well, they did end up destroying themselves. Humanity does that to itself. We don't need the Fae." I curl my nose up at his all-knowing bullshit.

"Fae are not like humans. Without the feudal society and our queen's control, we are ruled by wild. We would destroy all of Earth. I'm quite surprised humanity hasn't done it already. But then again, you always were an interesting creature. From the moment your kind were created, you fascinated us." Janice smiles.

I almost choked. *Created us?* "From the moment you created *us*, we fascinated you? What, as if you were there at the moment of creation?" I sputter.

"My lady, you don't have to like the words I say, but when I speak them to you, believe me, they are true. Humanity was created by Fae. One of our earliest queen's wanted workers for her mines to dig gold. When the Fae still ruled the surface, enjoying the daylight with all bending to our will, Lilith took a mammal and sang out its animalistic features—most of them anyway. Slowly, she worked in features of Fae. She attempted to make humanity beautiful, but it didn't take. I'm not implying humans aren't beautiful. Please do not be offended. You are simply not Fae. When I look at most humans, all I see is the mammal they originally were created from. Many of them are still heavily covered in hair, with the large ridged eyebrows. They do not strike me as one of beauty. You, on the other hand, were already beautiful before we took you. By human standards, you are an unbelievable specimen. Since you have embraced your Fae side, you've only become more so." His eyes shine with admiration while his face remains blank.

"Are you kidding me? Do you realize what a bigot you sound like? Now that I look more Fae, I'm beautiful. I was human, but somehow your weird magic is changing me. I didn't do this to myself. Do you really think I want to be a Fae? All I want to do is get the hell away from you and all of your crazy pointy-eared friends. You did this to me." I poke him in the chest with a pointy finger. "I didn't do this to myself. It's not like I want to stay here. I don't want to be one of you. I want to go home. I want to see my parents," *Crap, backpedal. No one can know they're alive.* "Wherever they are, if they're still live. You were there that night—did you kill them?" I demand, with my finger still presses into his chest, gaslighting is a great way to cover your own ass.

"No, I did not. I don't know where your parents are. Do you?" The truth rings in his words.

I close my eyes. I don't want him to see me rolling them in my head. I also didn't want him to see the lies pouring off my lips. "No, I don't know where they are. I didn't find their bodies in my house." *Stick as close to the truth as possible.* "They're gone, just gone." I force my shoulders to slump.

The elevator jolts, coming to a stop. It pulls me out of my angry bubble. I'd barely noticed the elevator moving.

Janice turns to me, his eyes searching my face. His hand removes my finger from indenting his chest. "He will ask you for fealty. Tell him you've switched courts, but you haven't decided which prince you wish to follow. Show him deference. Bow your head, slightly crossing your fingers as you did before. Fae are proud. We do not give our loyalty easily. He will understand you wish to weigh your choices and choose wisely. Tell him 'this is the first court you've been to and you still wish to compare it to Jacques'." Janice's eyes take in my face.

I demand, "And if he recognizes me?" The doors slide open.

"If he recognizes you, all Cernunnos can and will break loose. Unless of course, you came back on your own. Tell him you wanted to be with your own kind." His body stills. The box holds its breath. The wakes freeze in midair.

I turn to him. "I don't want to be with you. I want to be with my own kind, i.e. humanity." Whatever words he's about to say, they die on his lips as the doors fully seat themselves in the open position. I school my face into bland indifference. The other side of that door doesn't need to see my irritation or my disagreeing demeanor with Janice. I don't trust him. I don't trust any of the Fae, but he's my only ally. The first rule of secret infiltration is don't get caught and don't give yourself away.

Once again, the entry is completely vacant. I guess when you feel you're the all-powerful Oz in your domain, you don't need to watch the doors.

CHAPTER 17

Deston's chamber has all the same boring browns and greens—typical Fae. The hum is different here. I hadn't noticed the singing before. Last time I hadn't listened. I didn't know how. Sound wakes roll off everything, not just the ivy on the walls or the honeysuckle's around the doorways, but from the hyacinths, hollyhocks, morning glory—they all wake to me. Even the spiky leaves of daffodils do as well with their tongues' lolling out. In Fae, I expect there are flowers and leaves curling everywhere. Most plants are completely innocuous, normal everyday flowers. There's always poison among all that pretty; that's how Fae works. It isn't all going to be pretty. There has to be something to hurt you; something you wouldn't notice. The pretty blinds you right up to the moment it strikes and kills you. Fae draw people in with their pretty faces. You'll get just a little too close, and once they have you where they want you, they strike.

My trailing eyes linger over the individual wakes, but taken as a whole, the reason I don't like this room compared to the rest of the castle reveals itself. It's a prison, meant to draw you in to bring you closer to your own demise before it locks itself on you. The tips of fanged thorns hidden by green leaves wait to suck you dry of every last drop of your life's blood. I can almost feel the walls closing in on me. The flowers scream at me to be wary. The deeper we go into Deston's private domain, the heavier my feet grow. The magic wakes press me to leave. I want to escape the oppressive waking of the wall's magic; it batters at me. I glance at Janice, but he never wavers.

What if everything he told me about fairies is wrong? What if he'd been trying to deceive me the entire time to get me here to this room? Cold fear runs up my back. My heart beats frantically. This is a mistake. My instinct for fight-or-flight kicks in, and I'm inclined to try to run away. I might dive out the window and float down. Maybe call something to me or force a plant to grow. I'm not sure, anything. I swallow dried spittle. I run my tongue along my lips, hoping to calm myself. Both of Janice's friends are bowing to Deston with crossed fingers. As Deston lounges in his chair, it resembles a throne in front of the fireplace.

Everything here is made of wood. I can't understand why you'd have a fireplace. What if it burns the building to the ground? His fingers snap, and green fire leaps in the hearth. The temperature in Fae is comfortable. Why would you want a fire? I can't imagine. Janice lowers his head, crossing his fingers. He bends over in an honest to god bow. I'd never seen anyone in real life ease into a position of supplication with such grace.

"I see you have returned, bringing me my heart's desire, the human child, and who is this with you?" Deston's words scrape at me.

"I have returned, my lord. I'm afraid I was unable to locate the girl as you instructed. I've kidnapped her friend as you requested. Even now, she is here in the castle. The girl, Sarah, will come to us if she's capable, and if not, she will die amongst the humans." Janice's words trail a cold line down my back.

"Good! I would have liked it if you could've brought the resistor here. Who is this? Kar-ol tells me it's a new recruit."

"She's chosen to switch courts, my lord. She wishes to join our side." Janice repeats the story from before.

"Do you also wish to swear fealty now?" The query bumps me out of my alternate reality as I realize he is speaking directly to me.

"No, I wish to visit all the courts and decide which suits me best!" Too afraid to say anything more, I press my lips closed. The flash of Janice's eyes gives me the feeling he approves of my answer. The wakes coming off both of them are of satisfaction, smooth and clean.

"By all means, show her around my court. Make sure she fully understands that if she chooses us what she'd be gaining on the winning side. I intend to win." Deston's ease at announcing his ability to win grates on me. I hate that level of arrogance.

"Of course, my lord. Is there any doubt?" Janice's suck up, adds to my desire to smack them both.

"There's never any doubt. I'm always on the winning side. Are you sure that human girl will come for the child?" Deston asks again. The doubt, it always creeps in to gnaw away at you.

"Quite sure, my lord." Janice's reassurance is quick and practiced.

"Jacques has been tracking her." From my side angle, his eyes shift back and forth. He thinks he has an advantage. "I want you to go back to the human world and keep tracking this girl before the others get a hold of her. The entire fate of Fae may be up to her. They'll try to kill her just to stop her." The whole room has been cold and tilting the entire conversation.

It doesn't make any sense, the idea of Fae avidly searching for me in the human world and willing to kill whoever they came across just to find me. I'm just human or so they think. Janice knows I'm not or no longer appear to be. I can't understand why they'd be looking for me. I mean, if I could figure out how their magic worked, I'm sure any of the human girls can. It's not like I have special training in singing or know much about music. Everything I know is rudimentary. My mother is the songbird.

"Gather forces! Take them back to the surface with you after you've rested and eaten," Deston commands. "Be there as soon as twilight begins. If you must, hide out in the human world. Don't let this girl get away." Deston's hand clenches, and he pounds his fist into his chair.

"Of course, my lord." Janice regains his stance with both hands crossed before him.

Deston turns in his chair to take me in. Words die on his lips. His eyes widen as a slow smile curls his face. Both his hands come together, fingers steepling in the center. "I see perhaps there are somethings you do not see, Janice, but I most certainly do. Where did you find this Fae?" The cold of the room turns frigid.

"I found her near Puca's barn. She was examining the new stock." The lie rolls off his tongue so easily I could've believed it myself if I didn't know it wasn't true.

Deston turns full force on me. "So, Sarah, how long have you been in Fae?"

I recoil from his question. *Is this the part where all Cernunnos is supposed to break loose?*

My instant reaction is to turn and run, but there's only one way out. Unless I jump out a window, but I'd already established that might not be very smart.

I don't want to be a caged animal, but turning my head every which way, I resemble one. I call my powers of self-control to stare directly at him. Whatever is going to happen in the next few minutes will determine my fate. It sounds fatalistic and crazy, but the beating of my heart and the adrenaline pumping through my body tells me I'm not insane.

"Okay, you know who I am. What's the big deal? I've come to choose sides." It's an easy lie. I echo the words from before, releasing the breath I'd held.

He closes his eyes, tilting his head back and absorbing the moment. He enjoys it with a smile. "Those are the words I've waited to hear. Will you swear fealty to me?" His eyes are still closed, but I know in a second that if I don't answer him, they will be open.

Janice waves his pinky back and forth. I guess it's the universal symbol for 'don't do it.'

"No, like I said, I want to see which court is best before I decide what I'm going to do or where I want to be."

Deston's chin moves to rest on his chest, allowing his green hawk-like eyes to bore into me, down the bridge of his nose. "Have I not been kind? I have housed you, fed you, and taken care of you?" His words drip sticky sweet, but his body wakes with orange irritation.

Now the wakes have color? "Yeah, generally when you're being someone's friend, you don't kidnap their friends, like Olive, in an effort to force them back to you. That's a stalker ex-boyfriend move. I'm giving you a nine on the Creep-o-meter." I cross my arms, cocking my hip to one side.

"Oh, you're offended? This child, she's a human; she's just a thing," Deston replies. "Clearly, you're not any longer. You've changed and become something more. Why should this young human, Olive, matter to you at all? Soon you will have no humanity left. Humans will become irrelevant in your world." Deston waves his hand in dismissal.

Ugh, how can creatures like this survive? Why haven't they killed each other off by now?

"See when you talk like that, it makes me mad. I don't believe anyone is ever irrelevant. She might be young and completely human, and I'm not anymore, thanks to you and all your pointy-eared little friends. But she is still a person, and she deserves to live as much of a human life as she wants. Not stuck down here with a bunch of crazy pointy-eared bastards." My retort doesn't even make him flinch.

His laugh is dry as if he doesn't believe the words I say. To him, I'm a petulant child. "Sarah, the longer you're in Fae, the more you become one of us, and the less you're going to care about them. You will lose interest in the human world altogether and begin to forget you were ever human. Soon, the only thing you'll remember is being Fae, and before you were something else. But you won't remember what 'it' was." His benign smile fixes on his smug face with his eyebrows raised as a matter of fact. It reminds me of a politician's irritating reply to an ignorant constituent.

I want to smack his face off onto the floor and stomp on it. My lips curl back into a sneer. He's disgusting, as if nothing is more important than Fae. All they do is kill, maim, and create problems for every living creature on planet Earth. Or at least on the surface. Down here, they turn humans into creatures, and I can't get the taste of it out of my mouth. I keep seeing Brad withering on the ground as his body slowly changes from a six-foot human to the four-legged muscled flanks of a horse.

"Yeah, I don't think that's going to happen, Deston. I have every intention of never forgetting my own humanity. Anyway, didn't you say humans can't become Fae and Fae can't become human?" I raise an eyebrow at him. It's fun poking holes in his bullshit.

"Generally, you're right. Obviously, I was wrong. Apparently, under certain circumstances, it is possible. What's the saying? 'A Tiger cannot change its stripes.' Perhaps a tiger can, and I have been mistaken." He rubs the sides of his steepled fingers back and forth against his lips.

I'm amusing him in some way. "That's where you're clearly mistaken." With my hands on my hips, I shift to one foot.

Deston raises an eyebrow, "I wish to make you an offer. I will give you back your little human plaything. She's just a child, and as you say children are so important in every culture. I will give her back to you if you promise to stay with me. You could even stay at my side as my bride." His offer throws me.

I don't need Janice's help to know it's a terrible idea. I snarl my nose up on one side. "You're joking, right? Why would I stay here as your bride? I don't want to be Fae, let alone stuck married to one." I retort.

His smile leaps across his face. The magic wakes change into crests. "You need allies, Sarah. You cannot exist in Fae without them, however tenuous our alliance could possibly be. At least with me, you would have protection. I have an entire army at my disposal. I would be more than happy to put them at your disposal. They could defend you. You could lead them wherever you choose. We could rule Fae together, with the proper amount of incentive from others." His words strike me.

Why would I need an army to defend myself?

There's something missing. He's leaving something out, something important. Something I need to know. Janice looks pained, and the muscles on his neck rise. He strains against whatever holds him in check. He'd sworn allegiance to me. I don't know if fealty matters for anything down here. For all he'd said, it could be a lie, a big fat trick to get me to agree to be friends with Denny boy over there.

"I don't think I like that plan either. I agree everybody needs allies. For some reason, you want me bad. From the conversation I overheard a couple of moments ago, so does everybody else. I can't imagine why. There's nothing particularly interesting about me. In the human world, it's not like I'm some supermodel or a rocket scientist. But if you wish to truly be my ally, you'll release the humans. All of them, even the ones Puca has. Release the enchantments on them and send them back to the surface. Then sing some mumbo-jumbo so Fae can't find them or see them." It's my best bluff. "I don't know. Do whatever it is you can to keep them free. Then I'll agree to try to win the challenges. Right now, I don't believe you or him." I jab my thumb over my shoulder at Janice. "I don't believe anybody here. You're all liars and manipulators. And you're clearly doing something you don't want me to know about. Return the humans and come clean to me, or I'm gonna leave and I'm not sure you can stop me." I don't know if he's going to buy it or not.

Deston's entire body tightens. Clearly, I'd hit a mark, making him unsure of something. He wants me bad. As long as I say I'm his ally, he gets something from it. I don't know if I'm willing to hang around long enough to find out what it is, but I am willing to bargain for everyone else's freedom.

Deston fingers one of the trendles hanging down from his ear. He strokes it from top to tip and turns to face the green fire. He hunches and takes a deep breath a moment before he sits ramrod straight with a stick up his ass. "You drive a hard bargain. I do wish to prove myself to you. Clearly, you see yourself as my equal. I will not dissuade you at this time." His acquiescence is demeaning.

A laugh bursts from my lips. "Are you kidding? You're not gonna dissuade me from our equality at this time? You realize how pompous you sound? Yeah, I'm not sure I can be partners with somebody who clearly doesn't understand we're on equal footing. I have something you want—me." I tap my lip as I shift my weight from one foot to the other. "You have something I want. I'm willing to give myself over to you as a contender and work with you towards your ends, as soon as you tell me what they are. Give me all my people back in human form and send them back to the surface with whatever petty protections a Fae of your level can provide." *Now for the dig.* "Assuming you can even provide any." I know it's not really a good idea to insult people when you're trying to make a deal. Some are proud, stupid proud, and they think they're better than everyone, so of course they are going to think you know they can do everything, but I'm basically telling him I'm not even sure he can deliver it. I want what I want, that's it. He's either going to give it to me, or I'll go somewhere else. At least that's what I'm telling him.

"All right, I will tell you what I can, and I will release your people. Janice will return them to the surface with whatever protections we can provide them. We cannot make them invisible to the Fae. We see through allusions; it's one of our gifts. However, I can make them revolting, or less interesting. That sort of thing." Deston waves one of his hands in my general direction.

"Yeah, revolting doesn't sound good to me. I would rather them be less interesting or perhaps invisible." I shake my head from left to right, thinking perhaps he could do it or maybe he can't. But I know his pride won't put up with me challenging him at every step.

"Janice put a 'don't look here' on all her people. It makes them less noticeable. Most Fae will ignore them. Unlock Puca's belts." Deston palms a key to Janice.

I saunter over and sit down in one of the wing-backed chairs. I pop one foot up on the footrest. The other I throw over an armrest, kicking my steel-toed boots in his direction. "Well, let me know when you're done. I'll be waiting right here." I slap my hands together and then thrust them out at the fire as if to enjoy the warmth coming from it.

Deston raises an eyebrow. "What do you mean you will be waiting right here?" he sputters.

CHAPTER 18

"I mean exactly what I said. I'll be waiting right here until you're finished taking care of my demands. Come back and we will move forward with our plans, whatever they may be. Until I know my people are safe and, on the surface, I'm not going anywhere. I might stay right here and enjoy the pretty green fairy fire." I lean back and put my hands behind my head with my elbows up in the air.

A large O forms with his lips opening and closing like a guppy. He's nonplussed to say the least. "You cannot just stay in my private quarters. I must conduct business and manage my affairs, and I cannot have you lounging about eavesdropping." He sputters.

His outburst makes me laugh. I smile to myself at the sight of him standing in his own foyer, whispering to his minions after having been ousted from his private chambers by a human. "Not my problem. Get it done quickly, and I won't be interfering with your business anymore." I close my eyes and tilted my head back.

He grits his teeth and turns to Janice. "Do as I say! Do it quickly. Gather her people and return them to the surface now." His voice goes from that light sweet Fae tone he'd been using on me as if he was speaking to a child to a deep dark, Satanist quality. Tim Curry would've been proud.

I don't believe in fairy tales, I don't have any religious affiliations either. The tonal quality of his voice, which I suspect is probably his real one, makes fingernails run up and down my spine. It's like having the skin scraped off your back with a Barbecue brush. I stare into the fire and school my face. He doesn't need to know he has the ability to make my bowels quiver. I need to maintain the illusion of the upper hand in some fashion. I don't even turn my head to see Janice leave. Only the softened retreating footsteps inform me of his exit.

Great. Here I am sitting with a scary fairy prince, waiting for a different creepy fairy to return and tell me all my people were safe. Do I really want to stay here? I could go back with Janice. I'd get a chance to witness the return. Do I want him to take Nick, Tom, and Jake too? "All right, you convinced me. I changed my mind. I'll go with Janice and make sure you keep your end of the bargain." I twist in the chair, stomping both feet down on the floor and making bits of dirt and grim fall in my steps.

He sputters for a moment. "He's already left."

"I know. It will be an adventure to catch up with him, so I got a run. Catch you later, Denny boy." I jump up with a quick step and skip through the arches to the elevator, just in time to see Janice reach his hand out and stop the doors from closing.

His eyebrow shoots up.

"I can't let you go and return all my friends without me," I say. "Sorry, you're stuck with me. Besides, I have to make sure it gets done."

He bows his head ever so slightly, tilting his head in a downward motion as he steps back and off to the side. As soon as the doors close, I want to say something, but he shakes his head left and right a smidge. I hold my tongue. It becomes the longest elevator ride of all time. At some point in time, I think it'll never come to an end. Finally, we reach the seventh floor, and I unlock the door to my old room.

Nick stands slack-jawed.

"Do you want me to take him back with me? I could. He would never know. I can release him from his compulsion as soon as we land?" Janice inquires.

I look at Nick. I desperately want to take him back to the surface. He'll be safer there, but he's also the only person down here I can trust. Until I find Arty. *If I find Arty, do I want to send him back too?*

"No, Nick stays here. Anyway, I don't think you can take the enchantment off." I hear the ring of truth in my own words, and I internally cringe away from it. "I really don't care one way or the other if Jake and Tom stay or go. They don't belong here, but they said they wanted to kill some Fae. They seem pretty determined to get themselves killed."

Janice turns away from me and my harsh words. "As you say, my Lady, though I do not believe they will wish to leave. They did choose this path, and it's a one-way ticket without you."

"Take me to Olive." I grab Nick's hand, and we exit the room and begin the long descent to the ground floor of the castle proper.

Janice leads me back to the receiving room. In the center sits a flowered cage, woven together with blackberry vines. A small form cringes in the center, Olive. Fruit hangs from the cage as do leaves. Most of which are intertwined with a type of vining rose. Olive is alert. Her eyes are wide and terrified, and her body curls into a ball. I smell the fear coming off her as Fae walk by. Each one takes their turn to laugh and jeer at her.

"Why is she awake?" I grit out.

"We could not enchant her. We all tried, including Deston, but it is not possible. Whatever you did to wake her up, it's permanent." Janice puts everything so succinctly. "No one knows it was you. This makes it very dangerous for her here. They have her caged, and they're terrorizing her, hoping to break her mind."

Her whimpers echo around the chamber. I watch the leaves move in unison to carry the sound, amplifying it.

"Isn't it lucky we're here to take her? Why don't they make her a contender, like me?" I snarl it at him through clenched teeth. They really are barbarians. Anything they don't understand, they immediately have to terrorize, tease, and break. *God, I hate fucking Fairies.*

"She is too young," Janice replies quick and to the point.

Age matters?

"She wasn't too young to participate in the maze, but too young to be a contender. Huh?" I lift my foot to step forward.

Janice's hand thrusts out, holding me back. His lips breathe on my earlobe, sending tingles down my spine. "My lady, you were not instructed to free her. I was, and only I can. Stay back. You are nobody here. You don't want to be noticed." Janice says.

I freeze in place. Being statuesque isn't one of my strong suits. My fingers dig into my palms.

I hear the singing of the plants. I whisper to them under my breath. I can't help myself. The tune of the raspberries is cruel and cutting. I turn it sweet and encouraging, and its sharp thorns to flowers.

Janice freezes, turns, and gives me a sharp look. "Stop!" he mouths.

I do stop. It's hard. I want to continue, but if I keep going, I'll become a spectacle. Everyone would want to know exactly what I'd done and how I'd done it, so I cease. He sings his song, releasing the catch on the cage. A door forms and separates from the opening. Olive springs from it.

I crouch down, wrapping my arms around her. She struggles against my hold. Pressing my cheek against hers with my mouth next to her ear, I whisper, "Olive, stop fidgeting! I'm taking you back to Zoe."

She stills. "I don't believe you. You're all liars. Fairies look pretty, but inside you're really ugly." Her voice is small and determined. Several of the fairies around her twitter with amusement. I sing lightly into her ear, and an enchantment falls over her.

The room stills. Every Fae stops moving, and their voices die away. The musical notes of the walls cease as if everything has suddenly died and all sound has been stolen from the world.

"You enchanted her?" A tall white-haired Fae in the distance says. She's a fiercely beautiful woman, and her eyes are the color of freshly cracked acorns. Her skin is fine and delicate as orange blossom.

I recognize her from the dinner when I was first brought here. She's covered in leaves, but they can barely be called clothing. The necessary parts are covered, sort of.

"How did you enchant her? We have all tried. No one here has been able." She demands.

I falter.

Janice interjects, "She did not enchant her. I did." The woman turns her acorn brown eyes onto Janice.

"You lie, you did not. I watched the Fae. She whispered and sang into the child's ear, it was clear. Should we ask the walls what they heard?" She rebuts.

Stupid, stupid, everything in Fae is a tattletale.

"Yes, I enchanted her. I sang the same song you all sang. Perhaps my showing her some kindness relaxed her enough for me to enchant her." I turn my lips into a sneer when I say the word kindness, hoping they won't notice what I really mean.

The acorn-eyed woman continues. "If that is the only trick necessary to enchant humanity, they would've all been enchanted easily months ago. Kindness is not something Fae believe. It's only the strength and power of one's own song." Many nod in agreement.

"Having been out in the human world several times myself, I have seen how humans react to kindness," I retort. "It weakens them and makes them more predictable. I simply showed her enough of what she perceived to be human kindness for her to let down her guard." My belly rolls with my words. It sickens me to admit kindness is a weakness to be exploited. "I sang her the enchantment. It was nothing more. A simple trick I learned from watching my prey." The cruelty of my words burns in my mouth. Several of the Fae nod their heads, supporting my assessment of humanity.

"There is much to be learned from watching one's prey when you are the predator, spoken like a true Hunter." A male Fae turns his full attention on me. "The fairy's correct. I see the wisdom in your words. What is your name?"

I don't want to give them my name. Thinking quickly, I can't stutter. I have to give them any name. I give him the only name that comes to mind. "Sierra, my name is Sierra."

"She is lately from the other court. She is still choosing her new prince." Janice feigns boredom. "With your kind of intellect, Sierra, you would be wise to join Deston's court. He is the strongest prince. He will be Consort and end this reign of wild. I know it."

I choose to keep my thoughts to myself. *Reign of wild?* The land of Fae will take whatever you say and twist it around to their own ends. I simply tilt my head to the side, taking Olive's hand in my own. We turn and leave the receiving room. I keep my head high. I don't want anyone there to get the idea I am doing anything other than my duty.

Janice rustles up a carriage for us. I place Olive in the back next to Nick as Janice whips up the horses. Back to Puca's barn.

CHAPTER 19

The clicking of horse hooves on the ground echoes off the stone archway and rings from the drawbridge. Whipping my head around, I spy a second carriage. "Janice, what's the other carriage for?"

"You wanted all the human children, all your people. These were the humans in the castle and now there are none." He replies.

I don't say anything. It seems too good to be real, too easy. Deston wants me, I'm not sure what for, but I know he wants me. The way he said my name, almost as if caressing me, made my skin crawl. He still believes Janice works for him, and I still believe Janice works for him.

The clickity-clack of the horse hooves on the grounds is lolling. I find my eyes drooping. The last thing in the world I want is to fall asleep, not here in the open in a carriage. I rub my eyes, pushing the sleep back. It's a feeble effort. I pull air deep into my chest and push it out. Oxygen can awaken you. The wakes in the carriage hold no undertone of deception. It's plain exhaustion, nothing more. I hum, it's a nonsensical tune. The one I always heard my mother hum as she cleaned, it keeps me focused and awake. The lassitude recedes from my mind.

"Where did you learn the song you're humming?" Janice inquiry jars me back to our reality.

"It's something my mother always hums whenever she cleans house. She's kind of a neat freak. You know, a nervous cleaner." I play my fingers across my knees, keeping my eyes out the window for trouble.

"That is a song of cleaning—it's a Fae song."

Our eyes meet, and I tear them apart. *What's he talking about?*

He continues, "I told you before Fae possess their own music. They sing their own songs. The one you were using is a song of cleaning. Has your mother ever disappeared or gone on a long trip and no one saw her for a period of time?" His voice is inquisitive.

"No, my mother's a boring, nervous, stay-at-home mom. She's not really the adventurous type. I don't even think my mother went on an adventure even when she was young enough or stupid enough to want to. My mother's biggest adventure was meeting my dad and falling in love." I laugh at him, shifting my attention from the window to his face and back.

"Humans do not accidentally stumble upon our songs or music." His demeanor is intense.

"Are you suggesting my mother is Fae or knew someone who's Fae?" I scoff at him.

"What I am suggesting may be as simple as your mother met someone or knew someone who knew Fae. The song you hum, humans do not learn by accident. It is on purpose with repeated use. Someone taught it to her, or she picked it up through contact with the Fae world." His ambry hair sways with the rocking of the carriage, but his eyes never move.

"My mother is the most boring person in the world. She's nervous and jumpy and doesn't even like to sleep in the dark. She sleeps with a night-light for god's sake." I continue to laugh at his assertions. *Mom, a friend to Fae. What a joke. She doesn't even like Tinkerbell.*

Olive sits ramrod straight next to me, swaying in time with the carriage. Her unseeing milky eyes bore into the wall. I take her hand in mine, so small and soft. Children have perfect, smooth supple skin. Mine looks no different. Only the light iridescent quality singles me out. That and a light outline of day-glo design starting at my mid-arm. It glows just under the skin.

Janice's face shines with his marking everywhere the Fae light reaches. Two small lines between his brows are followed by two dots and arched tribal swirls up onto his forehead and down around his tilted almond eyes. It's an attractive combination. The purple-ish blue glow enhances the violet of his eyes, adding to the deep hollow of his cheeks. His eyes match my own in assessing each other. I turn away to stare out the window.

CHAPTER 20

I look down at Olive's glazed eyes. I feel terrible. It is the only way to get her out of the castle. The last thing in the world I need is for her to scream my name or give anyone a reason for a closer look as if I hadn't already given them one anyway. Taking away someone's free will is terrible. Their eyes glaze over, their mouth goes slack, the body relaxes. All facial expressions wash away along with their personality.

At some point, everything you don't want to happen ends up happening anyway. Your intent causes it. That's life. You must make a choice, or one gets made for you, not always the one you want. I had to make a choice. It wasn't the one I wanted, but it was the only one that was gonna get Olive back to Zoe like I promised. If only I can get Arty and be free of this place.

If I'd done my job to begin with, I wouldn't have had to come back here at all. I shake my head and look over at Nick.

I whistle the enchantment away. His eyes brighten and then narrow as they lock on me. I fill him in. "I need you to do something for me, Nick."

He coughs, closing his lips and whipping the drool away.

"I said I'd help you save your sister," I say. "I need you to go back with Olive and take care of the kids." It comes out weak, not the strong divisive voice I'd gone over in my head.

"No." He scowls and turns away from me, looking out the window.

"Even if I promise to save your sister myself?" I'm pleading with him.

"Nobody will take care of my family like I will. Sorry, Sarah, but I'm not saying you're a liar or you wouldn't try. I mean, obviously, you made a promise to Zoe and Olive, but it's my job to take care of my sister, not yours." His fingers comb through his hair.

"There's something bigger going on here than just your sister or you or what you want, Nick. If the Fae keep killing at this rate, this could end up being the extinction of the human race. Do you think the gangs on the surface care about the next generation?"

Janice's voice cuts through the air like a knife. "The human race will not go extinct. The queen won't let it happen."

I scowl over at him, making sure to inject as much sarcasm as possible into my voice. "Yeah, sure. Your fairy Queen? You mean like the one in all the stories? The one that's supposed to be so wonderful and loving and kind that she helps humanity?" I shoot Janice a cocked eyebrow.

"You know nothing about that which you speak, Sarah. If you did, you wouldn't say those things." His tone is cool and steady. It grates on me.

"I know enough about Fae to know your fairy Queen is an asshole. Instead of stopping her people from murdering the humans and treating us like cattle, she's probably sitting on her ass somewhere, eating fruit and having some stupid Fae do her hair. Then watching some humans run through a maze to kill each other. She was there watching all those girls die, wasn't she?" Acid rolls around in my belly and rises in my throat. The vision of that girl being chewed apart by the thorny vines fills my mind. I have to swallow back vitriol.

"No, Sarah. She wasn't there, and she wasn't watching. A true queen would never enjoy such sport." Janice retorts through his teeth.

"Yeah, sure. I know you've said you're vassal tied to me, or whatever it is you creepy bastards call it. But the truth is I haven't seen anything about you that's noble. You may be used to kneeling down in a knightly fashion, but you're just as happy to stab me with the sword as to look at me. I'm still wondering why you didn't." My retorts aren't helping us, but I couldn't stop myself.

Nick cuts in. "Yeah, why didn't you stab him, Sarah?"

I ignore Nick's jab.

"Maybe I'm growing weak in my old age," Janice mutters his droll reply.

I scowl and look the other way. No, I'm not just partners with Nick, but I'm starting to act like him.

We pull up along the side of the road where we'd left the Marines. I'm not sure if they are still there. They might have wandered off and found something to kill. On cue, they jump out, stopping the carriages.

"Looky what we got here. Sarah brought us lambs for the slaughter?" Tom's finger taps at the trigger, dancing over the safety and trigger guard.

I open my mouth, but Nick jumped in before I can speak. "She made a deal with the devil."

I shoot him a dirty look. "I didn't make a deal with the devil." I round on him. I see their eyes. It doesn't matter what I say. My shoulders slump. "Okay, so maybe I made a deal with the devil. I'm going to do whatever he wants me to do in exchange for all the humans in his castle and in Puca's stables."

Jake shakes his head. "You know you can't trust these guys? They're going to stab you in the back as soon as they get a chance. All he wants, is you?" Jake inquires.

"Yeah, me and my cooperation. They need me for something. I'm a contender of some kind..." I wave my hand at Janice.

Jake's eyes go wide. He blinks at me several times. "What do you mean you're a contender? In what?" he scoffs.

"Why don't you ask tight ass Janice? I'm sure he knows, but he can't tell me." I cross my arms. "He's not allowed to. I know it's some kind of contest or something. I think they're really just using humans for entertainment. It's not like I didn't make it through one of their tests or whatever the hell it was."

"You made it through one? Why don't you start from the beginning and tell me what exactly you did the last time you were here?" Jake's need for intel and my desire to discuss it doesn't meld.

"I don't want to talk about it. I watched a lot of girls die, and I was able to save some kids. The rest is really irrelevant." I clench my jaw, snapping it shut. No one is going to get me to talk about it. The screams rings in my mind.

CHAPTER 21

I turn my back on Jake. What I did with myself isn't his concern.

"You don't know why they want you and you're just gonna give yourself to them for their little competition?" Jake lets his carbine hang loose in front of him from the shoulder strap as he puts his hands up in frustration.

"Jake, I do not have to explain myself to you. It's very simple. Would you give your life to save your friends? Would you give your life to save any of the people that you've seen murdered needlessly?"

His eyes bore into me. I know he would. We both know.

"The price I have to pay for all these kids is me." I wave my arms around at the carriages. "They want me. I give Deston what he wants, and these kids get to go free, and you're going with them. I'll keep fighting from my side." I cross my arms. It's my best 'I dare you to stop me' pose.

"You want me to take all the kiddies and go home? I'm not a babysitter," he shouts.

"That's exactly what I want you to do. You're free to do whatever you want, Jake. You and Tom, you guys can hang out around here and kill a few fairies. Maybe get killed yourself. Most likely die because some crazy Fae plant decided to eat you because you got too close. Get caught by Puca and turn into a freaky horse. Or you can take all these kids. I just signed a deal with the devil for you to go back to the surface. Keep fighting there." It isn't working. I have to double down. "You both swore an oath to defend the United States from all enemies, foreign and domestic. Those kids need defending. Do your duty."

Tom leans over and whispers in Jake's ear. He's still as a statue. Jake doesn't like losing. He likes being in charge, in control. I just made a deal, and he had no control over that. It really chaps his hide. "These are it, just these kids?"

I shake my head. "No, Deston agreed to give us all the kids Puca has too." *Yes, I think I got him.*

Jake's mouth snaps with each word. "Are they all going to be fucked up like your little blue friend over there?"

I shake my head.

"No, Deston gave me a key." Janice cuts in an attempt to seal the deal. "If I unlock the harnesses, it'll cease their change and most will revert, because they didn't finish."

Come on, just a little more.

"What about your little blue friend over there? Can he revert back to a normal human boy?" Tom's inquiry surprises me.

I bite my lip. I don't know what will happen to Brad. "I don't know if this can help, but it's the best we can do. If we're lucky, he'll revert, and if not…" I heave a sigh. How do you tell a bunch of kids, 'I'm sorry you can't go back to your normal life'? It doesn't exist anymore because you look like a fucking freak?

Nick steps closer, keeping his voice low. "You know if they don't revert, they can't go back, and I don't think they'd want to stay."

I nod my head. They can't go back unless they're normal. Nick is right. Nobody's gonna want to stay here forever with the creepy day-glo plants and the pointy-eared freaks constantly reciting fairytale stories and lines. I wave Nick on.

"My choice is made. Make yours, Jake. You and Tom want to stay here and kill some Fae, go ahead. We're leaving. Get in the carriage, walk behind, I don't give a shit." I climb up onto the coachman seat.

Janice grabs the reins and smacks the back of the horses. The carriages lurch forward. We move on down the lane. The weight of the carriage shifts twice as Jake and Tom climb on. I sigh. Jake and Tom will go. One less burden to worry about.

The large flat plain isn't much to look at. It's as boring as the Midwest I'd grown up in. The only thing missing is a few tumbleweeds here and there. But off in the distance, I see the wake lines of Puca's protection field. The closer we get the barn, the more I realize what I need to sing to get back to the surface. I have an idea on how to protect the kids from the Fae. I don't know if it would work.

Puca's protection field automatically parts for the horses. There must be some kind of enchantment on the harnesses or the carriages themselves. It recognizes Deston's authority and allows him entry.

Jake, Tom, and Nick all leap off and dart into the barn. The stall doors slam. Various young men come running out of the stables with a wild, animistic roll in their eyes. It reminds me of Brad before his change, like the rolling in his eyes, the way the pupils on the irises became bigger and blacker, and the whites became smaller. Janice grabs each one in turn by their harnesses and unlocks them with the key.

When it comes time for Brad, I want to pray and cross myself like they taught in church. I'm not Catholic, and I'm not sure it'll do any good, but I'll do it if it helps. The magic will wear off or it won't. Brad still has human characteristics. Maybe the magic will fade. Maybe it can be like taking a shower where you just wash the dirt off.

Tom hands me the torn shreds of Brad's belt. Wakes still flow from it to Brad. It isn't changing him, but its power is still tethered him.

I touch the key to the lock, and it releases. His color lightens, becoming flesh toned, and his shape changes slightly. He doesn't revert, his form still half man half horse. He isn't human. The wake lines of enchantment wave around him digging into him. They aren't changing. They're weakened, but they're still there. There is enough residual magical energy to hold him.

I look at Nick. He shakes his head. I turn hopeful eyes to Janice. He pierces his lips, clenching his jaw. Fairies aren't as nice as humans. I don't believe they feel empathy like we do. Their whole existence is about disdain and selfishness. His black-tipped hair whips over his shoulder as he turns and stalks away.

My gun pulls easy from the holster. With the cool of the steel in my hand, I snick the safety off and raise it to Brad's temple, holding it there. My hand shakes, and I lower it, only to raise it again. *I can do this. This isn't what he would've wanted.* My eyes close, and all I can see is that day at the creek when everyone was swinging from the rope and dropping off into the water. Brad's laughing with our friends and then diving in through an inner tube. It could've been yesterday. The lump in my throat takes over, and the burning in my eyes race to my chest. The cold butt of the gun presses the side of my temple. I didn't even realize I'd moved it.

A warm hand lies on my shoulder, and soft words drift to me. "You don't have to kill him. As long as he's enchanted, he'll never understand what happened. He can stay here in Fae and live." Janice's words are gentle and soothing in my ear. *He came back just to stop me?*

"Back off, fairy boy." Nick shoves Janice away from me. The heat from his body radiates onto my back and the ache there. Nick's large hand covers mine over the gun. Nick's breath warms my ear, tickling down my neck. "You don't have to kill your friend, Sarah. I'll do it. It's okay. No one would want to live like this." He finishes.

I shake my head, feeling his face in my hair. I take a deep breath. The pain from my teeth digging into my fleshy lip tastes like copper. I'm going to live like this, changed by Fae. I'm no different from Brad, only I'm awake. *It's a band-aid. Pull it off fast, and it will hurt less.* I place my hand on the side of Brad's horse-shaped face. His eyes have returned to the blue I remember, no longer that soft horsey brown animal eye color. I pat his furry cheek, but the vibrations of the magic push me away. It doesn't want to be interfered with. *But it must be stopped.*

Something in me demands I touch the other side of his face. I relinquish the gun to Nick. The slide pulls back and locks into place.

"Move your hand, Sarah!" Nick's strong and determined words pour down my back like water on a duck, never touching me.

Of their own volition, both of my hands clasp Brad's elongated cheeks. If I could just pull it out of him or off of him, like sucking cobra venom from a wound. Or like it's a virus infecting your body and the right amount of antibiotics could kill the infection. I just need to provide the antidote. Closing my eyes, I don't need to see the wake waves to know what they look like. I feel them digging into him. Weaker than before, I pull them like a string in a seam. When you pull, the fabric separates as the seam unravels, falling apart. I feel the snapping here and there, and with each wave that snaps the magic falls away. Soon, the messy tangle of magic wrapped around him disappears. Falling to the ground dead inert, the wake waves locked in place. The spell is dead.

I open my eyes to a normal human face, Brad's. With blurred vision, I wrap my arms around him, hugging him. I had to sing the unlocking song and end the enchantment. By freeing him, maybe I could free myself.

"Brad, do you know who I am?" I ask.

He rears back for me. "No, I don't know you. Get away for me, fucking Fairy."

My hands drop to my side. Of course, he doesn't know me. I'm not me anymore. Nick steps between the two of us and puts his index finger square into Brad's chest, pushing him back. "She just saved your life. I think you owe her a thank you." Nick pushes him back in time with his words, like a bird pecking.

"Thank you for saving my life. If you did, I don't remember. Just stay the fuck away from me." He moves to the human boys hiding amongst the crowd.

My chest clench, and I wipe the tears from my face. I don't know what I'd expected. As a terrified life form being attacked by magic, he instinctively recognized me and looked for my help, but fully human and cured of the magical disease, he sees me for what I am. No longer like him, I'm not human in his eyes. I'm Fae, an evil creature out to kill everyone he ever loved. He can't see the humanity left in me. In his eyes, there isn't any. *Is being human biological or something you feel?* I don't feel Fae, even if I look it.

Nick remarks, "Don't let his behavior get to you. He is just some stupid teenage kid who got fucked up. You saved him. Don't lose sight of the prize." I latch onto Nick's words. Eyes on the prize, focus on what our true business is here. It isn't to make friends or just save friends. It's to save every human I can, and I saved Brad whether he likes me or not. I pull myself out of my own head. Running around and feeling sorry for myself isn't to get the job done.

Jake asks, "The barn's empty. Did we get them all?"

I hear Tom's voice off in the distance. "There's still one in the paddock. He's skittish. He won't come to me." Tom wouldn't be my first choice either.

"I'll be right there." I round the corner of the barn, heading to the paddock.

Prancing around inside the wooden fence post is a gorgeous black stallion. He is at least twenty-hands high with a massive chest and strong, stout legs. His main flows like it's made of liquid silk. It waves down one side of his neck, cascading into ringlets. His hooves wear a furry skirt of silky ringlets, resembling a hula skirt.

It's something out of a dream. He tosses his head and snorts while pawing the ground. The fringe of silky hair covering his eyes is tossed back, only to reveal the yellowy, golden eyes of Fae. They lock on to me. Everything in Fae is there to deceive you, to draw you to it so it can kill you or toy with you. His eyes release me as he prances away, circling the paddock.

"Tom, get out of here! Maybe, I can work my magic on it."
I feel silly using the word magic. I'm sure the guys think it's
magic. I mean it as a horse-whisperer, like humans do. The
farther my human friends recede, the closer the horse comes.
He paws the ground several times in between his tentative
steps. Then he prances around the paddock, jumping and
kicking in the air. It's a glorious show, and he knows it. Taking
one last flying leap, the air around him shivers as a magic wake
of bubbles shake off of him.

When he lands, it's a man.

CHAPTER 22

Why do the Fae have to fuck up everything? Why can't it just be a beautiful horse? A real horse? No, it has to be some Fae freak. A gorgeous freak. His Fae form isn't much different from his horse form. His shining, silky black hair cascades down his back into ringlets. Golden eyes stare into your mind, freezing you in place. Every inch of him is covered in muscles with every inch of those covered in black leather. Even his boots somehow look naturally part of his body.

He stands there for a moment, wagging his jaw back and forth, as if to fit it into place. He runs his fingers through his hair, starting at his brow, over the top, and down to the nap of his neck.

I'm still leaning against the paddock post. I have to pull back. I lean in, tasting the air. All of it is laced with his magic. It tastes of leather and musk. I pull myself out of the magic. It makes it easier to see the desire lining it.

He wants me to want him. "You must be the new one. I've seen you before." The gleam in his smile tells me he knows what he's up to. Only, I'm not game to become one of his fairy conquests.

"You can quit with the come-hither crap. I'm here to take these humans back to the surface." If he's surprised, it doesn't show.

"Really? What will you give me for them?" His left-hand toys with a ringlet, twirling it around his fingers. As his eyes tear into me, he rakes them up and down my body. I could have been standing there naked for how he makes me feel.

"Can you keep your slimy eyes to yourself, please? I'm not interested. Deston said I could take them, and I will." I reply.

He throws his head back, laughing. "Did he now? I don't suppose he explained that you would have to pay a price for them, did he?" He tosses a rock in the air, turning it into a flower and then bringing it back to a rock. "No, I thought not. Yes, Deston likes his games as much as I do. He said you could take them, or have them?"

I have to think. What had he said?

My heart falls. 'Take them' were his words. That means a fight. I can only have what I can take. *That fucker.* "What is your price?" I demand, through clenched teeth.

His eyes gleam with a golden flash. I hate players. "All you have to do is go for a ride, all night. Then I will give you all 'my humans.'" He tosses his hair. That doesn't sound too bad. He's easy on the eyes and riding a horse all night can't be that bad. His hand is outstretched, and I take it.

"Sarah, no." Janice's words hit me after the magic does. Time stands still.

Puca changes back into a gorgeous stallion. The magic wake waves off of him, popping bubbles. Every bubble has a different color. My hands reach for them. They float into the sky. Puca turns his head. I see one golden eye.

"Better hold on, Sarah." He lurches forward. I thread my fingers into the silky mane on his neck. The wind pushes my hair back. I throw my head back and laugh. A thrill runs up my spine, along with my adrenaline. I lean into his neck, keeping my eyes above his ears. The hills flash by. He leaps over creeks and rocks.

The horse begins to sing. A sound wake cuts the hill in front of us. It shimmers and splits. Puca jumps, and we dive through.

It's night, and we are surrounded by massive stones. In the back of my mind, I know this place, but I can't place it. Puca jumps over one of the cross-stones. His back legs collide with the stone, knocking it off the top of its supports.

I turn in my seat. "That was Stonehenge! You broke Stonehenge!"

He snorts and tosses his head. "Is that what you humans call it now? My people built that. Would you like to see what else we've built?" He shakes his head from side to side, snorting. My mouth goes dry with all the air rushing in as the landscape blurs by.

I had never been on a horse. I have no idea how fast they can go. Obviously, in the back of my mind, I realize cars equate to horsepower, but I don't have an actual number for that, an engine is a five-horsepower engine. I don't even know what one horsepower is. So, how would I figure out five?

It doesn't matter if he has one horsepower or five. He isn't a horse. He changed from a Fae to a horse. He's a shapeshifter. The only shape he doesn't seem to change are his ears. They stay long and pointy. But with every leap, he jumps over entire hills. From the time his back hooves leave the ground to the time his front regains it, he covers an entire field. He jumps over hedges from one side to the other.

Being in the human world, you would think everything has changed with the Fae attacking, but it all looks the same. I don't know if Fae killing humanity is good or bad. The truth is as humans, we're no better.

I see it coming. It's a cliff, and beyond is nothing but ocean. My stomach clenches, and the beating in my chest ramps up. *Where is he taking me?*

I have to believe he isn't going to kill himself. My legs grip his belly tighter as both hands wrap his silky mane around my hands. The cliff looms, but he never lessens his gait. In fact, I'm pretty sure we are picking up speed. I lean my head into the silky tresses of his mane. The musky scent fills my nostrils.

I scrunch my eyes shut as tight as possible. He's gonna jump off the cliff. I sure the fuck don't want to see it.

"Open your eyes, Sarah!" His voice is firm with the order.

I shake my head against his neck.

"Open your eyes or I'll dump you in the water," Puca says.

I pull my head back far enough to see over the top of his head. He sucks in a deep breath of air and pushes it out just as quickly. I pry my eyes open as we leap off the side of the cliff. I'd never heard a horse laugh, but then again, I'd never ridden a horse that could talk. His laugh is loud and booming. It echoes off the water as we glide over the channel, landing on a beachhead.

"Oh my God, where are we?" I release the breath I'd been holding.

"Normandy." He jumps from the sand to the cliff and continues across the French terrain.

He leaps over fences and bridges, rivers and towns until we finally come to a complete stop. "Where are we?" My eyes survey the landscape, gentle rolling hills with a few French cottages here and there. What strikes me the most is the number of standing stones, small and large. They cover at least a mile.

"You silly humans call it the Carnac stones. That's not what we call it. The Fae love their standing stones. We love circles. It used to represent the circle of life, at least for other creatures." He trails off.

"Are you saying all the stone circles were built by Fae?" I don't believe him.

"Of course, they're built by Fae. You, humans, aren't clever. You don't even know how old the stones are. Humans are just a stupid workforce, created by a Fae queen to clean and serve her. You're nothing more. I'm only indulging you because you're the cleverest human I've ever encountered." He snorts and paws at the ground.

"In case you hadn't noticed, I don't look very human anymore."

He tosses his head. "No, I noticed. You don't look human at all. But I can still smell the human on you. Whatever you are, Sarah, you haven't made your choice." He rears back. "Hold on." He leaps away. Again the landscape turns into a blur of mountains and rocks, cottages, châteaus, rivers, and lakes. Greens and grays blur everywhere. It's nighttime and yet the darkness doesn't pierce me as much as it would have a few short months ago.

I see everything. They aren't bright colors as if the sun is shining on it, though I hadn't seen the sun since my trip back inside the Hallowed Hills. My greatest change happened then. It hadn't occurred to me until now. I still looked pretty human before. But now I hardly look any different from the rest of Fae. I see my reflection, and I'm fiercely beautiful in a disturbing way. My eyes are more almond-shaped and tilted. Kelly green eyes so bright that it's unnatural, something only achieved with Photoshop. My skin is luminescence, like a pearl shooting off sparks of rainbows as the light glints off of it, a hint of the day-glo markings similar to the Fae.

My stomach clenches at the idea I will someday be like them. Will I become an asshole, a selfish creature toying with lesser life forms? The landscape changes to a dry, barren rocky outcropping. I watch as Puca jumps over a break in continents, adding to an aching suspicion of where we are, but I'm afraid to speak. Puca's gait slows and we come to a halt.

"The behold Gobekli Tepe, the most ancient of Fae circles. This is the birthplace of Fae. You, humans, have just recently discovered it. But if you walk around the monolithic stones, you'll see the story. What I find fascinating is long after the

Fae were tricked to live under the hills, humans continued to build temples on top of our stones and to worship us as gods. You, humans, are so stupid; you forget everything so quickly. Your short lives and short memories. If you had paid attention even a little, you would've known we were coming one day, and you would know why we're here. But you don't, stupid human. Hold on tight! I'm not done dragging you around the planet. Maybe I'll show you some more Fae stones. Or maybe I'll just toss you off into a volcano. I'm sure there's a few nearby." He turns his head right and left and flicks his tail.

The beating in my chest roars to a new rhythm, hammering out my human tune. His words shake me to my core. Will he toss me off? Can I stop him if he wants to chuck me into a volcano? My stomach clenches. The only volcano around here is in Sicily, Mount Etna. Puca could take me all the way to Hawaii and dump my ass in the Kilauea for all I know. *Think fast.*

"You won't dump me off, Puca. You want me to run around singing your praises to humans and Fae alike. You also want to be able to brag to Fae how you tricked me and gave me the wild ride of my life. You won't dump me off. You're just saying it because you're mad and you wish you could run during the daylight, free to do whatever you want. You hate humans. You think we usurped you. I don't know what happened between Fae and humanity or whether you created us or we're supposed to be friends and cousins. All I do know is I want to take my people and go, so finish our ride and I'll tell everyone you scared the shit out of me. Agreed?" I offer.

He tosses his head, snorts a few times, and paws the ground. He rears back. I hold on for dear life. He stomps down. We aren't even standing on the same ground he jumped from as he rears. We stand on the sands of an ocean of dry desert.

"I don't need a volcano to get rid of you, Sarah. I could dump you here. You'd be just as dead, and you'd feel the heat just as keenly. Although in a volcano, I have a feeling you'll die faster." His words race down my aching spin like cold fingers causing a shiver.

He lifts his front hooves and gallops away, crossing mountains off in the distance following the blur. I can make out the shape of a giant snake in the landscaping. In the back of my mind, I know the only thing that it could be is the Great Wall of China. I close my eyes. We are running too fast, and it's scaring me.

"Open your eyes, Sarah. If you can't handle riding my back, how can you possibly be a contender for Fae? No Fae would ever follow a coward or submit their fealty to one." He sneers.

"No Fae would ever follow a human, you moron. They only root for those they want to win because it'll keep them alive longer so you can watch them die slower. You're a bunch of sadistic freaks. I'll keep my eyes open if that's what it takes to save my friends. Leave me the fuck alone with your twisted Fae logic." I bite my lip at the harshness of my fearful words.

We gallop in silence. There's no way it can be night on both sides of the planet, and we certainly aren't following the sun or the night. We're going in the wrong direction. I think he's messing with me. It can't be night in Texas and China at the same time. The sky is devoid of a moon.

I spot wake waves. They split apart like a ripple in space-time. The closer we come, the easier it is for me to hear the song of Fae on the other side, calling to me and reaching for me. I lean in. I want it. I want to be in Fae and allow the sound to envelop me, to fill me. As we leap through, it's cleansing, like I'm washing all humanity from me and I'm enveloped in the warmth and beauty only Fae can provide. We slow to a casual walk before coming to a halt in front of Puca's barn.

Everyone is piled around sleeping. The ease of sleep even touches Janice's face. His back leans against the side of the barn, his hand on the pommel of his sword. Even resting, he anticipates war.

"You may take your humans and go, but I know you'll be back." He taunts.

I climb off of his back. The wake lines of the bubbles shift around Puca. He turns into a giant white rabbit with long ears. He hops around for a moment before shaking himself with bubbles to shift back into his Fae form. He winks at me and turns a dazzling smile on like a beam of light. "So, Sarah, you managed to ride me and hold on tight. Most humans would've lost their grip and fallen somewhere over the water. I should know; I've lost enough of them. The drunk ones are the easiest to dump. What's one or two humans every now and again when the planet has been infested by billions? Every so often what's happening now has to happen. The planet isn't meant to hold as much life as humanity gives it. And you're too stupid to figure out how to control yourselves. Maybe if you did build those spaceships that your people are always going on about and leave the planet, that might be good. Then you could infest the universe. As for Fae, we will be perfectly happy in our Hallowed Hills until you figure out how to get to them." He straightens his leather jacket and saunters away into his barn, slamming the door behind him.

His words ring in my mind. They remind me of someone. My mother had echoed the same thoughts, about humanity and overpopulation. I shake my head. *Na, couldn't be.*

CHAPTER 23

The sound of smashing wood awakens everyone.

"Sarah, you're alive! You're okay." Nick jumps up and wraps his arms around me, hugging me.

I pull back. "Yeah, I'm alive. I made a deal with Puca. We're free to go." I shove him off. I feel bad about it, but Nick always wants to protect me these days.

Nick steps back and locks both thumbs into his back pockets. He hangs his head and looks at me through his eyebrows. "I'm sorry I didn't mean to… or whatever. I'm glad you're okay."

I shake my head and smile. Yeah, he hugged me because he wants to make sure I help him find his sister. *Yeah, I believe that.*

Janice's reproving voice cuts my musings about Nick short. "You should not have made a deal with Puca. Luckily, you survived. Most humans don't. They are usually indebted to him for a lifetime. Did he ask you to swear anything?" he demands.

I shake my head and turn toward the deep voice.

"Well, wouldn't it have been nice if someone had mentioned how dangerous and weird Puca was, or that he's a creepy shapeshifter, *before* I approached the crazy black horse that no one could get a hold of. I mean, if I had known Puca was actually a horse too…" I let my words trail off for impact. "Yeah, your real forthcoming there, Janice. Great vassal you are. You think you could give me a little more information about Fae before we go wandering around and somebody else gets hurt? Or I make another deal that might cost everybody their lives?" I don't know why I'm so mad at him. I know Fae are dangerous. Nothing here is as it appears. I don't know why I trusted that horse. I thought it was a human forcibly being turned into one of Puca's toys. I'm angrier with myself than Janice. It isn't his fault. I'm not a child. Actually, I've been taking care of other people's children for months. I leaped when I should've looked. I shake my head. "I'm sorry. It's not your fault. I shouldn't yell at you. Is there anybody else we need to run into before we leave this wretched hole in the ground?"

Janice's eyebrows scrunch down, and his jaw sets as he speaks in a clipped tone. "We can leave now."

The round flattened space off to the side of the barn looks familiar. It's where we landed when I first came to the Hallowed Hills. It's a giant smooth stone, surrounded by mushrooms. Janice instructs us, "Gather all the humans and put them in the ring." My eyes lock with Nick, and I nod my head.

"Nick, we're all going, but we're not all staying," I reassure him.

He steps over the mushrooms onto the flat of the round, dragging with him a few of the younger boys. Jake and Tom take up position on the other side. All the kids crowd onto the ring. I take Olive's hand and lead her into the center. Janice takes up a position not far from me.

"Take us home, Sarah." Jake's words ring in my ears.

I raise my voice to sing, but the sound won't come out. I'd sung the US National Anthem before. It had worked, but now as the words reach my lips, they die as if they can't exit my mouth. I cough, clear my throat, and pull air deep into my lungs to try again.

"It won't work this time. You can't use that song to go back." Janice whispers.

My green eyes meet Janice's violet ones. "Why not?" I feel the lump forming in my throat. I know the answer, but I don't want to believe it.

"You're singing a song to go home. It's not your home anymore. You know that, don't you?" he whispers.

I shake my head and bite my lip. I feel the fire burning in my eyes. "It's not true! you're a fucking fairy! You're all goddamn liars. I don't believe you." I'm still holding Olive's hand, and I look down at her plump round face. I want to go home too. The anguish in Janice's eyes tells me it'll never happen.

"I'll take them home. We'll talk later." He whispers the words low enough that only I can hear.

"No, you won't. I'll take my people home, and you can't stop me." I have to find something to sing that will take me there, but the words never come. I can't create the magic wake necessary to blast us from this world up to the surface. I can't sing of home.

It can't be home because it isn't anymore. If music is all about intent, it doesn't matter what you sing, nor do you have to sing loud. You can hum or whistle. Nothing forms, and the tears tear down my face. I clench and unclench my hands.

"Go ahead, Janice. I can't do it." My voice barely whispers. I don't look up to see his face.

He raises his voice and sings a song of places I've never been. My shoulders sag as his voice rises. The words are about visiting. He won't live there. It's an adventure, a holiday, a short trip to the seaside, a drive through a forest. Words about a short-term visit but not a long-term stay.

Our ring lifts into the sky, and as he reaches the crescendo, we pop into the human world. I watch the wake waves wash away from us, reverberating out from our circle. We slowly lower back onto the ground.

We arrive outside the industrial district, close to the warehouse where Zoe and the rest of the kids are hidden.

"Jake, you and Tom take the kids." Every word tumbles out. I want this over quickly. Nick hands Jake a scrap of paper with the address and instructions on how to get into the hidden shelter. I put Olive's hand into Jake's so she'll follow. Then I sing them all awake.

Most slump to the ground. Some shake their heads. Olive stares up at me, frightened. "Where's Zoe?" Olive inquires.

I squeeze my eyes shut and kneel down in front of her. She rears back. "This is Jake, he's your friend. He's going to take you to your sister," I whisper the last part. *I'll never see Zoe again.*

Her eyes dart from Nick to me. "Nick, can't you take me to Zoe?" He shakes his head.

"No, kid. Go with Jake. He'll take you there. He and Tom are good guys. They'll take you right to Zoe. Then you can have some granola bars and a bottle of water." He kisses her forehead. She pushes her lower lip out. She doesn't recognize me. It's probably better this way. If humans don't know who I am, then neither do Fae.

"So, we're gonna take all these kids back to the little girl's mommy or her sister or whatever. And then what?" Tom retorts.

I cross my arms. "You protect them. Children are the future. If humanity's gonna survive this apocalypse of fairies, you'll have to protect them. Don't worry. Zoe will show you what to do. She'll show you what we've been doing so you can keep doing it. Tell Zoe I kept my promise."

Jake looks from me to Nick.

"And you're taking him back with you?" Jake demands.

Nick steps in front of me. I'm getting tired of the macho man crap.

"Yeah, I'm going back with her. You go take care of the kiddies while we go get my sister and her lover boyfriend." Nick waves his hand dismissively.

"Yeah, take the little boy with you. I'm sure he'll be great at defending you, Sarah. Leave with the child and the fairy. Tom and I will take care of the kiddies on our side."

I see the muscle working in Nick's jaw.

He stares into Jake's eyes, flaring his nostrils.

"Jake, everybody's got their part in this deal," I say. "Please do yours. I have to go back. I made a promise. One way or another, I wouldn't get to stay with you and the kids anyway. I'm poison. Look at me! I don't even look human anymore." I choke on the last few words. The lump in my throat is difficult to get by. Nick takes up sentinel by my side. His presence comforts me.

I whistle a few bars from Bridge over the River Kwai, putting a twist of Home on the Range in it. The air around the group shivers and wakes with the taste of flowers. I made it contagious. Any human they come into contact with would have the same magical appearance of flowers. Fae ignore plants.

Janice places his hand on my shoulder, and I shrug him off.

I step back over the mushrooms onto the fairy ring. "Nick, are you coming? Or are you going to stay and have it out with Jake?"

Nick turns his head slightly and throws a glance at me over his shoulder. He turns around and steps into the fairy ring. Janice never says a word.

They say you can never go home again. Those words always make me sad. The idea there'd be no place you could call home for real ever again, that it's just some kind of daydream—a fairy tale. A place of childhood, love, security, and safety. Here I am on the surface of planet Earth, but it's no longer my home. I can never go back to it. It wouldn't be allowed. The morning rays of the sun crest the hills in the distance. I know I have to go. If I stay this time, the sun will burn me like all Fae.

"Janice, I've got this." The mushrooms sing around me, and I hear the song clearly now. Fae calls to me. I lift my voice, and as the sound comes out, I know the truth of it. Fae is my home.

The tears roll down my face, and my voice shakes. I raise it and sing the song of home. Our circle rises into the air. My body sways with the music. I reach my crescendo, and a loud crack cuts the air. The day-glo light of Fae surrounds me everywhere.

CHAPTER 24

Home is a place that only exists in your childhood memories. That long-ago dreamworld where everything is safe and rimed in a rosy hue. There are hugs and cookies there, trips to the playground, the movie theater, video games, and explorations with your favorite pet. The sweet voice of Mom reading a book or singing you a lullaby while heavy eyes carry you off into dreams. It's a dream world children create, most of it never real to begin with.

The older you get, the further that dream fades, the more the reality of your world encroaches, pushing back that rosy glow. Until suddenly everywhere you look are fleeting moments of peace. You find a dull darkness lingers over everything. Corners hold sinister intentions, and books are only for knowledge and power. That's how adults see life, adult humans.

I will never see the world as an adult human. That's not how Fae see the world. I'm barely an adult now, and I ask myself, is it the magic doing this to me or is it something I did to myself? Or is it something that's always going to happen because it's who I am? I don't know. I don't have those answers. But in the back of my mind when I dream of home it has a rosy glow and a chocolate chip cookie.

Janice said I would have to compete. I'm already a contender. The numbers have been significantly whittled down. Of course, he doesn't say how many contenders there are to begin with. I don't suppose it matters. It's *fait accompli* to say the fate of the world rests on my shoulders. Like some bad dystopian novel.

I stand in Deston's room, half listening to his instructions. "The next challenge will be determined by a Seelie prince. His name is Bonn. We have three days to prepare. You missed the last challenge, perhaps that is for the best."

I'd barely catch Deston's words. *I missed one, and perhaps it's for the best. You think? What a dick.* He doesn't mention the prince's name the one in charge of the challenge. What difference does it make to me what a prince's name is or what court he belongs to? Not that I can figure out the court system here. But it made no sense. Seelie, UnSeelie. That's like saying dumb and dumber. Maybe they could call the courts Gog and Magog. The names are close enough and just as moronic.

I wish I'd paid attention when we were reading mythology and folklore in school. Fairies are supposed to be something all girls read about. All little girls love fairies, don't they? But my mother didn't. She hated Tinkerbell. No matter how many times I pleaded with her, she never let me get dressed-up or even watch the movies, but she was perfectly okay if I ran around talking about Pegasus and Greek mythology. I shake my head. The hypocrisy of it all makes me laugh.

"Okay, so what kind of contest do you think Bonn has in mind? Can't be any worse than a killer maze and save your friend or you both die, bullshit." I dart my eyes over, only to catch a glimpse of Janice. His face reveals nothing although his demeanor speaks volumes. I watch as his hands clench and unclench.

"This isn't a joke." Janice admonishes me. "The maze was extremely difficult. Few Fae would have made it through. You managed to make it out with thirty-seven people, which puts you in top running. You're a target, Sarah, and now you need to train. Every challenge after this will be increasingly more difficult." His eyes flash violet, and the color intensifies when they land on me.

"Great, so are we training with swords and knives? Now that you've discovered humanity has projectile bullets, perhaps we could train with a few guns. That's something I could really wrap my hand around and my head." I'm being flip, so what?

Janice replies, "You're thinking like a human. Stop thinking like a human. You don't even look human anymore. I highly doubt you are human anymore. You need to think in Fae terms. Do you think the Fae would have you do anything so pathetically sad as making you sword fight? If we just wanted to watch a sword fight, we would use our own people. At least they're trained. No one wants to watch a battle between two untrained oafs, bumbling around and stabbing at each other until they accidentally fall down and someone mysteriously dies. If someone's going to die in Fae from a dual, we expect to see true showmanship. Unfortunately, we don't have enough time to train you for that. No, in Fae, everything will be something you never expected. A flower which you must change its color and make it dance and sing. Or perhaps an animal you must tame. Or perhaps you need to rebuild an entire structure from scratch. It's anyone's guess, but whatever your challenge is, it will be something out of the ordinary. Something a human has never dreamed of. Change your thinking." His words sting me. Bumbling around in the dark and accidentally dying from a sword blow. Janice makes it sound as if I'm such a klutz like I'd trip and fall on my own weapon and kill myself.

Maybe he's right? I cross my arms and cock my hip to one side. I raise my eyebrow and snarl. "I have no finesse or grace, and clearly I'm not imaginative enough. Why do you want me in this contest?" I tap my index finger on my lower lip. "And can you please tell me more than 'the prize is the world'? What exactly is this charade about?"

Both Deston and Janice's faces slam closed like a door as if I'd kicked it shut in their minds. Muscles in Janice's neck bulge.

"All your needling, poking, and prodding will not bring you the answers you desire," Deston snaps. "If you wish to know what the competition is about, you must finish it and you must win. There will only be one winner, all other contenders will die. That is the Fae way, win or die. We do not take up competitions or challenges without being fully aware of what's involved, in case you missed that part in your first challenge. Anyone who didn't make it out of the maze with you died. All of them." Deston's words land like a blow to my belly.

My mouth goes dry. That's a lie. His answer had to be a lie. The rules said very clearly that as long as you freed whoever it was from the tree and had made it to the center of the maze, you'd live and so would your friend. His words make it sound like anyone I left behind, including Arty, is already dead. My head shakes as I step back.

"I left Arty in the garden, and I know he's still alive. I know you wouldn't kill him. I followed the rules and freed him." My jaw clenches shut.

Janice crosses his arms and turns his back on me, focusing instead on the licking green flames in the fireplace

"Everyone in the maze died, I believe that to be true," Deston says. "If your friend is still alive, someone is hiding him for their own purposes. There's only one way to find the answer. You must win." Deston reply is curt. He nods his head at Janice and then extends his arm to the archway, signaling my dismissal.

"Shall we train, Sarah?" Janice is always so calm, always in control. He behaves one way in front of Deston and another when we are alone.

Me, I feel like I'm gonna burst at any moment. In my mind, I jump on Deston, stabbing him through his green eyes and taking a knife to work each orb out of his head in turn before he can stop me.

My eyes trail over the walls. I watch as thorns grow and sharpen. Deston's domain would defend him, violently if necessary. I don't believe him. I think he'd lie about anything to get what he wants. He's probably holding Arty somewhere in this castle as a hostage, waiting to be used as leverage.

I'm happy to leave the study and the oppressive wakes of the walls. They push me to leave; it isn't my place. The moment Janice and I enter the elevator compartment, the wake waves ease, welcoming me, and peace descends again. "Why don't you ever say anything in there?" I demand.

"It's not necessary. Deston already has his plan of action. He's already decided what he wants to do. Our job is to play along. All we need to do is continue long enough in the competition for you to win." Janice's arms cross. It's the only sign of irritation I've ever seen from him.

"No matter who has to die?" My belly clenches. I don't want to kill humans.

"You know, that's true. They are going to die whether you participate or not. You already know the outcome of this can determine the fate of all. It determines the fate of humanity and Fae together." Janice drones on with the same drivel.

"Your ambiguous answers are so encouraging. Hold me back." I throw my snarky comment at him.

"We've discussed this, and I don't wish to go over it again. I have shared as much information as I can. You gave your word that you'd participate. Now we will go into the courtyard and train." His arms drop to his side.

I retort under my breath, "You and Deston said you would tell me what 'it' is all about. I'm still waiting."

Janice sighs. "Know this, Sarah. As soon as I'm able, I will tell you all. Until then, trust me." The low whisper of his voice slides over me like silk, clinging to my flesh. My skin rises with a slippery feel. The ring of truth colors his statement.

My head itches and aches in different spots. The blades on my shoulders ache every time I raise my arms, rubbing against something. Sharp pains shoot down my spine.

I follow Janice for my next ass kicking. *Joy.*

CHAPTER 25

The next three days consist of bumps, bruises, and pain. For every blow I land, Janice lands five. His face wrinkles in determination, constantly telling me to get back up and try harder. "You are faster and better than this." He remarks.

I don't know why he thinks I'm faster or better. I like to compete. I like to win, but it's not like I'd spent my entire life training for a fight to the death.

What Deston said sounded like a Battle Royale. However many go in, and only one comes out. I must be the one.

"Can't you just put some kind of enchantment on me or my clothes or a weapon? Let me use that and it magically makes me better?" I take a swig of water and swish it around my mouth. I spit the blood out while rolling my arm in its socket to stretch out the pain.

"You will have enchanted armor and weapons, but that's not going to be enough. If you want to win, you have to actually be good; you have to try. You must become something more than yourself. Whoever you thought you were when we took you off the surface, you must let that idea of self. Go!" Janice orders.

I glare up at him through my eyebrows. He'd just hit me with the side of his hand, not only knocking me down, but he plants my face firmly in the dirt. Tomorrow is the next challenge, and I still have no idea what it's going to be. Janice makes it sound like all I need to do is defend myself. Everything we'd gone over is hand-to-hand combat, and you don't master that in a day or two or three.

Hand-to-hand combat is about repetition, muscle memorization, and reacting without thinking. I'm not there. I'm never going to be there, not in three days. I don't understand why their magic doesn't work like that or maybe it does.

"So, you're saying I'll be given enchanted weapons and armor or whatever it is that I need. Why can't you enchant me?" I cross my arms, blowing hair out of my face.

"I can't enchant you. It's one of the rules of Fae. We cannot enchant each other." He shakes his head. He knows I don't understand the rules. I know he's frustrated. I'm frustrated. But it strikes me they can't enchant each other. That doesn't mean they can't enchant themselves.

"What if I enchanted myself? Can I do that?"

He stops walking away from me and pivots until his violet eyes land on me, a half-smile on his face. "Now you're not thinking like a human. I've beaten on you for three days hoping you would come up with an answer. These challenges aren't about who's the fastest or the strongest. They'll be about who's the smartest, who thinks the quickest. These challenges are all problem-solving, the Fae are extremely smart. We love tactics, to manipulate and play. It's a game. This is what we do. Once you understand that and the moment you stop thinking about the world like a human, that's the moment you will succeed." He stares me down with his conviction. "All the rest of the contenders will still be thinking as a human. It will be their downfall. I knew you'd figure it out for yourself. Now you want me to keep beating on you, or would you prefer to learn something that might actually help you?"

I blow air through my nose and huff. I'm not a toddler. I shouldn't be throwing a fit, but I'm a little-pissed off. He'd spent three days beating on me so I could figure this out for myself? He could've told me or given some kind of clue. But in the back of my mind, I know he already had. Deston said to stop thinking like a human, and I came down here and did just that. Guess I really did deserve to be beaten on for three days. I uncross my arms and let them fall limply to my side.

"All right, teach me how to enchant anything." I huff.

Janice bends down and picks up a rock. "If you want to enchant something, you first must understand what you want it to do. Learn what it does and then bend it to your will. You know magic is about intent, and it's also about manipulating the waves. I repeat the songs I've heard. I know I can make the stone float with a specific song." He holds up the stone and smiles with one eyebrow cocked. " 'Chickie bird, sitting on a wall, one named Peter, one named Paul, fly away, Peter, fly away, Paul.' If you want it to come." He removes his hand, and the stone floats in the air. He touches it with the tip of his finger, and it floats away. It doesn't exactly fly, but I get the drift. He made it float, and he can push it around. He pushes it toward me.

I thrust my hand up to stop it, but it singes me. I move out of the way. "You could at least warn me that the damn thing was gonna burn me. Why is it trial by fire with you?" I demand.

He blows air out through his nose. "I thought you would've learned by now from your encounter with the Puca's belt. Enchanted items, not enchanted by you or for you, will burn." His brows draw down into sharp check marks on his forehead.

"Okay, I get it. If I enchant something for myself, no one else will be able to pick it up and use it. It'll burn them. But if I enchant it for someone else or anyone else, it doesn't matter who touches it?" I ask.

"Exactly. 'Now come back, Peter, come back, Paul.' " The stone comes back to him, floating. He grabs it out of the air and whistles a sweet C. He tosses the stone to the ground. "Keep in mind, you can also enchant items so they work like a trap. It's inert until someone touches it or picks it up, but then you whistle a specific tone and awaken the item, causing the enchantment to harm them in some fashion."

My jaw sets as I grit my teeth. "Is that what they did in the maze to the plants? Is that how they made the ivy attack us? It was inert until someone touched it?" I see Janice is irritated with my anger over the traps in the maze.

"You must accept this is the way Fae is. It's not fair. I'm sure on the surface you have heard humans say life is not fair. If you are human, life will absolutely not be 'fair,' because you aren't. Somehow, you've made yourself a member of the Fae. You are fair folk. Life will be different for you." Janice's explanation sounds great and stupid.

I know life isn't fair. It doesn't mean I don't want it to be.

He continues, "Life is not fair. It isn't, and it won't be. You must accept that and move on. Stop obsessing over the past. Focus on the future. You only need to do one thing—win. Winning will resolve all the issues that anger you. Let your anger go, and simply focus on winning."

I don't like his answers or anything he says for the most part. He's right. Maybe obsessing over the past is a waste of my time. Understanding my new life is the quickest, best way to get what I want. "I'll make you a deal. I'll do my best to keep my obsessions with past wrongs to myself. And you do your best to make it sound less like you guys are fucking assholes. Deal?" I reply with a tight smile.

He crosses his arms. "Your deal sounds ambiguous at best, but if we're going to both put forth an effort, I will happily do my part." *Acquiescent, yes.*

I have to try this enchanting bit although I think the nursery rhyme he uses is rather cheesy. I can't think of a better rhyme. The nursery rhymes Fae use creep me out. I remember a Lenny Kravitz song my mom played a lot. I can't remember the words. Instead, I hum the tune. The rock rises in the air and floats nearby. I push it away, and it comes back. I think this magic thing is easier for me than him. "Why is it I can use any song I want and make the same thing happen, but you use the same old stuff?" I inquire.

He looks around and grabs me by my bicep. "I think we're done training for now. Let's go for a walk." He forcefully grips my arm and drags me. His fingers aren't digging in, but it still pains me. My shoulder is sore. Nervous wakes come off his body. I see his emotions, and my eyes dart around the courtyard. Every Fae creature here has its own wake. It reminds me of those psychics you see on television talking about people's auras. Is this what they meant? Can they see magic? Is an aura part of the magic that naturally surrounds us?

Where Janice grips my upper arm, I see my own wake—a white even glow. It doesn't have a shape or a color to it. I'm silver. Where it meets his hand, his dark purple glow becomes a light lavender. It fades away the longer he touches me, and the more my silvery glow overtakes his.

Soon enough, we walk out of the courtyard proper, and he leads me across the stone drawbridge. We stand in front of the castle with the moat between Deston's court and us.

He turns on me and begins talking. "Don't ever tell anyone you can make up your own rhymes. Our people use the same rhymes over and over. Let everyone think you're using the same rhymes they are. Don't tell anyone ever that you can make something new." He looks frightened. His entire wake changes to an almost black purple, deep like the void of space. It's thick with fear.

I touch my hand to his chest and watch the silvery white light of my own magic push the black away.

He closes his eyes and tilts his head back. "Sarah, you must stop. You cannot meddle with the emotions of others." He says through tight lips.

I snatch my hand back. "What do you mean? I'm not meddling with your emotions. I can see you're afraid. I'm not, so I tried to make you less afraid, or I don't know. I was watching my emotions melt with yours. I wasn't meddling or trying to manipulate you. I'm not like the Fae. I don't think you're a plaything." My voice hardens.

"You can see my emotions?" His eyes open wide in fascination.

"Yeah, can't you? Can't all Fae?" *I don't like new abilities.* I was just getting used to what I had become before I enchanted the stupid stone. The stone is probably still floating there. I hadn't returned it to its inert state. I whistle it to me and strip the magic from it, then toss it on the ground. "I'm not trying to manipulate you. I won't tell anybody that I can use my own rhymes and songs." I wave my arms around.

The place where I touched him on his chest remains white, and the black filters away to purple. I think it's his natural state of being.

His eyes pierce into mine and then down at my mouth. My mouth dries, and I lick my lips. I'd only done that maneuver once before when one of the boys I liked was going to kiss me, or at least I thought he was.

The boy had kissed me, and it was terrible. I get the distinct impression Janice wants to kiss me. I lean forward. My heart speeds up as he puts his hand on the side of my face. I tilt my head back, and as I close my eyes, he leans in.

"So, this is how you train, Sarah?" Nick demands.

My eyes fly open, and I step back. Standing off to the side is Nick with his arms crossed, lips pinched, and eyes hard.

"No, this isn't how I train. I don't. I don't. You know, Nick, it's really none of your business what I do. We have an agreement. As long as I fulfill my end of the bargain, what I do with my own time is my own business," I sputter at him. "And you should stop sneaking around. What are you spying on me stalker, creeper." I put some space between Janice and me.

Nick lets out a dry laugh. It sounds like a cough "Yes, lying is not usually your thing. Frankly, I don't give a shit if you kiss the purple-eyed freak. You do whatever you want with him after we get my sister. Let's get Nikki, and we leave or I leave with Nikki. You can do whatever works. You become more like them every day, and all I'm doing is sitting around waiting for something to happen." He shouts.

I feel guilty about that. I should've had Nick join us in training sessions. I'm not sure they would've let him train, but I should've at least tried. "Well, you don't have to worry about doing nothing. Tomorrow's a big, big day. I'm going to compete, probably against your sister and a bunch of other girls. At that point, we should be able to figure out who has her and then maybe we can actually get some movement forward and you can get the fuck out of Fae. Okay?" I turn to say something to Janice, but he's no longer standing there. I look around, and it's just Nick and I. I hadn't even heard him leave.

Did he want to kiss me or was it me messing with his emotions? I shake my head. *I don't have time for these kinds of distractions.*

But the memory brings euphoria. I think he was going to kiss me. I wanted it. Those violet eyes looking at me with so much desire, I liked it. My eyes turn away from the stone edifice of the castle only to land back on Nick. His color waves are bright orange and laced with reds. He's angry and deep in the heart of his aura as it leaves his skin there's a thin line of gray. *Why would he be gray? Gray always makes me think of storms and sadness, but we all have something to morn.* I push that thought to the side, a subject for another time.

"Let's go! I need to rest and eat. You probably need to eat too. Tomorrow a big day." I shake the depressing thoughts away.

"Just promise me whatever happens in the competition, you won't kill my sister." Nick's voice is thick with emotion.

"I already said I wouldn't. I promised I'd help you get your sister. I wasn't lying, and I won't go back on my word. I'll figure out how to send you back to the surface." I leave the life and death choice out of it.

"You won't choke like last time?" he whispers.

I shake my head. The lump forms in my throat again. I don't want to talk about it. I know how to send him back without me. That's all that matters. "Just promise me if we find Arty tomorrow, you'll take him with you no matter what. Don't let him stay. Knock him out and carry his ass into a mushroom round." I reply.

Nick raises an eyebrow but nods in agreement.

I implore him, "I don't care what you have to do. You can't let him stay. Take him home and tell him my parents found the room. He'll know where to go look."

We both walk back in silence into the safety of the castle walls. All I have to do now is choke down a meal and find a way to sleep tonight.

CHAPTER 26

Sleep eludes me. Tossing and turning is the only thing I do. My room is comfortable. The bed is like sleeping on a cloud. It doesn't matter which way I turn or how I close my eyes, I can't get the fear out of my mind. There's only one thing certain to happen tomorrow—more people will die. Light brightens the window, pushing back the dark purples of the night. Lavender enters my room, bustling about and twittering. I don't hear anything she says. I simply stumble out of bed and into the bathroom to splash water on my face. I wait for Lavender to dress me in whatever it is they deem appropriate for killing.

"Did you sleep, my lady?" she inquires in her sing-song voice.

I shake my head. What's the point of lying? Anyone who looks at my eyes can tell I hadn't slept a wink. The skin underneath my eyes is hauling around a fifteen-piece set of

Louis Vuitton luggage. I force a half-smile onto my face. "I know you're gonna be nice, Lavender; that's how you are. Honestly, I really don't want small talk or chitchat. My day's gonna suck, and I really don't want to think about it, but…" I leave the thank you to hang in the air.

She doesn't reply, only nodding her head and setting to work. She turns my hair into some magical coif of perfection. Who wants to go kill other humans unless they're perfectly dressed and looking appropriately snazzy?

"What kind of ridiculous get up are they putting me in today?" I query.

She produces a partial smile and holds up a black leather bodice crossed in back with a leather spaulder attached to one shoulder. It looks like something right out of the movie, *Gladiator*. 'We, who are about to die, salute you.'

"Is that it or do I get to wear something else with that? Maybe something underneath it? Maybe some britches?" I inquire.

She snickers, and really I hadn't decided to make her laugh. I was being sarcastic because that's how I like to deal with everything.

"No, my lady. Of course, they would send you in more than just a bodice. However, it's not just a bodice. Whatever you may think it's been made of or how it looks, I can assure you Deston enchanted it himself. All your clothing is enchanted. Deston made an allowance for me to touch it. But anyone else lays a hand on you, it will burn them to the core." She smiles brightly.

Great. What if I need help?

"So, it's hand-to-hand combat?" I'm hoping I heard her wrong. The last thing in the world I want to do is fight.

"I don't know. If anyone or anything in Fae touches you, they'll be burned. Having enchanted clothing is important. There are many creatures here that will happily kill you for a quick and easy meal. Many more people who would happily trick you so they could kill you just because it would be fun." She carries the conversation in a singsong tone.

"But not you, right, Lavender?" I snicker.

She puts on her sweet, cotton candy smile. The one she seems to always have for me as her ears tilt up at the sides. "You know I would never do anything to hurt you. I'm vassal tied to you." It's a matter of fact reply.

"No vassal has ever cheated or stabbed their liege lord in the back or anything like that?" I reply in a droll tone. Humans swear loyalty all the time but go back on their word.

"You have the free will to leave your liege. But if you're vassal tied to someone, it is impossible for you to work against them." Lavender always imparts the most interesting information at the most opportune times.

Sometimes I wonder if it's by design. She isn't stupid. Yet she's perfectly happy to impart an important piece of information at the most opportune time.

Therein lies the answer of why Deston desperately wants me to swear allegiance to him. He knows I can't work against him. By telling him I don't want to, I'd kept my free will.

I pat Lavender on the cheek. She holds up a black, peasant style shirt and a pair of black leather britches. Everything has buckles and straps of all kinds. It doesn't look like it's going to be comfortable. "Do I get any weapons?"

She slips the shirt over my head and shakes her head. "I can't give weapons. I'm not in charge of those sorts of things. However, if you'd like a hairpin, I could supply you one of those. I can leave it in your hair." My mouth pinches to the side with my barely repressed smile.

"Sure, I'll be the contender who stabs someone to death with a hairpin."

Lavender's eyes go wide. There's no mirth in her face. "My lady, you must take this seriously. Many a Fae have died from a hairpin stab, or they simply touched it, or someone grazed it across their skin. If you wish, I will hide twenty all over your hair. Then you can use them to stop anything you wish. It's not a toy. It's a tool, a tool that can very well save your life." The solemnity of her words strikes me.

Well, okay.

"As long as they don't stab me in the head or hurt me in any way, you can hide as many hairpins on my head as you want," I reply. "If it's a tool that I can use to save myself, you damn well better believe I'd like as many as I can get."

She smiles tightly and lowers her eyes. She knows something. I can tell she's holding back, but I don't have time to try to niggle it out of her. She gives me a drink of something resembling coffee along with a potion bottle labeled 'Drink Me'.

"There are no restrictions on this challenge today. I'm giving you something every Fae of the lower staff receives in the afternoon, a pick-me-up. In case you're tired and you need to keep working, I saved mine from yesterday for you. It'll give you energy, keep you going and alert. I didn't want you to go into battle alone." Her words touch me. She really cares, or is she like Deston and just wants me to win?

"What do I do with it? I mean, I don't have any pockets. Where will I put it? What if it breaks?"

"Oh, you have a small leather pouch on the back side of your belt so don't worry." She tips up on to her toes in delight.

I hold the thank you back again. "Lavender, I don't know what to say. I don't want you to become tired or be punished because you weren't awake."

"What you're doing is more important than what I do. If I'm punished for one day, but helped save the world... I'd hate to think that I could've helped you and didn't. They'll give me another one today. I don't use them every day, and they're not addictive."

I'm such a fool. Of course, I should've asked if it is addictive. Why would they give it to their servants if it isn't addictive? If she can go a whole day without it, maybe it isn't addictive. I pull the cork and sniff. It smells of dandelions and chamomile. I'd never been good with wildflowers. That was more my mother's thing. A drop falls onto my hand. I watch how it interacts with my aura. It doesn't burn, and its wake is pink like lavender's hair.

"Lavender, is your hair really pink?" I ask.

She bites her lower lip and laughs nervously. "No, of course not. My hair was white, and now it's black. But I dye it pink. I don't want anyone to know." She whispers in a conspiratorial tone.

If her hair had been white previously, she was vassal tied to Deston. But if it's black now, then she's indeed vassal tied to me. She changed sides. Is she dying her hair to protect me or to protect herself? It doesn't matter. She could be protecting herself or could be protecting me, it'd still be her protecting herself.

"When did your hair turn black?" I sip the drink and finger the leather straps on my clothes.

"About the same time you came." She never stops fiddling with my hair. She shrugs her shoulders and finishes weaving my hair. She places soft leather-like boots on my feet.

"You're not going to tell me, are you?" I muse.

Her large eyes gaze at me as she shakes her head. I know she won't tell me. It doesn't matter. *Let her have her secrets.*

She leads me to the top of the servant stairs. I snicker. I have an idea. There's no way I'm walking down all those stairs this time. I mulled over the process of enchanting all night long. The railing on the stairs is nothing more than a simple rope. The wakes are fuzzy like the fibers that make it. The song rises in my throat, and the music smoothens the wake waves into the fall of water. I grab Lavender by the arm and thrust my hand into the liquid. In a rush, it pulls me down the twisting stairwell. In a blink, we reach the ground floor.

For a moment, I forget all of my problems. My belly aches as I laugh.

Lavender laughs too, but her eyes grow wide. "You must put it back." She orders.

"No. Why? It's cruel to make you all run up and down the stairs. I think it works both ways." I reach out to test my theory.

"It doesn't matter. You're not allowed to change a castle without the Lord's approval." She informs me.

"Well, what part of 'I don't fucking care' do you think he'd have a problem with?" I snicker. A cough from behind tells me I'm being watched, and I know who is watching.

"Whatever you just did, you must undo. And you need to do it now!" I turn to see the disapproval filling Janice's violet eyes.

"No, I don't want to. Why should all these Fae have to run up and down the stairs as if they were nobody and nothing? It's cruel, just because they're 'lower' than you." I hip switch. He bites down, and I see his jaw grinding. His brow locks down onto his eyes.

"I don't care what it is you think or want. You cannot make changes in the Lord's house; it's impossible. What did I tell you? You can't be different." He grabs my hand and drags me away from the stairwell. His eyes dart left and right, and his whole stance takes on a demeanor of readiness. Fear wakes from him.

"What you're doing is dangerous. Stop playing with fire. Undo the enchantment. We must leave." Janice fears for me. My skin gives a tingled thrill where his hand clasp mine.

I huff. The air comes out my lips and puffs my bangs off of my face. Janice's eyes dart over to the Lavender. She steps in and pins them up and out of my eyes. I turn away from both of them.

Fairies are stupid. 'You can't make any changes. Everything must be the same. You can't do it because it's the Lord's house,' Nan-nan.

I hum a song, undoing the magic, and I keep shooting Janice dirty looks. I hadn't laid eyes on him since our almost-not kiss. My heart compresses as his lips flash through my mind. I'm angry at him. What does it matter whether the stairs are enchanted or not? He motions for me to follow. I huff as I do.

"Where's Nick?" My eyes search for him but find nothing but Fae.

"He's in the pen of humans we're bringing. Don't worry, he'll be there. So far I've managed to keep him out of Deston's sight, but if he does anything stupid today, I might not be able to protect him. You need to remind him who is in charge and what's at stake."

The muscles on my face relax with my smile. Nick will do whatever is necessary to save his sister. I climb into the carriage and plop down on the cushy seat. "Don't worry, Nick knows what's at stake. He's not stupid. He won't rush in." I'm not sure he wouldn't, but I need Janice to believe it.

"I know he won't because I want you to entrance him." He replies.

My mouth drops open. "No, I won't! It would be a betrayal. I promised Nick, and who the fuck are you to tell me what to do?" My chest twists when our eyes meet. The fear waking off of him grows in strength.

"He could betray you. I can't risk your safety." His hand reaches out to caress the side of my face.

My heart speeds up. I want him to touch me, but I snap, then slap his hand away. "Risk my safety? What a joke. So, it's okay to send me into some weird fairy thunder dome but Nick is too dangerous? I don't get your logic." My chest pounds with my own fear. I'd held it off, but now it threatens to overtake me. My hands are moist with sweat, and adrenalin blazes through my veins. "I am not yours to control. Nick is my problem, not yours. I'll handle him when and if the time comes. Until then, don't worry your pretty Fae head over my safety or Nick's." With every word, I move closer. Now my eyes line up with his. I hold his eyes for a moment before they lock onto my lips, only to dart back up. A thrill runs through me. I chance a glance at his lips, full and inviting. I want that kiss. My lips press together plumping up against my will as heat moves over my body.

The carriage lurches, and I bounce up, smacking my head into the ceiling. The spell is broken. I slouch back into my seat. The land of Fae speeds by outside the window. I pretend to find interest in it and ignore the violet eyes of the Fae man next to me.

We come to a halt, and the footman pops the door open while putting the foot pad down at the same time. I emerge to the full view of a hedge. *Great another hedge. What the fuck? Don't these creatures have an imagination? Please, don't let this be another killer maze.*

CHAPTER 27

"You don't look impressed." Deston's voice cuts through my thoughts. He must've arrived ahead of us in another carriage, flexing his 'I'm above your station' crap.

"It looks no different than the last challenge you brought me to. Big hedge with a garden on the other side?" I prod with a shrug. White teeth gleam in his mouth, but the smile never reaches his eyes. White hair falls down his back and over his shoulders, reaching almost to his waist.

"No, it's not a garden. This time I'm sure of it, but you can have weapons." He waves his hand, and Janice comes over and begins inserting daggers of all sizes all over my bodice and leather pants. "Give her the sword," Deston instructs.

A Fae I'd never seen before presents me a sword, out of a dream. The handle resembles small, intertwined vines. The blade itself gleams as if made of liquid metal. The light clings to the edge and glints off at the same time. My hand itches to grip the hilt.

"It's called Quicksilver, humans call it Mercury," Deston informs. "We enchant it to solid form. It will never lose its edge or become corrupted. Its specialty is death. Anyone you scratch with it will die, unless they are Fae. It will even kill Fomorians." Deston's description doesn't lessen my desire to hold it. My belly rolls with my hunger for the sword. It calls to me; the sword wakes out a bright line similar to starlight. The closer my hand comes to the hilt, the stronger the pull. I wrap my fingers around the grip, and the vines cling to my hand, encasing my grip—a perfect fit. A thrill runs up my arm to my mind. Instinct comes with it. It's balanced for me. I slash at the air in front of my face, cutting it in half and pushing stray wisps of hair back from my face. My heart pounds with the thrill. This sword makes me feel powerful.

"She's bonded with it; that's good." Deston winks at me and takes my free hand in his. He raises it to his lips. His green eyes never waver from my own. His lips vibrate on my skin, creating heat.

A fire races over me causing my heart rate rises as a flush climbs up my neck. He pulls my hand from his lips, and I open my mouth to protest.

"Don't worry, Sarah. Be safe! We can talk after you finish this challenge." Deston says.

The agitation that had been growing in me calms. The thrill of holding the sword is almost as powerful as the thrill I receive when I look into Deston's eyes.

Something about Deston and the feeling he evokes strike me as strange, not right. Looking at Janice pulled at every heart string I had, but it seems so long ago after Deston. I can't push this new desire away, no matter how strange it is.

"Have you heard what I've said, Sarah?" Janice's voice seeps through my dizzying fog.

I shake my head as if to throw something off. The sound of his voice is jarring. I shake myself again. Something is wrong with me, I'm about to go fight for my life, and I'm busy being dizzy over some stupid green-eyed Fae?

I remark. "No, I just. No, I'm fine. Thank you for asking."

Janice quirks his mouth to the side as if he doesn't believe me. He holds his hand open. "Give me the sword. I'll place it in your baldric," Janice requests.

I want to snicker. I'd only ever heard the term baldric in regards to some stupid British comedy my dad used to watch.

My eyes dart around, looking for exactly what he's talking about. "What's a baldric?" I ask.

"It's hanging from your belt. It's that leather thing with all the buckles and the scabbard." My eyes meet his, and my heart lurches anew then stills.

Strange, something is wrong with me. I shake my head again, trying to clear out whatever's fogging up my mind. As long as I don't look at either Deston or Janice in the eye or think about them too much, I feel normal.

Janice takes the sword and inserts it into the baldric. The weight of it pulls down on the side of my body, but it isn't an overly heavy. It feels natural.

I hear a low humming coming from Janice's lips. Through my teeth, I say, "What are you doing?"

He doesn't reply. He continues the low humming as he fiddles with all the buckles on my belt and bodice. Then he ceases. "I added an enchantment to your sword." I cock an eyebrow at him. He doesn't respond. Deston's here. Janice must be all business.

"Well, Sarah, I wish you all the best," Deston says. "Be safe. I would hate to see anything happen to you; it would affect me most deeply." Deston kisses my hand again, and the pounding in my chest speeds up. I tear my eyes away from his. A strange feeling settles over me, again something I just can't kick.

Deston saunters away with his retainers as if he doesn't have a care in the world. His words say I'm important to him, but his actions say something else. My eyes follow him. It feels impossible to tear them away.

A thumb and forefinger snap, breaking my line of vision and bringing me back to reality.

"Sarah, if this is how you behave inside the challenge, we're both dead." Nick grits his jaw. It's a relief to look at Nick. He doesn't make my heart pound with heat, nor does he give me strange longings. There's no unfulfilled need. It's just Nick. Good old, reliable Nick. A human with soft round ears, completely normal. We both have the same agenda, just different people. That's enough for me. He's more trustworthy than any Fae will ever be.

My eyes dart around. I don't see any other humans. "No, I'm good now. I think whatever it was, you snapped me out of it." I nod my head and give a half-hearted smile. Tilting his head to one side, he drags his eyes from the hedge over to me.

"Anything about this look familiar?" His sarcasm isn't lost on me.

"Yeah, another fucking hedge. Although I'm assured what's on the other side isn't the garden from hell this time." I give him a shove with my shoulder.

"The other one wasn't a garden either, Sarah. You were a mouse in a maze or a death trap. This is just a new way for them to try to kill you and me apparently." Nick shoulders me back.

I toe up on one foot to maintain my balance. "They're letting you inside?" My brows draw together. That doesn't make any sense. He isn't a challenger. Why would they let him inside?

"Janice told me this morning; every competitor gets a companion." He pokes his chest with a thumb.

"Well, that's just epic." I exclaim. This isn't part of my plan. I don't want to defend myself *and* Nick. "Whatever happens from here on out, it's super important you listen to everything I say. After the bullshit starts, we won't have a moment to do more than survive." *If we're lucky.*

He knows what I'm gonna say, but it still needs to be said. I plunge in. "Don't go all big brother if you see Nikki. You don't know if she's enchanted or not."

Nick tilts his head down and looks at me through his eyebrows. "I'll try."

Janice cuts Nick off. "If you two are done muttering between yourselves, it's time for the competitors to hear the rules."

There had been thousands of competitors the last time. Now, it looks like there are hundreds of girls and boys everywhere. Every girl is with her human companion, waiting for our latest death game. They move in pairs. I guess they are kind of like Nick and I, the challenger and their minion. I give a half-smile. How would Nick feel if he knew I was calling in my minion?

I hear the snick of the gate as it slips closed. Janice's hand remains on the rail with his lilac-colored fingernails and the day-glo markings indicative of all Fae. I want to reach out and place my hand on top of his. Instead, I settle for next to his on the railing.

I have my own markings, similar to Deston's—green with swirls and dots. The outline of leaves are so faint; it's almost imperceptible. My eyes travel up Janise's arm meeting his face. My heart speeds up, and a flush rolls through me.

Janice says, "You will be safe, you will survive." I can't tell if it's a statement, a request, or if he's pleading. My feelings are muddled. I can't drag myself from him. *What's wrong with me?*

Just because some violet-eyed, pointy-eared motherfucker attempts to kiss me and then doesn't, that doesn't mean I should be all googly-eyed in front of him. But I can't help it. Something between us has changed. I want to survive whatever this is, and I hadn't been afraid until this very moment. With a dry mouth and moist hands, I take a deep breath to study myself. "Don't worry, I'm smarter than the average bear." I nod my head and turn slightly, throwing a glance over my shoulder at Nick. "Let's go get a picnic basket!" Nick puts his hands on my shoulders and gives me a quick rub.

Nick replies to my banter. "All right, boss. Let's go!" Janice's nostrils flare at the contact between Nick and I. *What the hell would he care if Nick rubs my shoulders...unless he does?* I smile to myself.

I turn my back on Janice and the burning brick in my belly. I hadn't paid attention to our trip through the hedge or the human cattle pen we're now trapped in. What spans out in front of me is a wooden, top rail fence. It goes on for miles in every direction, encircling and enclosing hills. A forest stands off in the distance and the crevasse of the creek cuts through the area. Fifty flags dot the landscape in a multitude of colors. I could say they're a rainbow, but there are more colors here than I've ever seen in any rainbow. More like something you'd find at the paint shop. One of them looks like it's Catalina blue.

Hovering in front of us is an exquisite looking male Fae. His hair is so black, it is as dark as a void in space. His amber eyes, fleck with black, are large almonds, framed in black lashes. Day-glo Fae tattooing covers his body also in a deep amber. He stands on a floating mushroom platform, and when he speaks, his voice booms. I tear my eyes away from him to look behind the pens.

A rainbow of Fae colors flood bleachers infested with easily a million creatures sitting, lounging, and standing. Thrones and platforms float in the air. They're clumped together. I guess even in Fae, there are cliques. As if on cue, they turn and face our pen.

"I am Bonn, Prince of the Seelie court, Defender of the Queen, and leader of the Fae war machines. Welcome to my game zone, challengers." The crowd roars with wild anticipation or bloodlust. I can't tell with the Fae.

His title is a mouthful of meaningless nothings. *Why bother?* I'm sure all the Fae know who he is. We lowly humans don't give a crap.

"You are all here because you survived the last two challenges. In some cases, you impressed us. In other ways, you were allowed to pass onto this challenge." I feel all eyes on me. The murmuring around my shoulders tells me that even the human girls know exactly who I am.

Upon closer inspection, the girls are less human and more Fae. Opalescent skin and pointed ears peek out from the hair in varying stages of turning white and black, all laced with flashing eyes. I still see the human in all of them. Their faces are round and plump with mortality. Not one of them is as far along as I am.

Bonn's amber orbs laugh at my discomfort. *How is it I'm so oblivious to this? Is there some kind of Fae twitter feed I'm missing?*

"Each flag represents a station. You can either defend it, or you can try to capture it. When you enter the game zone, you'll be given a squad of Fomorians. They are at your beck and call. You are to instruct them in what you wish. They can protect you, defend a flag, or kill another competitor—whatever you wish. They are your own private army. Keep in mind, you're welcome to kill your competitors as well or band together with them. We really don't care. At the end, only fifty will leave this game zone. In case you're wondering what your odds are, there are 872 competitors. Good luck." He laughs in his snickering Fae fashion. The mushroom ring floats down and places him on what can't be anything other than a throne.

A whistling rises from the background, signaling the opening of the gates. Nick grabs my wrist and drags me towards the entrance as butterflies and bile rise up from my belly to my throat. "If it's capture the flag, we need to get one. *Now*." Nick's hand tightens on my arm.

"That is not what he said. He said there would only be fifty contenders at the end and you are welcome to kill as many of your competitors as you wish. He said you could capture the flag or you could defend it. He didn't say that is the way to win." I stumble over a rock and regain my balance. "Nick, stop for a moment!" I pull my arm back, but he holds firm.

Nick doesn't care. He isn't listening. As soon as we step through the gate, something changes. Wake waves cover the rail fencing all the way around the game zone. In every direction, it's a blue-bubble reaching toward the sky, creating a dome over the top of us. Bodies of girls jostle us back and forth. Whispering fear wakes surround each of them, along with their companions. Nick drags me off to the side. His words are lost to me as he shakes my shoulder.

"Sarah, head in the game. They won't listen to me. You're the only one who can instruct them. Tell them to come with us, and let's get the fuck out of here." He waves his hand at the Fomorians standing by my side. *What's wrong with me? I can't seem to focus.*

"What is your name?" I inquire to the largest Fomorians and shake my head to clear the mental fog.

"Bull." The Fomorian grunts while shrugging his single shoulder.

"Well, Bull, get your guys and let's go," I order.

He slaps his one hand against his chest with crossed fingers. With a closed fist, he beats his chest several times. The rest of his crew join us. They are ugly and smelly, but each carries a cross-slung baldric with a short sword. Other than the leather skirt that hangs from their waist, they are naked.

Bull eyes me. "We ready, we go."

I whip my head around and head towards the farthest flag. "What color should we go for?" I inquire.

"Only a girl would care what color the flag is," Nick says. "I just want to go for the one that's farthest away from here. It'll take everybody the longest to get there. Most people aren't willing to travel far. If we double-time it, we'll make it there before anybody else. Then set up a defensive perimeter and defend the flag and win the game." Nick's answer makes sense.

Defend the flag, win the challenge. But that's not what Bonn said. He said there'd be fifty contenders, and we were welcome to kill each other. He didn't say we had to have a flag. He said we could defend or capture, but he didn't say that any of those ways would win the challenge.

My eyes keep scanning the area around us for an attack. Different groups are heading in a multitude of directions. *Only fifty will leave the game-zone.*

That's when the screaming starts; it always does. "Pick up the pace people." I raise my feet and lower them down as fast as I can. Nick falls behind, and only the Fomorians are able to keep up. I stop and pull one of the daggers from my bodice "Nick, take this. Bull, you and your crew create a perimeter around us. We need two minutes."

They close ranks, creating a protective wall around Nick and I. I squat down and sing to his shoes. He needs an enchantment to make him run faster. If I lose him in the middle of this, I don't know what I'll do.

His shoes are the ones he'd worn on the surface, typical steel-toed biker boots. They looked great, capable of walking long distances, but the truth is they weigh him down. The wake lines coming off them are weak. They do their job, but that's about it. It's the best I can expect for human construction.

The Nancy Sinatra song about walking boots comes to mind. I sing the chorus, quickly increasing the shoes power by a hundred. I add 'the float like a feather, sting like a bee.' Nick needs to strike to live. "Let's move!" I dust my hands, giving Nick a half-smile.

CHAPTER 28

Screams fill the air over my shoulder. I'm not the only one to realize fifty means fifty. One way or another, we aren't all getting out of here.

"Sarah, turn left. I hear a stream." Nick's ears pick up almost as much as a Fae's or my ears.

I absently tuck a stray hair behind my ear, letting my finger linger on the point; it's longer. I don't have time to daydream about my looks. I shake my head. A dull aching encircles my cranium, and it itches like a son of a bitch. My fingernails scrape over my scalp with no relief.

"You got lice, Sarah?" Nick quips.

I shoot Nick a slit-eyed glance. I can't stop myself— the burning itch is never sated. I roll my shoulders; they too itch. A pressure focuses on either side of my spine near my shoulder blades. I reach my arm back and scratch through my shirt. I slow my pace. "I don't have lice, but thanks for your concern. Are you going to ditch me if you see Nikki?" I shout.

His pace slows as he shakes his head. "No, you're our best chance of getting out of here. She comes with us." His slight nod is enough for me.

"We may not have a choice in the matter," I respond.

He stops dead. I almost run into his back. He turns on me. "I'll never leave you, Sarah. Nikki will listen to me for once and leave with us." He means *us*.

"You know, I can't go back. I can take you there, but I can't stay." The lump in my throat forms again, but I swallow it down. I don't have time to think about my parents or my old life.

"I know you can't, but I won't leave you here alone." He pivots on his heel and keeps moving. *What does he mean he won't leave me here? Is every male on the planet making a pass at me?* I shake my head. My ego must be getting as big as every other Fae.

Between the itching and my head shaking, I feel out of step. I follow the tinkling of water over stones to find the stream. Nick is already poised at the edge. My enchantment made him into a Speedy Gonzales. His cupped hand extends to the water. The smacking sound of his lips reaches me. I shake my head to clear my eyes, only to have them land on the water and its magic wakes. They're wrong. Sharp dagger-like points move over the surface, clawing at the bank. The tips move like the teeth of a saw, working back and forth and chewing into rocks and plants.

The roots of the trees bordering the stream pull back. Steam rises from withered dry leaves. "Nick, stop!" I scream, it tears at my throat.

He freezes, fingers just above the water level. One splash and it would have him. He snatches his hand back. His wide eyes turn on me. "What is it?"

The air catches in my throat. "We'll get water elsewhere. I don't like the look of this stream. It's not right." On instinct, I pull a dagger from one of the many sheathes in my breeches.

Nick stands up and stalks back to me. His eyes surrounded by dark lashes meet mine. He reaches his hand out to touch my face.

I slap it away. "What's with you? Why are you trying to touch me?" I reposition my footing.

"I love you, Sarah." He moves in closer, tilting his head down.

I back away. "Um, you aren't going to kiss me, Nick." I give him a nervous laugh. *Now is not the time, dummy.*

A toothy grin spreads across his face. "You don't want me to?" He turns on what I can only guess is his best smolder.

"Umm, no. I don't. Back off, beefcake. Look Nick, I'm not interested and we don't have time for this."

He laughs.

I place one foot after the other behind me. I move into the grouping of Fomorians. "Bull, encircle me!" They move to a defensive formation, surrounding me.

Nick's forward movements cease. "All this time why else do you think I've stayed so close to you?" The hair on the back of my neck stands up as cold air finds its way down my back.

I inquire, "What about Nikki?" His words make no sense. Not ten minutes ago all he could talk about was saving Nikki, but now she's forgotten? My belly pinches and I run my hands over my bodice. They find handles of all kinds sticking out. I pull another one. The aura surrounding him is puke yellow, the sour color milk becomes when it's gone bad. The wake waves move slow as molasses on a cold winter's day.

He's under a spell.

I see sick rot emanating from his hand. The same hand I'd touched right after we entered the game zone. "Bull, step aside," I order.

The smile on Nick's face returns. His shoulders puff, and an eyebrow cocks up on one side. I extend my hand. My eyes lock on my hand. The rot is there. It came from me. I'd spelled him, but how? The rustling in the distance brings the danger back to mind.

"Bull, defend!" I hum out the Fae cleaning song and the rot on my hand dries up, melting away and returning my aura to its natural silvery white. I grab Nick's hand.

"They have to be over here somewhere," a light woman's voice says. "I saw him, it couldn't be anyone else." She retorts.

"How can you be so sure?" Another voice freezes me to my core—Arty.

"You think I wouldn't know my own twin?" she scoffs back at Arty.

I hum to counter the magical rot on Nick's hand and watch his aura return to its green brilliance. I meet his eyes as the magic flows over him. His goofy smile turns to a focused scowl. It's my turn for the goofy smile. I huff in relief. "Feeling better?" The knot in my tummy fades.

"Yes, what the fuck was that?" Whatever he was going to say dies.

"I told you, it was my brother. Now kill him!" Nikki orders.

Both Nick and I gasp.

I blink twice. "Arty, no, don't! He's my friend." I move to block Nick's bulky frame. Arty holds a sword in one hand and a dagger in the other. Nick only has my dagger. Arty's eyes blaze forth with no glasses to block the view. His face is covered in blood spray. I wonder who he killed on Nikki's orders. The Fomorians close in on us. "Bull, no, don't hurt him!" I scream, as my heart pounds its way out of my chest.

"Tell them to subdue him." Nick's wording is right. I have to be precise.

"Bull, subdue Arty and Nikki only! Kill the rest." I order.

The Fomorians line up to face off with each other. Nikki's group is already one short. I have the advantage of numbers. Now all I need is magic. I throw Nick another dagger. It grows to its full size and then some as the music reverberates away from my lips, turning a dagger into a sword. The air fills my lungs for another enchantment when a blow lands in my gut.

I'd shut my eyes, I never saw it coming. Landing hard, I fall to the ground and roll to my side. The air around me pushes back as Nikki's sword crashes into the rock next to my face. *Why hadn't I trained more? Why did I close my eyes?*

"Sarah, watch out! She has a sword like yours." Nick's words shoot ice and fire through my veins. I'm loath to unsheathe Quicksilver. I don't want to kill anyone, but the sword calls to me. It wants to fight and draw blood.

"That's right, *Sarah*. I have a sword too. Can you use yours, or are you just playing at winning?" Nikki's laugh sends shivers down my spine with the icy cold it contains. I leap to my feet, floating up and then down like flotsam. I kick out before touching down. My toe connects with her chin. I watch in slow motion as her head snaps back. She hangs in the air for an eternity before crashing onto the forest floor.

From the corner of my eye, Arty moves in on Nick with his sword raised to attack. I take the few extra moments to sing an enchantment over Arty. Arty's eyes glaze white, and his aura changes from the sickly yellow to a dull brown. His hand drops to his side, still gripping his weapons. I add a note at the end. He's a trap. No one can touch him without paying the fairy price of pain.

I refocus in time for Nikki's next charge. Her roar vibrates, changing the air around me. I'm caught in slow jelly, and every movement is an effort. I tumble over in the gelatinous bubble.

As I hum, ten rocks rise out of the stream. I hurl them at Nikki with breakneck speed. Each one pelts her in a different place. Her body reels as each stone connects with the soft tissues on her torso. The water is acidic and burns her leather armor away, reddening the exposed skin underneath. She screams in a rage, stomping a foot on the ground. "I'll kill you, little girl! You think you're the only one who's figured out Fae magic?"

My eyes search for Nick as my voice hums the jelly trap away.

"If I can't kill you, maybe I should kill my traitorous twin. You should never have turned against me, Nick." She pivots on her left foot, moving swiftly to where Nick stands. Nikki screams 'roses are red'.... But I sing, encasing Nick in a bubble that rises into the sky. His mouth opens wide, but he's trapped in his own world. I watch him pound against the protection of the iridescent sphere.

Nikki rounds on me. Her aura is still the putrid yellow of rot, like Arty's. I hum the counter for the enchantment, but it's too late. Her foot connects with my stomach, forcing me back into a tree. My head bounces off the bark. Little yellow birds float around my head. I blink to clear them away, only to have one land on my nose. The bird tweets in my face and pecks at my forehead. I slap it to the ground and wave the others off.

Nikki's wicked laugh cuts the air.

She's close, too close. I whip my head left and right, pushing off the tree. A new blow lands on my lower back. I tumble forward, tucking my head under and embracing the roll. My feet meet the forest floor. I jump up, turning in the air at the same time.

The sound of clashing swords in the background ceases. I have just enough time to see Bull fall. His great eye is opened and fixed.

"Oh, Sarah, you can roll in the dirt. How cute," Nikki says. "Did you think I'd just leave with you? Is that what Nick told you? You could go home with my brother, taking him away from me. That will never happen. Nick is mine forever. We will always be together." She rushes at me, but I dodge left and then right. She hacks at me moments after I vacate the space.

I throw one of my daggers at her chest. It glances off, cutting her forearm on the way to the ground. I hum the counter spell for the putrid enchantment, but ducking her blade ends the magic prematurely.

"If I can't have him, neither can you." Nikki turns and dashes at Nick's floating bubble. I whistle a breeze to raise the enchanted sphere. Nick's eyes widen as he pounds his fist against the bottom of the bubble. She jumps, thrusting her sword and piercing the bubble. The tip scratches Nick's palm. My mouth goes dry. Nick's body tumbles to the ground, landing hard on his back as the last note leaves my lips.

"Sarah, Nikki." Nick chokes and then grasps his left hand with his right, cradling it to his body. The flesh wilts around the wound, sinking in on itself. It slowly creeps outward. I choke on my tears and leap to his side.

"No, Nick! Don't die, please! We need to save your sister and Arty." My pleading voice comes out as a croak. He releases a dry laugh, followed by a cough. Nikki's feet take up residence next to Nick's shoulder. Rage rises in my chest as my eyes do. My nostrils flare and a snarl curls up one side of my face.

"How could you? Your own brother, your twin!" The dingy brown hair on her head slowly turns a crisp white.

"Sarah, it's not her. It's not Nikki." Nick coughs again. The desiccation creeps up his arm. My eyes dart back to his face as the tears tear at my eyes. A brick takes up location in my throat, working its way down my esophagus.

"Look around you? Would Arty ever not know you?" Nick says. "Nikki could never hurt me. It's not in her; it's a trick. I can't believe you can't see it." His eyes close, creasing in pain.

I swallow the brick back. "Fae can't enchant each other." It's a weak argument. I'm not completely Fae, just mostly.

He laughs. "Sarah, you aren't Fae yet. A little more and I think you'll be there." His jaw clenches as he grinds his teeth. His eyes go wide with pain. The withering reaches his shoulder. "I wasn't faking when I said I loved you. You're the sister I always wanted. I love Nikki, but she was never very nice to me. We've had our issues. You wouldn't leave me behind, ever. The magic twisted my feelings to make me do things I wouldn't normally do. I can't use the magic, but I understand how it works." He murmurs.

The spell is moving faster now. It stops at his clavicle and moves down his body. He gives me a half-smile.

"Nick, don't go. I can't do this alone." I want to say, *I trust you.*

His good hand touches my face. I close my own over it. He breathes, "Yes, you can. Go find the real Arty and Nikki and save them. Don't worry about humanity. They can save themselves. Don't lose yourself, and don't trust Deston. Fifty is fifty." His legs melt into the soil around us. He's disintegrating in front of me.

I try to sing, anything to breathe life back into his fading body. The music doesn't turn to magic; it sounds flat. The sound waves butt against his body and reverberate back at me.

I press my hand to his chest, but his aura is fading. The rock lodges in my belly, burning in my gut. Every part of me shakes, and my teeth rattle. A river of tears runs down my face, seeping into my blouse. Heat burns through me.

Nick smile up at me as his good hand fades from my face into dust and floats away. I gulp at the air as a vice tightens around my ribcage.

"Don't go, Nick!" I plead.

His beautiful eyes blink open and closed. He breathes out and disappears. I tilt my head back and scream. I drag my fingers over the soil, digging my nails down and scratching. There's nothing left, not even his clothes. The outline of my dagger lies on the ground, nothing more than ash.

My eyes shift all around the clearing. I'm alone. All the bodies have disappeared, leaving the stream bank clean and empty. As if they'd never existed.

The rocks dig into my knees, and my hands hold clods of dirt. Hysteria is close. It toys with me, and I play back. My screams echo off the trees, bouncing back in my face and laughing at me. The pain in my head sharpens before the scream in my raw throat subsides. I squeeze my eyes shut, pushing the liquid out.

My vision clears, and the ache around my head throbs. My fingers rub the aching ring, only to run across itchy bumps. They encircle my head, ending at my temples. My back is in agony, either side of my spine on fire. Why can't the aching stop? Why can't the killing stop? Tears threaten to wash over me, and a whimper escapes my lips.

I sit back on my heels, and my eyes search everywhere for answers. What had Nick said? *It's not real, but he's dead. It must be.*

CHAPTER 29

The forest is quiet, too quiet. Tilting my head back, I scan the sky, peeking through the forest canopy. It's a sky, but not the Fae iridescent cavern—impossible. My hands rub the moisture from my eyes. The mind fog I'd had since entering the game zone falls away. Squinting, I see minute wakes.

This isn't real. Nick had seen it. How could I have missed it? I jump to my feet and waver with weakness. I run my hand over my bodice and land on my belt pouch. I pop the snap open, and my fingers shift around, searching until the cold smooth exterior of a vial meets the tip on my thumb— Lavender's energy potion. It doesn't look to have more than a dram at best.

The squeak of wood pulling apart followed by splashing water dripping on rocks. A cold wind blows my hair forward into my face. Every hair on my body stands straight up. I turn to the sound of rocks crashing together. They all laugh, each reeking with disdain.

"She doesn't look like much to me. Can't we just kill her and be done with it, Terra?" The misty shape curls around the other three. The body is nothing more than a hint of a breast and flowing hair, pierced by icy white eyes. Her pouty lips hitch to one side.

"You know we can't, Aer. We need to test her mettle. We must find the Aether." Rocky lips spark with each word. Aer humphs, blowing her hair around.

"I could give her a watery embrace, and then we'd be done. Easy as falling over a cliff into a deep pool." Steely blue eyes reflect the color of deep blue cold ocean water. Her skin pills with scales like a fish as iridescent as a rainbow trout.

"No, Aqualis. Her roots are deep in Fae. She will either bend like a sapling or break like a heavy branch. You know the rules we test for Aether." The tree has the body of a woman naked and grained. She could've been carved straight from a single tree. The hair hanging from her head resembles a weeping willow. Leaves cluster over her breasts and groin. Her eyes are the color of a Japanese maple leaf. Her lips are the red of turning fall leaves. Her hand points a branchy finger at the watery woman—Aqualis.

A breeze pushes down my nostrils and over my tongue. I smack my lips together, searching for the moisture that is wicked away. "What the fuck are you?" I say. Fae sight is excellent, but my eyes aren't big enough to take it all in. Fear roots me to the forest floor much like the tree woman in front of me.

"Elemental Nymphs, human." The words from the craggy mouth shoot tinder on to the forest floor. The flame takes and rises high, spreading in a circle around all of us. I sing to the rocks to rise, but they keep their place.

"You can't use my children against me, stupid half-ling." The rocks I called all fly at me, slamming into my chest and head. An old-fashion stoning. Humming vibrates in my chest, pulling the wind to my command.

"Perhaps she doesn't understand how the game is played, Ignis? Do you even know what an element is? Surface dwellers are too thick. You must lighten your mind." The force of Aer's words throws me out of the fiery circle and into a tree. It knocks away every breath in my body with the impact.

The four of them circle around my new location. I hear the slap of water before it splashes part of my chest and face. A scream tears from my lips, and the acid in the water burns half my face, disintegrating my chemise and melting my leather bodice into the jelly that I once called skin. Smoke rises around my head. The scent of burning hair fills my nose and mouth. Salty tears stream from my eyes, stinging the wounds wherever they fall. I lift my head, pushing off the tree trunk. My chest clenches from the vice grip of branches and vines closing around me. Roots hold my feet in place. I'm trapped like the kids in the maze.

"She's not the one! Look how easy it is to subdue her. Ignis, we should use her to feed the forest. The mushrooms from her blood will strengthen us all. Aqualis don't burn her anymore, it sours the food." My eyes shift from side to side, searching for a way out, pushing against the vine that holds my head firmly to the tree. What did she say? My blood, and mushrooms?

The acid water burns away the sheath of a dagger. My hand is so close. I fold my thumb into my palm. Finally, being double-jointed pays off. I can practically pull my hand out of anything.

My hand pulls free from the branches wrapped around my wrist. I grab the blade. Before they can stop me, I bring it down, stabbing my thigh. I pull it free, only to have Terra's vines wrap around my wrist, wrenching my arm behind the tree and overextending my shoulder in the process.

"Look! She knows it's a lost cause. She kills herself. It is better to feed Fae than be ruled by this. Don't you think, Ignis?" Aer caresses the side of my face with the warmth of a summer breeze. My heart pounds in my chest, along with the fire of hate. They're toying with me. If I die here, Nick died for nothing, and Arty will be lost to this place.

I angle my head down, pressing my brow into the bark of the branch that holds me in place. I see the mushrooms growing where my blood dripped on the forest floor. It isn't enough. The wake lines coming off my blood move slowly. I'll never bleed enough. Harnessing the ache in my chest, I turn it into a vibrating sound, emanating from my heart. It raises blood from my thigh down to the forest floor, and I fling it around my body.

"Aqualis, stop her!" Ignis crashes her words out, spewing flames. Three sparks land on my legs, catching on the leather straps. A whimper escapes from my lips. I continue humming the droplets into place.

"I can't take her water. She's too Fae. There isn't enough left. The human side is too far gone." Aqualis rages her scales, turning white like angry water. My lips chap with moisture loss, but I smack them together.

"I'll stop her. Even Fae must breathe." Aer moans as she pulls the air from my lungs. My chest caves with the loss of oxygen and air pressure.

The magic wake comes from my chest, not my lungs or throat. The sick sound of stone impacting flesh hits my ears before the pain reaches my mind. Ignis pelts my upper body. One stone crashes into the melted skin of my head, pulling it farther from my skull. Panting takes over, and the throbbing beat of my heart fills my ears. I bite down on my cracked lips, and the coppery taste of blood fills my mouth. I spit it to the side of the tree and watch the tiny fungi grow. Every blood drop I move falls in place, and mushrooms grow. My whimpering sways reverberations over the forest floor, slamming into the nymphs. I push them back with only my cries.

The magic wake bounces back to the mushrooms. It supercharges their growth, turning them purple and becoming small trees surrounding me.

The vibrations in my chest shake the vines and branches into dust, freeing me. I sag away from the tree trunk.

At my feet lies Lavender's vial. In one motion, I scoop it up and pour it down my throat.

The blast of energy flees through my body as if all the energy from a supernova exploded in my chest traveling outward. Magic wakes move out at the speed of a tsunami. It tears down all in my way, pushing the nymphs to their knees.

"We have a contender, ladies! The test is over. We have our Aether." Ignis sparks fire from her mouth with words. I push harder, dousing the flames. In unison, they all regain their feet and move in. I stand my ground. It isn't real.

With magic wakes, I grab Aqualis and push her watery body into the unyielding rock of Ignis. I pick up the willowy form of Terra, and I twirl her in a circle like a cyclone and tangle Aer in the vine-like branches.

"You cannot use the elements against each other." Ignis stamps her rocks together. It amuses me.

"The elements only work, if you use them in order," I shout. "Otherwise they cancel each other out. Nature has a balance. It's called the cycle of destruction. Not all surface dwellers are dumb, asshole." My voice rises as does the mushroom round. I sing myself above the nymphs. They wriggle and scream in frustration. The ring carries me to the fence where I'd entered the game zone. I lower my voice, landing in the grass with a soft bump.

There it is, the entrance and the magic line of bubbles floating up over my head arching into a dome. Extending my index finger, I touch one bubble. It pops. The world around me tilts, and I stagger to right, waiting for the movement of the earth to settle. Then pop another bubble, and a fence post falls. Beyond the post, there's a clamor of clapping and laughter. My lips press together, and I clench my teeth. They are watching, those bastards. They watched Nick die and laughed about it. I follow the laughter's source with one foot in front of the other, and I storm to a tear I created in the magic. Inserting both hands into the opening, I pull with all my might ripping it apart.

The game zone melts away with the wind and a laugh. "That's thirty-two." Bonn's voice fills my ears as do heat from my anger. *It's all just a game to them.* I open my mouth to sing, but my leg gives out from under me. My hip hits the ground hard. Two hands wrap around my arms, pulling me up and hugging me.

"You made it! I was so worried." Deston pulls back, staring deep into my eyes. The green of his eyes is so perfect and bright. I want to stay there forever. His hands move over my body, sending thrills into my battered muscles. The goofy smile returns, along with a perplexing fog. "Let's get you back to the castle before you faint," Deston informs me.

I nod vigorously. I want to answer, but the words don't come.

"You bitch, you killed him! It's your fault." Nikki's voice runs down my nerves like nails on a chalkboard.

"You killed him, Nikki. I tried to save him. You killed your own twin." I choke on the words. My chest wavers with the cries I want to scream.

"No, Sarah. You killed him." Arty's words cut me. He stands with his arm around her protectively.

"Nick was my friend. Why would I kill him?" I turn to face Nikki. "He only came here to save you, you ungrateful cow. How could you? You didn't deserve a brother like Nick. He died trying to find you, and you killed him in cold blood." The words lodge in my throat.

Her hair is white from tip to root. Points from her ears peek out between her long hair. Arty's aura wakes the sickly yellow of rot. Under my breath, I hum the counter to the rot. Arty's eyes mist over and clear before widening.

"Sarah, where have you been?" He leaps over to my side and hugs me with his big bear style, rocking me from side to side. He pulls back, meeting my eyes.

I sputter. "Your safe, I wasn't sure. No one had seen you. Deston told me everyone from the maze died." I clamp onto him, squeezing with all my might. I bury my face into his chest and breathe in a scent wholly Arty.

"I fell from the circle. I sat there, listening to your voice, and then there was a loud crack. You were gone. Nikki and I met, and she helped me." He smiles back at her.

Nikki whispers, "Arty, come with me." Nikki's hand grips his bicep to pull him away. I see the magical influence she has over him.

Arty's wide eyes trail over my acid washed face. I cringe at what I must look like. Arty had said I was pretty, once. I doubt he'd say that now.

"It was an enchanted world, you dimwit," I snap at Nikki. "In my world, you killed Nick and in yours I did. One way or another, he's dead and he's never coming back." My voice wavers as heat burns my eyes and chest with a pain that will never go away.

Nikki cuts me off. "No, you killed him, Sarah! You came back and brought him with you. You did it!" The rumble in the back of her throat is all the warning I get before Janice's shield blocks my vision. The magic slams into the magic shield, glancing off. I wish I'd left Nick on the surface with Jake and Tom. At least then he'd still be alive.

"Time to go, Sarah." His eyes mesmerized me and I blink to find clarity

Nikki's right. I'd killed Nick. I saved him from the maze only to kill him. The weight of it slams down on me, bowing my back. My hand finds Arty's. Arty smiles and squeezes my hand in return. I draw comfort from the contact. I pull him along with me, heading toward Deston's carriages.

"You know the rules, Deston. You can't take my slave with you. He's mine." Jacques floats over Arty and I. His wicked smile flashes white, shiny teeth.

Deston quips back. "I have no intention of taking your slave. I have my contender; that is enough for me. You heard what the nymphs said. She's too Fae. Today has been a double win for me." Deston's words burn my ears the same way the acid had burned one side of my face. Nick is dead, and it's a double win for him? The ache in my throat radiates, reaching my eyes to wash over with tears. I press my lips into a tight line. I swallow the pain, and it slithers back to my belly, lodging itself there.

Hot breath moves over my un-scared ear. "Let it go, my Lady. This is a long game," Janice whispers.

My chest shutters and nostrils flare. All the blinking in the world will never make the tears or the pain stop. I hadn't just lost Nick. Now I had to watch Arty walk away too.

"Come, slave!" Jacques orders Arty to his side.

I watch Arty's pained expression. He strains against the magic. My eyes search Arty's, tracing down to our laced fingers. I lock on the leather bracers on his forearms. They glow with magic, forcing his hand from mine. His shoes emanate the same enchantments, dragging his feet toward his master and away from me.

I choke out an "Arty," but my whispering desperation can't change the magic. I grab his hand with both of mine only to have, his fingers slip from mine. My eyes meet his. Only his glasses aren't there to reflect the light or block part of his face. His goofy half-smile scrunches up one side and he runs his fingers through his shaggy hair.

"Don't worry, Sarah. I'll be safe. I've made friends." His eyes dart to Nikki and someone behind her.

I shake my head. His eyes narrow with a slight nod. He throws me Scout's Honor.

"Don't' go, Arty." I choke back a sob. The pain in my leg overwhelms me along with blood loss. Blood on my face has coagulated and dried, causing the skin to contract and itch. My head aches and itches too.

My body sags to the ground as strong hands lock around my shoulders. My legs sweep into the air. My head rests against the rhythmic beating of a heart pressed to my good ear. I embrace the oblivion of black on the back side of my eyelids.

CHAPTER 30

"Don't leave her side," Janice whispers.

"No, my lord, never. Can we not treat her?" Lavender pleads.

"No, Deston would be alerted. She must heal on her own." Janice's reply is bitter.

"As you say, Lord Janice. However, I will not let her die, even if it costs me my own immortality. I may be a lower caste of Fae, but I have the same stake you do," Lavender retorts.

Their words wash over and through me. I hear and understand, but I don't care. Arty, Nick, Pastor Rollins, the girls from the maze, and their haunted faces rush in to scream at me. Olive's eyes stare, pleading for Nick to take her back to Zoe. The bloody grass in Arty's front yard, his headless father, the crumpled form of his mother. Everywhere I look is covered in blood with giant pools pouring into the cracks of my enchanted bubble of body pieces and hell. Girls scream in the background as vines climb up my legs, digging their thorns into my flesh. The vines inject a paralyzing poison into my limbs. My hands rip at the vines, but the thorns turn into teeth chewing away at my limbs. Water sears my flesh, and branches pull my appendages from their sockets.

Slowly, the bloody pool surrounds me, climbing up to reach my neck. I open my mouth to scream, and the fleshy warm coppery taste pours in. I'm choking on it as it slithers down my throat, bubbling up into my nose. My hands flail and dig at my throat for air. I whip at my eyes, pushing the blood back. The world turns red and then black.

The raw meat of my throat from blood curdling screams is all I feel as my fingers grip the sheets. I'm in bed. Sweat beads on my forehead and under my arms.

"My lady, you are safe. I am here." Lavender's voice is soft and soothing.

"Lavender, are you alive?" Tears threaten, but I blink them back.

"Yes, of course. I'm alive and so are you." Her hand smooths my hair back on one side.

My hand races to my face. Fingers trail over withered, rippled skin where my ear should have been, only to encounter a melted stump and a sticky cold hole. My hair no longer warms one side of my head or the pointy ear that once lived there.

"I want a mirror, please." my scratchy voice caws at her.

"Oh, my Lady, I think you should wait for Deston. He may heal you." Her eyes shift from left to right as she stands up, nervously fluffing my pillows and straightening the bedding.

A fog comes with Deston's name, settling over my mind along with a warm liquid in my belly.

I shake my head, but I can't find the clarity I desire. "I still want the mirror. Don't pacify me or I'll get it myself." I flip the covers back, revealing the gash in my leg. The cut, a straightforward stab wound, but black rot radiates down my leg, shooting ugly veins in all directions. "Why hasn't my leg been treated?" I ask. Throbbing pain from the wound rages back at me, shooting and vibrating with my pulse.

"Lord Deston forbade it." Lavender moves back to the wall. Her fear wakes from her, reaching me at breakneck speed before it slams into my senses.

My leg refuses to obey my wishes. I hum my limp leg over the side of the bed while the other one follows. Licking my lips, I pierce them together and whistle up a mirror. My naked body is a forest of black and blue. Other than my right forearm, every part of me had been beaten. The watery acid leaves red patches all over my legs, along with my wound, which is leaking blood. Speckles of red dots my chest. The real damage is the side of my face, but it doesn't stop there. Melted skin drips down my neck, flowing over my shoulder to my upper chest. My right eyelid sags with the skin pulling and distorting the once almond shape. It missed my lips and the eye itself. The image conjures up a vision of the Phantom of the Opera. *Is this what I look like now?* My nostrils flare with hot air.

"Lavender, please leave me alone." I push her. Magic has its uses. She hurries from the room. I'd compelled her, and I did it on purpose.

I can't tear my eyes from the mirror. I devour every scar, and I slowly cry for Nick and every other person who isn't alive to cry for their own scars. My hands grasp the sides of the mirror, willing it to change.

Kelly green eyes glow at me with the almond shape of the Faes—it's my own. I push the hair back on my left side, revealing my intact ear, long and pointed, angling out from my head. My legs had grown along with my arms. My waist is long and thin. Now on one side, I'm beautiful, but the other is a monster coming to kill you. *I truly look Fae, two-faces and all.*

Air can't fill my lungs. The muscles in my throat quiver in protest. I lean in and crash face first into the floor. The mirror disappears. Pushing up from the floor, I work my legs under my body and try to stand, but I'm too weak. The world tilts, spinning with the sudden movement. A hum rises in my chest. My body rises with it, moving back to the bed.

Magic wakes emanate out to batter the walls. A withering pushes out from my position, engulfing the room in dead silvery rot. Leaves drop, drifting down to clatter like rocks on the floor. I gasp for air that never reaches me. My arms cross, gripping each bicep and digging with my nails.

The remains of my clothes lie on the floor with knives still sheathed in their scabbards. The rumble in my chest draws one to me.

My hand aches for it, to draw cold steel across my skin, freeing the blood held there. I want to see the color. Is it red or blue? The T-shaped handle nestles between my index and middle fingers, ready to slash whatever my heart desires. Poised to cut, the blade glimmers at me, calling to me. My lips curl into a cruel smile.

"Sarah, stop," Janice pleads.

I don't want to stop. I want to die with everyone else. My chest burns with anguish while my eyes smolder. The only one left is Arty, and I can't even help him.

"That way is the UnSeelie way. That is what he wants." Janice moves into my line of vision and kneels down to eye level. Janice's eyes meet mine.

I dart away. I want to scream.

The blade clatters to the floor. I watch it in fascination as the tip lodges itself in the wood. The floor wakes back its irritation at the metallic intrusion. I wish it had stabbed me.

Nails dig into palms, tightening into a fist. My eyes meet Janice's smoky amethyst pools. Raising my fist, I lower it, adding a wake of power for an extra push. The blow slams his shoulder, forcing him back.

I hear his exhale and ignore it. Instead of following it with another, I scream in frustration. "Why, Why, Why?"

Janice takes the pummeling, his eyes never wavering from mine. "Don't give up! What's inside is what matters, not out." He whispers.

My hands falter midair. *This isn't me. I'm mad, but Janice isn't my enemy, is he?*

His hand cups my scarred cheek, and his magic encircles me like honey. Slow, warm, and sticky sweet, Janice sings. White gauze floats around my form, encasing my breast and hiding my wounds. His eyes never waver from mine.

"What's inside is what makes you so precious. All the world will fight and kill to possess it." His eye moves from mine to my lips.

My heart speeds up, as my tongue plays across my lips. His warm hand rests on the smooth side of my face, sending shivers down my neck.

"Deston is coming. You need to be ready. Ask him to heal you." In one swift motion, he's across the room, near the door. He tips his head, his eyes grazing over me. Then he looks away.

His eyes pull me in every direction at once, stretching my chest tight over my bones. Pain evaporates with the flight of butterflies in my belly. Bruises and bleeding melt into the background with one gaze from him. The silver of the walls bloom with life, flowering into a drunken perfume. So thick is the foliage I can't make out the walls for the blooms and leaves.

His gaze settles back on me. His full lips melt from a thin line to a broad smile. My damaged skin wrinkles and cracks with the force of my grin. "Happy is all I want for you, Sarah." His husky admission is all I want.

The door swings open, revealing Deston, followed by Lavender. Janice's eyes tear from me to stare at the wall. His smile is gone.

"I'm so relieved you're awake. The next challenge is in two weeks, and we need you at full strength," Deston exclaims and then lays his hand over mine.

The fog returns full force, muddling a mind only moments ago sharp and clear. I shake my head, but it does nothing more than add a dizzying effect to the mix.

Deston's touch locks me in place, moving from dizzy to drowning in a split second. Is this how enchantment feels? Why is this happening? My heart pounds with his touch. I only feel this way when Deston is around. Somehow, he's has a power over me but I can't see it. If I can't see it, I can't break it.

It's different than when Janice touches me.

Deston licks his lips. My eyes follow the movement unbidden, no matter how hard I try I can't tear myself away. I physically want to kiss him. Mentally, I recoil from the idea. Why do I only feel this way when Deston's around?

Janice told me Fae can't enchant each other. Is this how Lavender feels when I compel her?

"I'll have an apothecary to look you over and treat that wound." Deston steps back, removing his hand and releasing me from whatever power he has over me. That's it—a power.

Janice's words run through my mind.

"Can't you heal me?" I plead, showing only the unmarred side of my face. *Why am I behaving like this?*

Deston's eyes widen as he pulls his hand from mine. "I can't, my love. Even in Fae, healing takes time." The lie leaves his lips so easily. I heard it, but which was the lie? The love or the healing?

"Then I hope to heal fast." Leaning back into the pillows, I close my eyes. I don't want to look at Deston's beautiful lying face anymore.

"I'll check on you tomorrow." With that, he turns and leaves the room. The fog recedes with him.

CHAPTER 31

Lavender flitters around, touching and smoothing every wrinkle on the bed. A sound from the door produces another white-haired Fae with a case. He turns his orange eyes to my leg, pinching his lips to one side.

"I can only put a poultice on the cut. The burn will need a salve. Keep it moist or you'll lose the flexibility in the skin." The apothecary's eyes dart to Janice and Lavender. He never meets my gaze, but he focuses on the task at hand with efficiency. His aura reeks of nerves and fear.

"What's your name?" I inquire.

The man's fingers still, and there's an intake of breath. "Kag'a, my Lady."

I'd compelled him. I shouldn't have done that. "Kag'a, your work is acceptable." *Can't say thank you.*

The breath he holds slips away. Placing his supplies back in his box, he leaves as does Lavender. The room sighs with the release of tension.

I glare at Janice. "How can you stand there and act like you're here to help me? Like you're on my side when everything the Fae say is a lie? Whatever it is the Fae say, it means the exact opposite," I snap.

Janice crosses his hands in front, clasping them together. "Have you learned nothing about the courts? The Unseelie, the Seelie? Black is white, white is black." His words stun me to the core. The acid in my belly rises in my throat. I know what he means, but that can't be true. Deston is on my side. He's my ally. Just the thought of Deston brings the fog back. *He'd always been my ally; he's never done anything to hurt me.*

Those words came unbidden. "You're lying. It isn't backward. I don't have it wrong. Deston's on my side. He's fighting for us, all of us." As I say it, I know them for the lie they are. Deston isn't fighting for all of us. Deston is fighting for himself.

Black is white, white is black. Deston is white. How could I have been so stupid? Blood fills my ears, raging through me. The songs of every building, leaf, and tree rage with me. The shape of the room morphs around me, distorting and changing. Everywhere my green eyes look, flowers wilt with the leaves fading away. I rake Janice over, inspecting him. His hair is almost completely black now.

"You changed," I say. "You were white when I met you, but now your hair is black. Tell me what that means."

The ends of his lips curve up as satisfaction fills his eyes. "It means exactly what you think it means. I switched sides. In Fae, we can't lie about which court we belong to. Black is white, and white is black."

I look down and around the walls are no longer rich, shining, or humming with life. They're no longer a living tree. They'd turned to that dark gray with the silver shot through, the color only dead trees get. I killed this whole room. My anger did that. I don't need to sing anymore to make my will happen.

"What does that make me? My hair is black. It's growing out black. Why didn't Lavender dye it white when she first had the chance?" Both eyebrows pinch in the middle, pulling down on my scalp and the new scar.

"Lavender didn't dye your hair at all. Lavender revealed your true colors, nothing more nothing less. In Fae, you can lie about many things. You can lie about love, you can lie about family. You can lie about who your friends and allies are. You can lie and say you love flowers when in truth you love monsters. But you cannot lie about which court you answer to. Lavender revealed which court you belonged to. You were so filthy when I brought you in, almost no one could tell your hair was brown. I'd made sure of that when I dragged you through the mud. I protected you. You belong to the Seelie court, not the Unseelie Court. Deston doesn't know, and that is how you can win."

I feel the air slide into my nostrils, filling my chest. With every breath in and out of my body, I'm relieved knowing to which court I belong to. I didn't understand how important it is. The heavyweight I'd been carrying is gone. It floats away with every breath like the fairy dust I'd always dreamed about as a little girl. The gray of the trees comes back to life, and leaves scream and bloom with flowers. The heady scent of honeysuckle fills the air, my favorite.

I smile. "Why is it so important to hide what I truly am? What does it matter? If you can't lie about it, why is it so important to hide it?" I demand.

His stance changes, his legs apart and his arms crossed, but open for a fight. "You hear, but you don't listen. Your eyes behold, but do not see. Sarah, I was charged with finding a new Queen." His body flexes, leaning forward with his admission straining against some unseen force.

There, that was the missing piece—the part Deston had been hiding.

"We were all charged with finding a new Queen, by any means necessary to push back the rule of Wyld," Janice continues. "If the Fae don't have a Queen, we're not controlled. Only a Queen has the power to stop the death and slaughter. We're a bloodthirsty lot. We like to play tricks on humans. We all enjoy it, and it's so easy to do. Our Queens fade away; it's hard work controlling the Fae. Eventually, we suck them dry of all their immortality. What should've lasted for time eternal disappears quickly while we outlast the Queens. Every one of us schemes and hopes that our desires will live beyond hers so we can fulfill them when she's gone. Finding a new Queen, controlling her, manipulating her, and pleasing her. We live for it. We're like a hive of bees searching for that one perfect Queen."

My mouth dries with astonishment.

He continues. "We feed her the royal jelly until she blossoms. Then, we want to control her. He, who controls the

Queen, controls Fae and the fate of humans. I know my cousin. I can never let him control a Queen. I had to let you get away. I had to let Lavender teach you what little she did, and it was just enough. I don't want to control you. I never did, and as you can see, I have changed my allegiance. For you, Sarah." He finishes.

My eyes widen at his omission.

"When I said the prize was the fate of the world, I meant it," Janice says. "I have killed. I may be every bit of the bastard that you humans think I am, but I did everything to preserve the balance. A balance only you can provide." The truth of his words wakes over me. "Take up your mantle. Become Queen. We need you. The world needs you. Do it for humanity. Do it for your friends. Do it for the little girl you insisted upon saving. Do it for all those other girls who didn't survive. Do it because if you don't, someone will come and kill you and do it for you."

I turn from him and his entreaties. Every breath in my chest shutters, and tears threaten.

Janice rushes on. "None of them will be nearly as good as you are. It comes so easily to you. Don't look away." His hand cups my chin moving my face back to meet his eyes.

Queen. I'll never lie on the living room floor watching TV and eating pizza with Arty, go to prom, or graduate from high school or college. For as long as I exist, I'll be surrounded by conniving, manipulative, strange creatures. Not like me, and every bit like me. My eyes burn, and I blink back tears. Moisture drips down the walls, and they cry for me.

"Have your cry, Sarah. Remember, it needs to be the last one anyone ever sees. If you want to cry in the future, it needs to be in private. Only when you're alone. You can't let anyone see weakness. They prey on it." He whispers.

My lower lip presses to the upper as I keep my mouth closed to stop the trembling. Working the muscles in my throat, I swallow. My chest muscles shutter.

I want to scream, but I don't. Hot tears roll down my face, burning their path to reach the end of my chin and dripping down between my breasts. I dig my nails into the palms of my hands to feel the pain of it. I said I'd do anything to end this battle, to make the Fae stop killing us—humans. I thought it'd be simple. Something like finding out who's in charge and killing them. I guess I hadn't thought it through.

My father calls it blow-back—unintended consequences of a decision. My mother calls it hindsight; it's 20/20. You can look behind you and see every choice you made and how it brought you to the point where you're now. If you'd done one thing differently, you wouldn't be here.

Yet I know if I'd done one thing different and I wasn't here, where would humanity be? I hadn't done it all right. Find me an eighteen-year-old kid who has. If I go out there and I take up the mantle of their Queen, that'd make me one of them. I don't know if I can do that. My stomach muscles quiver with the burning inside of me.

"And there's no other way?" I whisper and gaze up at him tentatively, pleading. "You'll just keep killing until there's a Queen?"

"Depends on the Queen. A good Queen would make us stop. A bad Queen would continue. I think we both know what kind of Queen you would be."

I have no choice. The decision was made for me the moment I stood in the street and saw Janice. I can't let Nikki win. She'll rain down death on the whole world for a perceived wrong, keeping Arty by her side. She'll enchant him and find my parents. I can't let any of that happen.

"Tell me what I have to do." This isn't just about saving Arty. It hasn't been for a while. It's about saving everyone.

The End

Thanks for reading! I hope you enjoyed Test of Fae.

Make sure to get your copy of the next installment of These

Hallowed Hills - Thorns of Fae

Take a sneak peek of Thorns of Fae.

THORNS OF FAE
CHAPTER 1

Little girls want to be a princess, a fairy, or a mermaid. No one wants to be Queen. I certainly didn't. Queens are evil step mothers who spend all their time trying to kill the young beautiful girl—me.

Humming under my breath, I watch the enchantment settle over the rope handrail on the stairs. I'm not walking 700-plus steps just because Deston's a dick.

A rush of wind fills my nostrils as the magic pulls me to the ground floor. Humming again, I reverse the enchantment while planting my feet on the stone floor to study myself. The wound on my leg itches, along with my head and back. Nick was right—it does feel like lice.

The knot in my throat that won't go away forms, and only grows as his voice echoes in my mind. I wish my dad was here. He would say something to help me over it. Something to ease the ache of Nick's loss.

Off in the distance, lower Fae clean the castle, humming the cleaning songs, reminding me of my mother. She hums all the time. The castle could have cleaned itself, but Deston didn't want that either, the dick.

I tear my mind from its wandering journey and force my feet out to the training yard. "You're awake. Are you ready to train?" Janice inquires while standing next to other nameless, faceless Fae, all waiting for me, apparently.

My heart jumps with the timbre of his voice, it's nothing compared to the swooping butterflies in my belly. Who wouldn't get hot and bothered? Janice's jet-black hair hangs down to his mid-back in soft waves, covering muscles honed to kick your ass over a thousand years. And now he was willing to kick mine.

"Yes, and yes," I announce to him, along with all his pretty Fae friends.

Janice began the lesson of the day. "Holding a sword is not like wielding a butter knife or fork. It's a weapon and should be treated with proper respect."

My eyes roll. I don't know how old he assumes I am, or if he actually thinks I'm a moron. But I do know the difference between a sword and a butter knife.

"Can we get past the baby shit?" I ask and pretend to examine my fingernails, over-dramatizing my boredom.

"Sarah," He says with a sigh. "I understand in the human world you learned a thing or two about weapons. But those are your modern-day, projectile-shooting weapons. What I'm about to show you is a classic weapon. One invented by Fae. Somehow humans managed to wield them with a monochrome of proficiency, but they gained no true mastery." He waves his sword around a few times. I'm sure he considered it some kind of flourish. Don't get me wrong, it resembled something from The Last Samurai. "The actual use of it comes nowhere near to the level of proficiency of the Fae. Very rarely does a student surpass its master." He finishes with a thrust and a slash along with a bit of fancy footwork.

I just don't have any interest in waving around a poisonous sword. It isn't poisonous to Fae, only humans, and I don't want to carry it. I don't want to be someone who kills my own kind. Whether I was human anymore or not, deep down I still feel human.

I uncross my arms, I'm telegraphing my irritation and it's not a good idea to tell your enemies exactly what you're feeling or thinking. I'm working on it. Is this how it's gonna be for the rest of my life? Having to carefully orchestrate every move, every facial expression?

"Sarah, are you listening?" Janice asks, sheathing his sword and moving to stand in front of me with both hands on his hips.

Janice's voice pulls me back into my new reality, forcing my participation. I respond. "Sorry, I know I should be listening. I just don't want to kill anybody. And I don't want to get anybody killed. I don't... I don't want to become like you." I bite my lip at my own words, wishing I could chew my tongue off and somehow take them back.

His aura visibly changes, the bright purple fading to pale lilac.

I could kick myself. I rush on, "I'm... I'm, I didn't mean it like that, Janice." I swallow back my apology. "I just meant...

I don't want to be a killer. Fae seemed to kill because they like it." It comes out feeble.

He doesn't turn his back on me, but the cold chill waking off of him is unmistakable. Me and my stupid big mouth.

He continues, "If you're done whining like a Fae-ling, can we begin? I'm not teaching you this so you can become a killer, Sarah. I'm teaching you this so you don't get killed." His aura wakes back as chilly as the cold color it gives off.

"Oh, you mean Fae and the Hallowed Hills aren't done trying to kill me?" One hip cocks to the side with my hand on it, and I raise an eyebrow. I just can't control my mouth.

"No, the Fae aren't done trying to kill you and there's a great deal in The Hallowed Hills you've never dreamed of, heard, seen, or could have possibly imagined. And yes, some of it is going to try and kill you. My job is to make sure you survive. Now, are you going to work with me? Or should I just send you into the next challenge unprepared so that you can be slaughtered like all those other girls?" Janice's cutting retort burns my ears.

I hate it when he's right. My hand finds the grip of my sword and it naturally fits my palm as if it was made for only me. Silver slides from its scabbard soundlessly. It is infused with magic to help me wield it. And truthfully, I love the feel of the tang in my hand. It didn't feel like I was holding a sword, but an extension of myself.

Janice's cold instructor voice drones on. "When you wield your weapon, it should feel as if it's a part of you." He raises his blade holding it with two hands to demonstrate.

Check.

"How is it your sword can be wielded with one hand? My dad took me to the Metropolitan Museum in New York. They had swords with different grips. Some were longer than others, and they were specifically listed as single-handed or double-handed swords. Some were so long and large I couldn't imagine anybody waving it around with just one arm. Yet I watch you and you're able to wave your sword with one hand or two hands as you choose." My inquiry is an attempt to lighten the mood.

A dry laugh issues from between his lips. "Why don't you answer your own question? How is it possible that I am capable of wielding a two-handed sword with one hand?" He volleys my query back at me.

I hate the question, with a question answer, but sometimes I'm an idiot. The wake lines coming off of his sword whisper different kinds of magic. Spells layered over spells each imparting a special ability. I'm a moron, why did I ask such a stupid question? "It's enchanted," I say with a half huff.

He turned just enough for me to catch the curve of his cheek hinting at a smile. "Yes, everything in Fae is enchanted. That's why humans have those huge grips they can only wield them one way or the other not both at will. In Fae, swords are crafted to be wielded any way the bearer chooses and still have perfect balance. The grip adjusts to your desire." He turns to face me and flips his sword in the air, letting go before it drifts back down to his waiting hand. "Also, we're not weighed down by the constraints of mass. A sword can be made as light as a bubble and float on air." He slashes at the empty space before him, then sheathes the blade.

"Okay, that's pretty cool. Can you enchant a sword so that it will only go to your hand or always return to your hands when you want, like a boomerang?" I inquire.

He scratches his chin, something he never used to do. The shadow on his otherwise pure, opalescent face is disturbing, almost as if he is growing hair. That's silly, as the only Fae I've ever met with facial hair is Puca. And that's only when he turns into a horse or rabbit or something.

"There was once a song capable of forcing an item to always return to its owner, but I have never heard it and I know of no one who knows it. With your abilities, Sarah, I'm sure you'll be able to figure something out. Shouldn't be too difficult—after all, you seemed to do the impossible quite often these days." He smiles with his full and inviting lips.

I quirk an eyebrow at him, then hitch my mouth to one side. "How comforting to know that you can't help me, but that doesn't mean I can't solve it all on my own. Thanks for nothing, Janice. No offense, but you're supposed to be training me, yet you don't even seem to know half of what I'm asking about." Just when I thought we were going to make nice, nice my mouth gets in the way, again.

He sighs and twirls a strand of hair. "Sarah, the questions you ask, most Fae would never think of. We know what we learned as young Fae-lings. Your questions baffle me. I don't know how to make new magic. All I know is the magic I was taught. I listen to you, you create as you go. It happens without you willing it. It's simply an instinct in use, 'I want this' and your desire makes it happen. I can mimic you but I cannot re-create what you do. I don't know any Fae that can. So, when I tell you I've heard of something, but I don't know how to do it, it's simply because I haven't been taught." He crosses his arms in defense. "It disappeared with time, or perhaps it was something only one Fae knew and never shared with another. We don't create magic, we recreate it — that is our true weakness." He takes a breath and charges on, "It limits us and binds us. We all know the same spells, we can only attack each other the same way. Everything in Fae is old and repetitive. You are the first person I've ever met able to create magic from thin air, never having encountered it before." Janice uncrosses his arms and moves toward me. "All of Fae knows it, and many will try to kill you to stop you from using it. They don't want anyone wielding that kind of power. It frightens them." His brows draw together and his eyes grow dark. "Instead of feeling hope, they feel nothing but fear, anger, and jealousy. So, pick up your sword and learn how to defend yourself, or someone will come along and chop off your head to stop you." The tone of his voice grew cold and desperate. Before I have a chance to reply, he unsheathes his sword and slams it down towards my head.

Without thinking, I immediately hum a bit of Bohemian Rhapsody and a magic shield closes around my crouching form to avoid meeting his blow. His sword crashes against my shield several times.

His eyes widened in shock and pride. "That is what I'm talking about, on instinct alone you protected yourself. There are others that don't want you to do that. They don't want this to happen. They want everything in Fae to continue on as before, with a Queen they're capable of controlling, one who knows nothing more than they know. It's what they understand."

Janice bashes his sword on the flat side against my shield. I lose focus and my shield cracks, allowing the flat of the blade to smack me in the head, shooting stars in every direction.

"You bastard." I leap up to hit him and realize it isn't me hitting him, it's my sword. Silver is in my hand, the sharp edge angled toward him. I watch in horror as I slam the sword down with all my might. Only to clash against the edge of his blade.

"Hate me all you want, Sarah. But if it means you survive, then I did my job and I'll live with your hate for as long as you're Queen." His eyes harden to the deep purple of a stone.

Stepping back, I ask myself. What am I doing? I don't want to kill him. Why am I so angry?

"Why do I suddenly hate everything you say?" I scratch at the bumps encircling my head.

Janice's reply is slow and filled with innuendo. "It is not always easy to hear the truth. Sometimes facing it makes your choices difficult. One way or another, you must learn the truth about yourself, your abilities, and all of Fae. You're right, we are evil creatures hiding behind pretty faces. And every one of the pretty faces here, unless you get a sworn allegiance, will do nothing but try to kill you." He moves in closer, lowering his voice. "I guarantee you will not get a sworn allegiance unless you can defeat the best by force. Besting one of us will be difficult, to say the least." He lowers his sword and steps back, sliding it into the waiting scabbard.

"Do you see those two Fae over there?" Janice indicates two males loitering across the courtyard.

I nod my head.

"They're young, I know all Fae look young, but they are young. Not much older than you. They're learning to fight with a sword." He extends his arm, pointing to a female Fae whose face holds a long scar from cheek to chin with white hair and poppy-colored eyes. "That is their sword master. Go train with them. Follow the instructions of the swordmaster. I'll be back later to check on you. Do not become distracted by those around you. Some of the Fae here will come to talk or to watch. Focus on what's important. Surviving that is the only thing you need to work on today survival and swordplay." he states.

I nod my head. I said I'd end this. What if killing is what I have to do to end it? Then that is what I'll do. I join the other trainees, mimicking their stance. Then, I pull my sword from the scabbard, take up position, and begin the movements.

The swordmaster stares at me with cold eyes and hard-pressed lips. I don't need her approval, only her knowledge.

CHAPTER 2

Days go by before I lay eyes on Janice again. My life settles into a new kind of rhythm. But one look at Janice and the rhythm begins to race along with my heart. His black hair fans out behind him as he strides into the courtyard on a path straight for me. He hands me a coiled rope and a dagger.

Janice's first instructions. "Tie Titom up over there, using only magic."

He indicates one of my fellow students. Titom relaxes his fighting stance and nods his head in acknowledgment to Janice. Then, he presents himself to us. "It is my honor to serve His Grace in any way Deston sees fit." Titom crosses his fingers and arm over his chest and lowers his head.

I shoot Janice a narrow look. Everyone knows I can make up my own magic. The enchanted game zone where Nick died showed them. I purse my lips, sucking in the air to whistle.

Janice cuts me off. "No whistling, no sound, only your desire. What if you can't make a sound, or stealth is necessary?"

Ugh, I hate him. Then, I close my eyes and start to feel the magic around me. The wakes behind me feel off. I turn to face the anomaly, as pain ripples across my face.

Janice's voice slams into me just like his hand. "Keep your eyes open."

Stumbling back, I shift my weight to my bad leg and fall, crashing to the ground and landing on my butt. My eyes are wide open now, and I plant both hands in the dirt next to my aching tail-bone.

"Why didn't you say open your eyes? What the fuck? If you touch me again, I'll... make your clothes burn you for days," I threaten.

He tilts his head back and laughs. "I'll take them off, problem solved." Janice's eyes twinkle with mischief.

My cheeks redden at the thought of him taking his clothes off. Why am I acting like this? No matter what I think, everyone in Fae is beautiful, and I'm not — not anymore. My hand unconsciously lifts toward my face and the scar I know is there, but then stops mid-air.

Janice offers me his hand. Instead, I scoff and push off with my other hand on to the balls of my feet, jumping into a standing position.

Janice laughs out. "Try again, Sarah! Never take your eyes from your opponent and be mindful of the landscape around you. An attack can come from anywhere, even a friend." The double meaning in his words isn't lost on me.

I retort, "I have no friends, and I'm certainly not friends with you." I let the disdain, I didn't feel hang in the air. I was mad he hit me in the head, but it's a long game and I know I have to play it.

I dust my hand on my leather leggings and bend over, and grab the rope and dagger. My irritation fuels the power in my chest. I turn it into magic; the rope creates a slipknot at one end and tightens on the handle of the dagger. At breakneck speed it flies and coils around Titom, crossing over his body up to his neck before pulling him to the ground.

"For my next trick, I shall unravel him." I hum a Bruno Mars song as I spin Titom in the air and dump him in the dirt.

Titom pushes up from the dusty ground, shaking his head. "You don't need to rub my face in it. I'm here at Deston's order to help you train, not to become your plaything," Titom says, seething at me.

The irony of his words isn't lost on me. "Fae don't have a problem turning humans into a plaything—don't like it when the tables are turned, do you?" I laugh under my breath and cross my arms.

He hisses. Now that just makes me want to smash his face in the dirt again. But now isn't the time for a lesson in manners.

"Titom, get up and stop whining! Sarah, try to keep the grime to a minimum." Janice's attempt at diplomacy only spurs me on.

"Funny, I thought Fae didn't mind a fight. I'm only here as Deston's plaything, so why should you be any better? Suck it up, buttercup, let's dance!" My leg itches as the muscle flexes around my wound. I change my stance, dancing on the balls of my feet.

Titom eyes light up to a glowing ember of fiery yellow-orange. His aura wakes change from a glowing orange, to burning fire to match, with muscles coiled he charges me. I pirouette to the side, spinning on my good leg. As he passes, I hum, creating a bubble of jelly, which makes him bounce across the yard. I bend in half, laughing at his body as it topples over with each impact on the ground.

"Sarah, remove the charm. We are working on hand to hand and magic." Janice's voice was laced with amusement. I humpf, then, hum a counter-charm. The bubble pops, splattering jelly-like goo in a puddle of Titom. I hold my belly laughing as Titom squeezes the clear jelly out of his hair.

"You will pay for making a fool of me." His words barely leave his lips before the song starts. The wakes began in his chest, radiating out from there, in a rosie-orange color. The magic wakes race toward me at lightning speed. I brace my good leg behind me and raise my hand.

Calmly I ordered, "Stop!" the magic wake blasts around me. The force pushes my hair back. The wakes had moved around me like water around a stone. I grab the wakes with my hand crushing them like tinfoil. The force of the magic pulls my arm back, so I turn the momentum back on him and watch in fascination as the magic returns to its caster.

The wake smashes into Titom's chest, hurling him back into the stone wall of the castle. His body slumps to the ground.

"Sarah," Janice's voice is laced with horror and concern. "How did you do that?" Janice runs to Titom side, where he checks Titom's vitals while he studies me through his brows. "We're done for today," Janice orders.

Then, he turns his back on me. I'm dismissed. Faltering for a moment, I quickly whirl around and storm out of the courtyard, only to linger in the arched opening of the stairwell.

Lavender appeared and remarks, "My Lady, Titom will be fine, come away. You will give the wrong impression," while pulling gently at my arm.

I turn at Lavender's words and raise an eyebrow. "Wrong impression? What impression is that?" I demand.

"Concern over the injury of a house servant is beneath you." Her reply is quick and to the point.

"You Fae and your class bullshit. I just slammed him into a wall and, yet I'm not supposed to be concerned? How *should* I act?" I retort, with no interest in hearing the reply. I whistle the enchantment on the rope and disappear to the seventh floor and the sanctuary of my rooms.

I didn't intend to hurt Titom, I didn't even know I could throw magic back as a weapon. Janice said magic was dangerous and could rebound —is that what I'd done?

Concern is a human emotion, but my actions resemble Fae more than human. I don't want to become like the Fae. But maybe Deston had been right: over time my human sensibilities will fade away like the Queens of Fae. Will I become one of them? I already look like one.

If you've enjoyed what you've read here please give

it a little love and leave a review and feel free to follow me

on Amazon Or send me an email slmason1889@gmail.com

or follow me on Instagram @s.l.mason_author

For the most up to date information on the Killing

Gods Universe or These Hallowed Hills visit:

Quickquillpublishing.com